D1615522

NARCOMANIA

NARCOMANIA
On Heroin

Marek Kohn

faber and faber

LONDON · BOSTON

First published in 1987 by
Faber and Faber Limited
3 Queen Square London WC1N 3AU

Photoset by Wilmaset Birkenhead Wirral
Printed in Great Britain by
Richard Clay Ltd Bungay Suffolk
All rights reserved

British Library Cataloguing in Publication Data

Kohn, Marek
Narcomania : On Heroin.
1. Heroin habit
I. Title
362.2'93   HV5822.H4
ISBN 0–571–14506–X

For Roxanne

Any important disease whose causality is murky, and for which treatment is ineffectual, tends to be awash in significance. First the subjects of deepest dread (corruption, decay, pollution, anomie, weakness) are identified with the disease. The disease itself becomes a metaphor.

Susan Sontag, *Illness As Metaphor*

Contents

Foreword

''Eroin? I don't know what all this fuss is about.'

That was the opening line of the government-sponsored television 'commercial' which first appeared in the spring of 1985. The complete script was an adroit précis of one form of self-directed braggadocio that leads to heroin dependency. As far as the first line went, though, it summed up a feeling I had had since the heroin panic first appeared on the horizon like a cloud no bigger than a man's hand.

In the autumn of 1984 I realized that sooner or later *The Face* magazine was going to run a heroin feature. At that point, I was fed up with reading articles about the drug that merely shuffled around the same received opinions on the subject. I decided that it was time that somebody wrote *the* article on heroin, and that that somebody should be me. One of the props for my misplaced conceit was a university training in neurobiology that had included writing a dissertation on the endorphins, the natural chemicals whose proper place in the nervous system opiates usurp. But I quickly realized that the question I was really addressing was not that of the 'heroin problem', but that of *what all the fuss was about..*

The essence of my case was and remains that not only does heroin have a singular power to dominate the lives of individuals, but it also has an extraordinary symbolic force in the life of British society. It acts as a sign under which some of the deepest concerns of a people can gather. It creates channels for the transmission and discharge of anxieties far more massive than the actual issue of heroin use would merit. Heroin, particularly in a culture so dazzled by mass media, is like a creature scuttling across a dimly lit floor.

The darkness of the shadow, many times more massive than the animal itself, is more frightening and mysterious than the real thing. It is more difficult to take appropriate action against the creature if one is transfixed by the image it trails.

This book's intention is not to provide a primer for dealing with heroin abuse, nor to discuss practical tactics for its treatment and control. It attempts to string together a chain of voices which will cut across the chorus of accepted ideas; one that will question received wisdom and help cast a different light on the issue of drugs in Britain in the 1980s. I was given the opportunity to attempt this task after writing the original piece in *The Face*. Books call a writer's bluff a hundred times more than magazine articles. The ideal writer for this book would perhaps be historian, sociologist, psychoanalyst, literary critic. Instead, this essay is written by me, with the word's etymology (*essayer*, to try) in mind. It has, therefore, no pretensions to being a textbook, a survey of the scientific literature, a comprehensive text, or a 'closed' one. It is a polemic.

One of the principles that inform it is an understanding of the drug issue in terms of what is said or written about it – a massive flow of discourse swelled by several major streams. There are, for instance, the law, medicine, and the popular press. From such a perspective, the texts themselves are the proper object of study, rather than their authors. The prime aim of this particular text is to speak about the way heroin is represented, the connotations and meanings that attach to it, how it came to acquire those meanings, and how at other times it, or its cousins, have had different meanings. The objective details of, for example, a court case are thus mainly of importance as a way of commenting upon the *representation* of the events in question, and of emphasizing the complex nature of the forces that shape the discourse on drugs. That discourse is like a mighty current: this is an attempt not to swim against it but to cut across it; to create a few illuminating ripples and eddies.

Since a text is a web of re-readings of other texts, it is necessary to give especially prominent acknowledgement to several vital building-blocks of this volume that were written by Virginia Berridge, David Courtwright, Terry Parssinen, and Jonas Hanway.

Susan Sontag's *Illness As Metaphor* – and *there's* a closed text – stands to one side, awesome in its confidence, erudition and power.

Jonas Hanway, dead some two hundred years, is in some ways the presiding spirit of this text. Like his 'Essay On Tea', referred to in Chapter 2, this essay both is and isn't about its ostensible subject. It too finds itself spilling over on to its neighbours: it has to take account of heroin's predecessors and its present companions in the drug panic; it is centrally concerned with Britain's relationship with opiates, but has to consider the experience of other places. And it is fundamentally political.

One problem with writing about heroin in the middle of a highly charged crusade against the forces ranged under the banner of 'Heroin' is that a loyalty oath is insisted upon. In innumerable conversations I seem to have perplexed people by not assuming a posture of anxiety or censure. My feeling is that in the drug panic, emotionalism too often passes itself off as morality. I think that an apparently 'amoral' text may rest upon, and express, a far sounder moral foundation than other tracts anxious to demonstrate their responsibility and civic virtue. It is certainly of more use than the posturing of media crusaders whose righteous anger is unlimited by any knowledge of the subject beyond what they read in the *Daily Mail*.

For the record, I think that heroin addiction – a monomanic dependency which threatens an individual's intricate and multiple relationships with the world – is a dreadful thing. But it need not be absolute, and it can be ended. I am in favour neither of the punishment by the criminal law of such individuals, nor of the drug's free availability. I also believe that drugs must ultimately be controlled by culture; by customs and conventions behind which the law waits as a recourse of last resort. It seems that opium in some cultures is a drug whose benefits can be enjoyed, and its ill-effects kept to a level considered acceptable, by learning from experience how to live with it. Heroin is an opiate optimized for twentieth-century needs for instant gratification and sudden impact: this and the sorry histories of its appearance in various cultures around the world suggest that the culture that can handle heroin does not exist. And if one evolved that could, it wouldn't want to.

As this book is being written, the signs are that heroin has served as the spearhead of a larger drugs campaign, and is shouldering less of the burden of attention as its companions catch up with it. Heroin is now a vital part of a complex called 'drugs', whose absolute menace and horror goes largely unquestioned. The momentum of the anti-drugs juggernaut provides justification for, among other things, restrictions on civil liberties and interference by northern powers in the affairs of southern nations, yet the premises for such acts are rarely examined. It is not simply a question of putting together an interesting essay out of a contemplation upon the place of opiates in British history. The irony and anger that shape this book are not present just for rhetorical effect.

When I started this, it seemed necessary, as a matter of urgency, to unveil the underlying meanings of heroin. As the rhetoric, raids and scandals pile up, the drug seems to be getting more meaningful by the week.

MAREK KOHN
August 1986

Acknowledgements

My thanks go to all those who have helped me with this project, including Radehey Bentley, Heather Black, Aidan Bucknall, Mark Cooper, the Institute for the Study of Drug Dependence, Angela McRobbie, Bill Nelles, St Mary's Hospital Drug Dependency Unit, Jon Savage, David Skinner, the Wellcome Institute for the History of Medicine, and John Witton.

ONE

Cough Mixture and Race Mixing

Black, dark blue, light blue, grey, pink, red, gold. Each of these has a value; a social value, at that. Each corresponds to a social class. Gold, of course, stands for the wealthy. Red is the colour of the middle class, and pink that of the 'fairly comfortable'. At the other end of the spectrum, light blue denotes a level of poverty where eighteen to twenty-one shillings a week supports a modest family. Grey indicates a mixture of comfort and poverty. The dark blue signifies chronic want. This is the colour of the casual labourers. And black is the mark of the 'vicious' class.

Here is all London, graded street by street. Thanks to social reformer Charles Booth, these social strata of London are arranged horizontally, each street illuminated according to status. The Descriptive Map of London Poverty preserves a kaleidoscopic moment in the class history of the metropolis.

The year of the map's compilation is 1889. Our focus is upon the outer north-west of the city, a district galvanized at the turn of the nineteenth century by the passing of a canal through it, and established some years later by the terminating of a great railway in its heart. By the time Booth's cartographers reached it, Paddington had achieved, in their terms, a healthy rosy glow. The stigmata of black-edged blue marked a sizeable area on the other side of Edgware Road, and slightly to the north. Praed Street, on which St Mary's Hospital stands, provided a respectable locale for the nativity of heroin.

Nowadays, a plaque set at a suitable height for passing bus passengers points out the window in the block a few yards along from Paddington Station through which, medical legend has it, wafted the spores that landed on Alexander Fleming's culture plate and introduced him to penicillin. The hospital that gave this to the world, as well as the electrocardiograph, typhoid inoculations, and the Princes William and Harry, has drawn a veil over its other less salubrious offspring. There is certainly no plaque commemorating the moment in 1874 when C. R. Alder Wright boiled morphine with acetic anhydride and created diacetylmorphine. (Labouring under the contemporary misapprehension that morphine was a double molecule, he named it tetra-ethyl morphine. It acquired its common name in a later incarnation.) All that remains in St Mary's Medical School Library of the erstwhile Lecturer on Chemistry and Physics is a book of educational experiments for the inquisitive schoolboy. The copy is signed by the hand that first created heroin. Among the recipes is a painstakingly detailed account of how to make a phosphorus incendiary device called 'Fenian Fire'.[1] Whatever else he may have been, Alder Wright was not a great one for the social implications of chemistry.

In fact, this original synthesis is of little more than genealogical significance. Like his more illustrious successor Fleming, Alder Wright was better at happening upon significance than recognizing it. Both penicillin and heroin were developed and tested elsewhere. But it is necessary to start somewhere. For in this book, heroin is recognized in its supernatural aspect. The awful significance of the imagery that attaches itself to the word heroin is seen to be much more than merely a way to sell newspapers and create drama. The power of heroin does not lie simply in the arrangement of atoms that first formed under Alder Wright's hand. It is also a matter of the powerful but veiled concepts that shape the *idea* of heroin.

A science which was elaborated some time after heroin made its laboratory début conceived of the fundamentals of matter as items which under some circumstances it was more useful to think of as particles and under others as waves. Heroin is a powder, but in the imagination it becomes and is spoken of as a fluid: a 'flood' of heroin, a 'rising tide' – these are the images that arise in an insecure island nation.

Like the quarry of physicists and other scientists who investigate the invisible, heroin has to be inferred more often than it is captured. Statistics, supposition and hearsay are what detect this elusive flood. It is said to be rooted in the housing estates; and also to span the classes. Measurement, assertion and anxiety are at the heart of the heroin problem. Heroin is something that resists pinning down and fixing on a grid. Booth's map, and for that matter its popular descendant, the A to Z, do not capture heroin.

Diacetylmorphine is merely a new configuration among other opium alkaloids. It fell to F. M. Pierce, at Owens College, to begin the interminable exercise of ascribing properties to the new compound. Pierce found that it induced sleepiness in dogs, dilated their pupils, caused their mouths to water, and made them vomit.[2] The first papers to take it as their subject appeared in 1887. They identified it as a narcotic, more powerful than ethylated or methylated morphine. Its true nature, that of a single molecule, was established in 1890. The pharmacological débutante was then left on the shelf until 1898, when the German Heinrich Dreser re-examined it and christened it 'Heroin', derived from *heroisch*: 'heroic' in the sense of 'mighty'.

It seems a curious name on which to market a cough mixture. Bayer Pharmaceuticals felt able to disregard the common name which the prescient Dreser had bestowed upon diamorphine. As a useful alternative to its opiate cousin codeine, it had its 'antitussive' action singled out as its selling point. Its 'heroism' – or rather, its anti-heroism, its place as the Hamlet among drugs – was not to develop for some time. The drama of the heroin saga is heightened by the initial presumption of its innocence. Pharmacology's relatively immutable laws do not allow a chemical to become a tragic hero, who falls from early purity to diabolic maturity. In this account of a Fall within the domain of science, the reason for it lies not in the chemical itself but in a mistake made by its attendant scientists. They are said to have blithely assumed heroin's innocence until it was proved guilty, thinking it non-addictive and even going to the extent of promoting it as a cure for morphine addiction. Freud's comparable enthusiasm for that supreme foster of vanity, cocaine, led him to make a cocaine addict out of his formerly morphine-addicted friend Fleischl.[3] Freud abandoned his advocacy of cocaine, and the folly of its use as a 'cure' for morphinism became notorious.

Such accounts play a part behind the scenes of the debate on the social control of drugs. Thus the prohibition of cannabis, with its implications for heroin's position in society, is a result of the principle of scientific caution. If alcohol or tobacco were introduced today, the argument runs, there would be no question but that they should be prohibited. A débutante drug is an elusive and deceitful creature, capable of leading scientists astray. A classical allusion exists in modern speech, ready to compound the image of plagues irreversibly unleashed upon the world by the folly and pride of scientists: that of Pandora's box. In British society, the disaster of thalidomide would, no doubt, spring very readily to people's minds in support of this line of thought.

In the case of heroin, however, at least one historical investigation[4] fails to support the idea of an initial misreading of heroin that, by implication, let the scourge fly out of the box. Searching the scientific literature of the turn of the century, its author could find only four proponents of heroin as an agent for use in assisting withdrawal from morphine. A review published as early as 1900 had noted reports of tolerance (the phenomenon in which larger and larger doses of a drug are needed to produce a given effect) and addiction. Its pain-relieving powers are recognized, but were thought to be inferior to those of morphine and cocaine. Three reports from France, published between 1902 and 1905, expressed concern about using heroin in the treatment of morphinism. A very small tide of heroin misuse had already been turned.

Heroin was, however, still used in the treatment of narcotic addiction some years later. It served as bait to lure young addicts through the doors of a New York City clinic, in 1918–19. There was no medical or pharmacological justification for the choice of heroin as the lure. It was simply that, in the space of a decade or two, heroin was already on the way to its unique place in drug-taking subcultures. Properties of little interest to the first scientific scouts who reconnoitred it had come into play.

Science had failed to recognize in heroin that which gives it its place in the illicit pharmacopoeia. Opium, and latterly morphine, had been *universal* panaceas, sufficiently comprehensive in their actions – upon the respiratory and digestive systems, on the relief of

4

pain, and crucially but covertly, upon the sensations of pleasure – for their use to be indicated for pretty much anything. A substance with such profound and all-pervading effects upon body and, apparently, soul must surely be touched with the aura of divinity. 'I'll die young, but it's like kissing God', the comedian Lenny Bruce would say, many years later, of the habit which was indeed to kill him. But medicine had moved far away from the divine. It was securely ensconced in the scientific domain based on refinement, differentiation, categorization and reductionism. The mystical and imprecise idea of universality threatened instability. In any case, if the ghost of a universal panacea made physicians feel that their pharmacopoeia was complete, morphine served this purpose and they saw little need to learn to work with a new and poorly known derivative. Medicine's use for heroin was summarized thus, in 1906, by the Journal of the American Medical Association:

> (It is) recommended chiefly for the treatment of diseases of the air passages attended with cough, difficult breathing, and spasm, such as the different forms of bronchitis, pneumonia, consumption, asthma, whooping cough, laryngitis, and certain forms of hay fever. It has also been recommended as an analgesic, in the place of morphine in various painful affections.[5]

Some reports had actually denied heroin's analgesic powers. In any case, the fact that it is more powerful, weight for weight, than morphine in this respect was of little interest to a legitimate profession. There must have seemed little point in performing a chemical complication upon morphine so as to fit more doses into the jars in the pharmacies. Perhaps much more significant was the influence of capitalism. Bayer had chosen to trade upon the respiratory benefits of heroin, and that company was the first agency significantly to shape the brand image of a product which would later become the object of advertising campaigns aimed at *stopping* people from buying it.

Reduced by the medical profession, heroin could never have achieved heroic greatness (the image derives from Dreser's choice of name). However, it was introduced at a time when the United States was instigating and shaping the pattern of international drug controls that persists to this day. One of the first effects of these controls within the US was to lessen not the medically acknowledged qualities, but the quantities of opium for smoking (its import was banned) and of cocaine. Heroin was cheaper than morphine. Those selling it found it easier to adulterate; and the greater potency of the drug was an increasingly significant factor as international trafficking developed: compactness and concealment, irrelevant to medicine, are crucial factors in smuggling. There was, however, one pharmacological element in the expansion of the use of heroin: time. Heroin turns to morphine in the bloodstream within minutes, so much of the effect of heroin is literally that of morphine. However, heroin is more soluble in fats than its parent molecule, and therefore it enters the central nervous system more quickly.[6] In users' terms, this is the buzz, the lure of a sudden moment of pleasure – no question of medicine, of relief from discomfort, but of hedonism and sensuality. In nineteenth-century England, licentiousness and vice were a continuous shadowy presence in the opium world. For most of the course of the century, however, pleasure was so submerged by the overwhelming physical misery and hardship which underlay opiate use that any brief pulses of euphoria were seen only as side-effects, like those experienced in the course of procreational duty. Heroin's pharmacological nature thrust the crucial question of pleasure to the fore. Not only was this an opiate in its fullness, but one in which its most unconfinable properties were at their sharpest.

The tragedy of drug addiction, however, lies in the confusion between its two elements: drug plus addict. There is a medico-scientific story to be told about heroin, but perhaps much more important, and more elusive, is the social and political saga that shaped the opiate phenomenon. Timing, again, is of the essence. This book is being written during a political epoch in which a myth evoked by the code phrase 'Victorian values' has become a basis for political debate in Britain. The book is in part a riposte to this myth. The current British government has successfully surrounded itself in an ideological mist inscribed with the image of a Golden Age. To most British people, this golden age is probably synonymous with the whole Victorian era. By current standards, any troughs in the

6

course of Victorian achievement or morale seem quite negligible. Yet textbooks suggest otherwise, revealing a conflict in the era. It was the 1850s and 1860s that threw up Samuel Smiles, self-help, optimism, enterprise and the confident prospect of indefinite expansion and increase. But in tension with the outward-bound middle classes was what those middle classes perceived as 'the failure of the working classes to acquire the essential virtues of thrift, temperance, industry and family responsibility'.[7] These four qualities are implicit in the social struggle over drug use, and they are especially well developed in the British heroin panic of the 1980s.

1870 is a convenient date at which to divide textbook chapters on the Victorian age. Before, the glory days of optimism; after, a draining of morale, the disappearance of Britain's undisputed supremacy in the world, and a series of economic hardships. Underneath the boom of the previous two decades lay a second industrial revolution.[8] The industries upon which the seemingly unchanging heyday economy had been built were, in fact, on the point of decline. Coal, iron, the cotton industry and cereal farming had peaked by the early 1870s. The disappointments of that decade were not body-blows, but their psychological impact gave rise to the 'Great Depression'. There were bad harvests, troubles in Ireland, and an influx of cheap imports as the Americans opened up their hinterland and created the Midwest grain belt. Later in the 1870s came bankruptcies and a sharp rise in unemployment. The Great Depression is generally given an inaugural date of 1873. Into this familiar-sounding world came heroin.

In 1874 also was founded an agency which helped to create the human element to complement the drug: the drug fiend. The Anglo-Oriental Society for the Suppression of the Opium Trade devoted most of its energies to campaigning against the trafficking enforced against the Chinese by a coalition of the British government and private British commercial interests. This unpleasant repercussion of imperialism was to prefigure a social unease to be linked forever with fears about drugs. As British supremacy over the global economy and on the seas (of which the coerced opium trade was a particularly brutal instance) was seen to be vulnerable and possibly transient, the island's preoccupation with an alien invasion began to stir in a hitherto untroubled area. As subsequent chapters will illustrate, opiates and their users have evoked very different reactions in different times and places. It was in the last quarter of the nineteenth century that they began to evoke terror and hatred rather than complacent concern.

It was the Anglo-Oriental Society which helped to introduce the notion of the devil's cauldron out of which the drug fiend sprang: the opium den. It has proved a powerful and durable invention, both as a hazily conceived figment in the popular imagination, and as a literary device for introducing the idea of evil. Much of Victorian London was a *terra incognita* for the classes on the warmer-coloured stretches of Booth's spectrum. The distance between the elements of the social order was poignantly expressed some years into the twentieth century in a notorious trial involving the East End immigrant Jewish community, with heavy undertones of political radicalism and English racism:

> *Mr Justice Darling*: I do not exactly know where Whitechapel is.
> *Mr Muir*, KC: Beyond Aldgate, my lord.[9]

Beyond Aldgate, awaiting Booth's reconnaissance, lay Poplar and Stepney, and the Chinese. Most of the Chinese in Britain lived in London, and most of them occupied these boroughs. Yet the numbers were tiny: in 1881, the estimate for the total throughout the country was 665. This was, however, a huge advance on the 147 estimated to have been resident twenty years earlier. The heart of the Chinese community lay in just two streets, Limehouse Causeway and Pennyfields. The imagination of middle-class Victorian society invested a world of fears in this tiny kernel.

> Between a slop-shop and a gin-shop, approached by a steep flight of steps leading down to a black gap like the mouth of a cave, I found the den of which I was in search. Ordering my cab to wait, I passed down the steps, worn hollow in the centre by the ceaseless tread of drunken feet; and by the light of a flickering oil-lamp above the door I found the latch and made my way into a long, low room, thick and heavy with the brown opium smoke, and terraced with wooden berths, like the forecastle of an emigrant ship.

8

Through the gloom one could dimly catch a glimpse of bodies lying in strange fantastic poses, bowed shoulders, bent knees, heads thrown back, and chins pointing upwards, with here and there a dark, lack-lustre eye turned upon the newcomer. Out of the black shadows there glimmered little red circles of light, now bright, now faint, as the burning poison waxed or waned in the bowls of the metal pipes. The most lay silent, but some muttered to themselves, and others talked together in a strange, low, monotonous voice, their conversation coming in gushes, and then suddenly tailing off into silence, each mumbling out his own thoughts and paying little heed to the words of his neighbour. At the farther end was a small brazier of burning charcoal, beside which on a three-legged wooden stool there sat a tall, thin old man, with his jaw resting upon his two fists, and his elbows upon his knees, staring into the fire.[10]

In this magical chiaroscuro, all is not what it appears.

It took all my self-control to prevent me from breaking out into a cry of astonishment. He had turned his back so that none could see him but I. His form had filled out, his wrinkles were gone, the dull eyes had regained their fire, and there, sitting by the fire and grinning at my surprise, was none other than Sherlock Holmes.

Holmes was one of many outsiders, fictional and real, who were drawn by business, curiosity or vice to the opium dens. The Victorian enthusiasm for exploring 'darkest England' drew voyeurs and slummers (the expression dates from this period) on an itinerary which took in the dens. There were those for whom the spectacle was entirely Other, in whom no spark was struck by the fancied tableaux of bodies frozen in fantastic postures, who had no wish to suspend themselves in this zone; these folk caused no concern. It was the emergence of the West End rakes towards the *fin de siècle* and persisting into the First World War, who fanned fears about the spread of degeneracy – *racial* degeneracy. A deeper anxiety perceived the mysterious dens as the equivalent of disturbing regions in the psyches of respectable men. Holmes, with his hypodermic, cocaine and lapses into chronic depression, was no true Englishman.

In another, the pilgrimage to the den was more than a nearly sinister weakness. It was the setting for the dramatic, blasphemous revelation of inner evil:

> 'To cure the soul by means of the senses, and the senses by means of the soul.' Yes, that was the secret. He had often tried it, and would try it again now. There were opium-dens, where one could buy oblivion, dens of horror where the memory of old sins could be destroyed by the madness of sins that were new.
>
> The moon hung low in the sky like a yellow skull. From time to time a huge misshapen cloud stretched a long arm across and hid it. The gas-lamps grew fewer, and the streets more narrow and gloomy. Once the man lost his way, and had to drive back half a mile. A steam rose from the horse as it splashed up the puddles. The side-windows of the hansom were clogged up with a grey-flannel mist.
>
> 'To cure the soul by means of the senses, and the senses by means of the soul'! How the words rang in his ears! His soul, certainly, was sick to death. Was it true that the senses could cure it?[11]

Dorian Gray's condition was unquestionably incurable, but alarm at the prospect of lesser sinners finding sensuality or mere sensation by such means gave rise to a plethora of rumours. There were stories of 'opium establishments' catering exclusively to the racy West End trade. According to Virginia Berridge, the publication of Dickens' last work, *The Mystery of Edwin Drood*, in 1870 introduced a new note of sharpness and intolerance into representations of the opium den. Dickens's unfinished story could be said to inaugurate a period in which a new seriousness entered what had hitherto been only a marginal source of anxiety.

Whereas social mobility was a condition for the golden Victorian period of self-help, retrenchment only reinforced the defences of that island within an island, the privileged classes of Britain. Some of the new sciences, like the theory that disease was caused by germs suggested that a source of foreign infection might be found deep in the unmapped slums, in the opium dens.[12] Much more directly, the dens threw fears of racial degeneracy into relief. National decline was coming to be seen as a consequence of the decline of the racial stock, and contact with foreignness was seen as a potentially degenerative contact with racial pollution. While Sherlock Holmes was no more than an atypical Englishman whose melancholic, intellectual temperament gave him some rather Continental tendencies, less controllable foreignness could threaten the most hallowed Englishness. *Edwin Drood* opens with the wicked Jasper's opium hallucination:

> An ancient English Cathedral town? How can the ancient English Cathedral town be here! The well-known massive grey square tower of its old Cathedral? How can that be here! There is no spike of rusty iron in the air, between the eye and it, from any point of the real prospect. What is the spike that intervenes, and who has set it up? Maybe, it is set up by the Sultan's orders for the impaling of a horde of Turkish nobles, one by one. It is so, for cymbals clash, and the Sultan goes by to his palace in long procession. Ten thousand scimitars flash in the sunlight, and thrice ten thousand dancing-girls strew flowers. Then, follow white elephants caparisoned in countless gorgeous colours, and infinite in number and attendants. Still, the Cathedral tower rises in the background, where it cannot be, and still no writhing figure is on the grim spike. Stay! Is the spike so low a thing as the rusty spike on the top of a post of an old bedstead that has turned all awry? Some vague period of drowsy laughter must be devoted to the consideration of this possibility.[13]

So the battle of Vienna, not to mention the Crusades, were all in vain, for the hordes of Islam have overwhelmed the English cathedral. The dreamer whose vice permits the hallucinated internal dissolution of England and Christendom is John Jasper, choirmaster of Cloisterham Cathedral. He has awoken in an East End opium den, presided over by an aged Englishwoman. The universal panacea has now acquired a terrible new capacity:

> He notices that the woman has opium-smoked herself into a strange likeness of the Chinaman. His form of cheek, eye, and temple, and his colour, are repeated in her. Said Chinaman convulsively wrestles with one of his many Gods, or Devils, perhaps, and snarls horribly. The Lascar laughs and dribbles at the mouth. The hostess is still.

To poisoning and addiction is added the power to turn English folk

Chinese – the power to act as a fluid medium for the transmission of foreignness.

What of the reality of the opium dens? As a member of the Royal Family will nowadays be treated to displays of local custom while inspecting the various segments and outcrops of the Commonwealth, no less a personage than the Prince of Wales paid a visit to the house of Chi Ki and his English wife during a tour of East London in the 1860s. A contemporary report found the premises to be 'mean and miserable', but not sinister. Other observers were able to describe opium smoking in level-headed and sympathetic terms. Some questioned the existence of dens, suggesting that the smoking of opium was simply part of the Chinese way of life. To call these shabby dwellings 'opium dens' would be no more appropriate than to call the living-room of an ordinary twentieth-century family, among whose members are cigarette smokers, a 'tobacco den'. 'As for the so-called "dens", they seemed to me simply poorly fitted social clubs, and certainly as free from anything visibly objectionable, as to say the least of it, public-houses of the same class,' was the verdict of a visitor who stopped to smoke, and was undeterred by hallucinating a large centipede with a chain round it walking up his leg.

The actual practice of opium smoking, then, seems to have been a prosaic matter of relaxation after work, and perhaps fortification during it, among a small and highly localized immigrant community. Yet in the miasma around it formed the germ of a new perception of drug-taking as deviant and alien. By the 1890s, a nascent 'bohemian' subculture was absorbing this image and taking drug-taking for pleasure to its bosom as a token of deviance. Heroin was in its infancy, and its human counterpart, the drug fiend, was also being formed.

In fact, it was America where the true notorious fiend was made flesh. The period was the same, the racial encounter the same, but class and numbers made the difference. While in Britain the Chinese immigrants amounted to little more than a few hundred individuals washed up by the tide of international trade, who made a living by catering to their kinsfolk passing through on the ships, the Chinese population of America was a classic migrant proletariat in its tens of thousands. They dug for gold and built railroads, labouring under the burden of repaying the loans which had paid their passages. Opium dens provided a place of relief – while helping to maintain the labourers' impoverishment and delaying their return home. For some twenty years, from the discovery of Californian gold in 1848, the practice of opium smoking, like the Chinese community itself, remained secluded from white society. The honour of breaking the barrier between the communities has been ascribed to one Clendenyn, a 'sporting character'. He is said to have been the first white person to smoke opium in America: the place was California, and the year 1868.

Clendenyn represented a vitally important section of white society: the criminal classes. 'Sporting characters' – gamblers – could find plenty of sport in the Chinatowns, which also provided a crowded and ready market for prostitutes. Shunned and isolated by a hostile white society, the Chinese found themselves playing host only to this very select section of the white population. In what one opium smoker from Colorado called the 'sacred sanctum' of the opium den, a subculture was born. The companionship of opium and the hostility of outsiders crystallized the drug-takers' exclusion. The Colorado testimony makes this clear: 'Another feature of the "hop" fiend is his absolute aversion to the society of everybody, save and except the fiend or Chinaman ... They are a society in themselves and care nothing for the outside world.'

The more intense, dynamic character of the Chinatowns in America, and the terror and hatred felt by whites there, seem to have stimulated a rather livelier imagination than the phlegmatic English visions of decay and paralysis. If English middle classes saw degeneracy as slow decline, the younger, more energetic society of the United States was appalled by a more vigorous miscegenation. The San Francisco doctor, Winslow Anderson, was to take his place early on in a long tradition which linked racism, drugs and sex. He described the 'sickening sight of young white girls from sixteen to twenty years of age lying half-undressed on the floor or couches, smoking with their "lovers". Men and women, Chinese and white people, mix in Chinatown smoking houses.' The city was quick to respond to the meeting of the white underworld and the

Chinese workers through the medium of opium. It passed an ordinance against opium smoking as early as 1875.

The problem of opiates – for which, today, one may read 'heroin' – is a compound of the deepest Victorian and contemporary concerns: work, the control of money, and the family. Once xenophobia entered the opiate equation, a group of relatively separate concerns began to shape itself into a complex.

Notes

The bulk of the material concerning the history of opium in Britain is drawn from the work of Virginia Berridge, particularly *Opium and the People*, by Virginia Berridge and Griffith Edwards (London, Allen Lane, 1981). The main source for the accounts of opiate use in the United States is David T. Courtwright's *Dark Paradise* (Harvard University Press, 1982). For the sake of simplicity, the number of specific references to these books is limited.

1   C. R. Alder Wright, *The Threshold of Science* (London, Charles Griffin, 1892).
2   John C. Kramer, 'Heroin in the treatment of morphine addiction', *Journal of Psychedelic Drugs* 9, (3) (1977), pp. 193–7.
3   Frank J. Sulloway, *Freud, Biologist of the Mind* (London, Fontana, 1980), p. 26.
4   Kramer, 'Heroin', ibid.
5   Courtwright, *Dark Paradise*, p. 93.
6   Kramer, 'Heroin', ibid.
7   Vieda Skultans, *Madness & Morals* (London, Routledge & Kegan Paul, 1975).
8   Richard Shannon, *The Crisis of Imperialism 1865–1915* (London, Paladin, 1976), p. 109.
9   Andrew Rose, *Stinie: Murder on the Common* (London, Bodley Head, 1985), p. 71. 'Muir's reply blandly defined the boundaries of civilization within the Empire's capital,' the author drily observes.
10   Sir Arthur Conan Doyle, 'The Man with the Twisted Lip' in *The Complete Penguin Sherlock Holmes*, (London, 1981), pp. 230–1.
11   Oscar Wilde, *The Picture of Dorian Gray* (London, Penguin, 1985), p. 220.

12 See Terry M. Parssinen, *Secret Passions, Secret Remedies*
    (Manchester, Manchester University Press, 1983).
13 Charles Dickens, *The Mystery of Edwin Drood* (London, Penguin,
    1974).

TWO

The Welfare of the State

Jonas Hanway was a man ready to respond to innovations from overseas. He was the first Englishman to carry an umbrella through the streets of London.[1] But his perceptions of abroad were not untroubled. He saw danger lurking in an Oriental fluid and, in the course of twenty-five letters, expounded upon the menace.

> Madam,
> MANKIND have given themselves up so much to their senses, that REASON seems to be considered rather as a SERVANT, than a MASTER. Even this custom of sipping tea, affords a gratification, which becomes so habitual, as hardly to be resisted. It has prevailed indeed over a great part of the world; but the most effeminate people on the face of the whole earth, whose example we, as a WISE, ACTIVE, and WARLIKE nation, would least desire to imitate, are the greatest sippers; I mean the CHINESE, among whom the first ranks of the people have adopted it as a kind of principle, that it is below their dignity to perform any MANLY labor, or indeed any labor at all: and yet, with regard to this custom of sipping tea, we seem to act more wantonly and absurdly than the Chinese themselves.[2]

Hanway spins the sorry tale of the introduction of the leaf from Holland in the eventful year of 1666, its diffusion among the plebeian classes, and the woes that it brought with it. His indictment was received with a similar lack of reverence to that which would meet it today. Samuel Johnson mocked it in the *Literary Magazine*, and Oliver Goldsmith took particular exception to the great eighteenth-century philanthropist's desire to keep tea from the lower classes.

Hanway's literary style was not much admired, and the general reception of 'An Essay on Tea' deterred him from attempting similar dissertations in the future. But in its concern for public health, and in one other of its arguments, it touched upon social concerns that were far from being considered eccentric in the middle of the eighteenth century. And 'An Essay On Tea' is an endearing classic of its kind, a prototype drug panic text as far ahead of its time in its anxieties as it was far away from identifying their proper causes. In it can be seen the lines of a thousand latter-day anti-drug discourses.

Like this book, and the panic during which it is being written, 'An Essay On Tea' is not really about its ostensible subject at all. Tea is the sign under which Hanway gathers together his fears and opinions; the central point from which his arguments radiate out into the great wide realm of civic and public concern. As he puts it, 'You will easily perceive that this TREATISE upon TEA is a DISSERTATION ON PUBLIC LOVE.'

This glorious pronouncement comes later on. First he must start, as must his successors, by rooting his polemic in the body. His assertions have the ring of duty in them, as though perhaps the thought of tea's toxicity is not really what he is worried about. He sees tea as an agent of relaxation that saps what is nowadays identified as the immune system by weakening the alert posture of the body and its organs. Fluids in general, hot ones anyway, seem to be a menace. Hot water, he says, damages the teeth, weakens the nerves and prevents sleep. If the digestion is damaged by tea, then womankind will be prey to 'low spirits, lassitudes, melancholy, and twenty disorders, which in spite of the FACULTY have yet no names, except the general one of NERVOUS COMPLAINTS'. There is the typical drug-panic tactic of conjuring up a rhetoric appealing over the head of reason (or REASON, as Hanway would render it) in the name of common sense. 'Every thinking person in this island,' he says, will acknowledge that never have 'PARALI-TIC' or 'NERVOUS' disorders been so prevalent. As the obligatory supporting argument, he implies that tea-drinkers are the section of the population most prone to such ailments, but his basic intention is to correlate an alleged increase in the disorders with an increase in tea-drinking, and to deduce a causal relationship from this correlation.

In fact, Hanway's references to wisdom and reason show that, for him, tea represents the mortal terror of the Age of Enlightenment – unreason.[3] Tea-drinking is a frivolous activity. It interrupts industry, and wastes both time and money. Sipping is the occasion for chit-chat and vanity, and the practice is folly, which is one of the foothills of unreason. 'Will the sons and daughters of this happy isle, this reputed abode of sense and liberty, for ever submit to the bondage of so tyrannical a custom? Must the young and old, and middle aged, the sickly and the strong, in warm weather and cold, in moist and dry, with one common consent, employ so many precious hours, and RISK their health in so low a gratification as DRINKING TEA?'

His temper quickens. Now he asks, 'can any reasonable person doubt that this flatulent liquor shortens the lives of great numbers of people?' By this point, the rhetoric renders supporting evidence superfluous. And it is round about here that the semblance of evidence appears in the guise of hypothetical statistics: what has entered today's vocabulary, when applied to the British 'immigration problem', as the 'numbers game'. Like his spiritual successors in discourse, he uses the lack of accurate information to conjure up a nightmare by the use of arithmetic. This was a speciality of Hanway's. In an excess of enthusiasm for cost-effectiveness (which would have put the zealots who entered government at the end of the 1970s to shame) he once calculated that the average labourer returned a profit of £184 3s. 3d. to the State, which had 'invested' some of its limited public spending in him.

When the question of immigration does arise, it differs from today in that Hanway actually supports it as a countermeasure against the ravages of the 'ridiculous customs' of the time – in his ready reckonings, he avoids a serious examination of the proposition that tea is directly responsible for those ravages by lumping it together with gin and wine:

What an ARMY has GIN and TEA destroyed! Figure to yourself

the progress of this destruction from the father, or mother's drinking liquid fire, to the birth and death of the child; and how often the spirits of both parents and children, have been forced to quit their bodies, when these are set in a blaze with GIN; or the springs of life lose their powers by the enervating powers of TEA.

Two hundred years later, the illegal drugs grouped together are a far more fearful invisible army than each individual agent. Gin and tea, heroin and cannabis; taking them together obscures the properties of each. The enervating, feminizing influence of China tea will reappear in the torpor of the opium smoker, and in the image of the heroin addict's despairing lethargy that touches a raw nerve in a society characterized by mass unemployment today.

By now, deep in his Essay, Hanway's commentaries are proliferating well beyond the bounds of the tea question. He is concerned about the condition ('intemperate and debauched') of the common people, especially in comparison with Britain's Continental competitors. 'PUBLIC LOVE' presents itself as, overwhelmingly, a concern to improve the vitality of the body politic – to keep the population up, and to improve the bloodstock. He turns his attention to the appalling child mortality rates in certain workhouses, and the effects of tea and gin on the nurses who dissipate their time and allowances on these vices, to the detriment of the children with whose care they are charged.

One of Hanway's most charming traits is his gift of combining a level of overexcitement which even his contemporaries apparently considered eccentric with light touches of level-headed insight. A lot of people talk about declining standards and the depths to which society has sunk, he notes, as though he were writing for today's *Daily Mirror*, but, he feels, his age is not more wicked than those which preceded it: rather, it is an 'AGE OF IDLENESS AND PUERILITY'. The circle of ladies sipping their tea and gossiping are the tip of an iceberg of infantilism, which leads to an enervating, potentially lethal, lack of productivity. His remedy for the erring poor: 'Endevor to find them constant employment, and they will have the less time to drink tea or gin: keep them out of idleness, and half the business is done.' Had he spoken on Michael Parkinson's *Saving the Skag Kids* programme, or Esther Rantzen's *Drugwatch*, nobody would have thought his general perspective anything out of the ordinary.

Certain elements of his thinking would not receive a sympathetic audience in today's polite society, though. One such would be his notion of developing a foundling hospital to improve the quality of the class ('we can introduce a LESS vicious race of working poor'), which embraced a policy of whipping beggars found with children and removing the young as foundlings to the hospital. Tea was not for those loitering at the lower stations of life. It was a substance to be disseminated only under specific conditions, which included the quality of the persons fit to drink it.

> If there are any rare properties in tea to brighten the intellects, and enliven conversation, it ought to be confined to those choice SPIRITS who soar above COMMON mortals. A cup or two as a BITTER, could do no great injury to the body natural or political: if the choice tea of CHINA was drank only in small quantities, not hot, not strong, and confined to the higher orders of the people, it could do no GREAT MISCHIEF. But it is the CURSE of this nation, that the laborer and mechanic will APE the LORD; and therefore I can discover no way of abolishing the use of tea, unless it be done by the irresistible force of EXAMPLE. It is as EPIDEMICAL disease; if any seeds of it remain, it will engender an universal infection.

Hanway's ghost was surely the invisible celebrity guest on *Drugwatch*. Two hundred and twenty-nine years later, with his metaphorical 'epidemic' and 'infection' now taken as a literal description of the heroin problem, *Drugwatch* would assemble a troupe of choice spirits, from Princess Diana to the peaked pop star Adam Ant, to set an EXAMPLE for their inferiors, who were thought to be universally at risk. Hanway's Essay laid down a class polarization which has endured in drug discourse to the present day. Drug use by those of high social status could be taken in its individual complexity. As the conditions for its use – 'not hot, not strong' – could be specified, so could the circumstances leading to what might be perceived as drug misuse. In the nineteenth century, a middle-class aesthete's lapse into addiction might be considered in terms of its origins in medical treatment, for instance. Such a case would engender both sympathy and analysis in depth. What caused a less controlled welter of feelings was the prospect of drug use by the mass of common people: the semi-submerged fear of a submerged, indistinct class persists today. Drug use by the glamorous or the disco aristocracy is of concern mainly because of the EXAMPLE it sets: that is why the newspapers are so full of cases of fallen stars and disastrous histories of drug abuse. Beneath them will be a pitiful subterranean host of nameless slaves, neglecting not just human feelings but animal drives in their bondage to the drug. 'Look into all the cellars in LONDON, you will find men or women sipping their tea, in the morning or afternoon, and very often both morning AND afternoon: those will have TEA who have not BREAD.'

The energetic Hanway is not done yet, though. His rhetoric has still to get to grips with a far nearer and more pressing threat from abroad: France. 'Were they the sons of TEA-SIPPERS, who won the fields of CRESSY and AGINCOURT, or dyed the DANUBE's streams with GALLIC BLOOD? What will be the end of such EFFEMINATE customs extended to those persons, who must get their bread by the labors of the field!' And what would he have made of Tommy Atkins with his mug of char fighting in the trenches alongside his French allies?

Hanway is prepared to look at the positive side of the tea traffic. In a way that is entirely recognizable to late-twentieth-century British eyes, he allows the importance of the employment created. Six hundred seamen, he estimates, make their living by transporting the commodity. The consumption of tea encourages that of sugar, and this builds up the stock of seamen – a strategic resource, whose prime importance lies in holding off the French menace. But, he argues, the tea industry is far from being an ideal generator of economic and military strength. The shipyards are building vessels for transporting tea instead of warships. Export earnings are being lost because too much sugar is being absorbed by the home market, and that is weakening Britain's position in her economic rivalry with France. And then there is the economic cost of tea-drinking itself. That 'it occasions LAZINESS, and FRUITLESS discourse' is bad enough, but Hanway is not a man to leave rhetoric unsupported by arithmetic. As a final flourish, he reckons up the accounts, taking in every possible expense from the cost of tea and the cost of kettles to the loss of servants' time (FINE ladies' and gentlemen's time is considered invaluable.) The total comes to £2,691,665 per year,[4] a lot of money in those days.

As a true patriot, Hanway is keenly informed about his country's foreign competitors. As a true Briton, he has a sense of the heart of the national character that is valiant and second to none when it has a chance to show its true colours in battle, a sense which he combines with an equally British vision of a surrounding world which has managed to order its affairs and produce more efficient systems than have the sons and daughters of Albion. He blames the daughters, actually, for women are the vessels not of reason but FOLLY, which is what tea-sipping is and encourages. Abroad, tea plays the moderate role proper to a respectable commodity. The British, though, have allowed their relationship with LUXURY to escape the grasp of reason, leading to a dangerous distortion in their spiritual and material economies.

Other countries drink tea as well, Hanway allows, but they have integrated the practice so that it benefits the nation. Or they drink coffee, which they buy in Turkey in exchange for cloth. What in other countries is a normal element in the rich web of foreign trade, an agreeable system which enriches the countries of Europe, causes a potentially lethal haemorrhage in the British body politic. Perhaps Hanway's ghost is also present today looking over the shoulders of the columnists who each week pour out thousands of words on the subject of Britain's inability to learn from Japan, or her failure to maintain her edge over France in the development of high technology, or the way that a clutch of European countries have succeeded, unlike Britain, in combining steady economic growth with bountiful and healthy welfare states.

For the twentieth-century reader used to reading between the lines of rhetoric which makes lofty moral declarations based on the individual, Hanway has a special charm. His era allowed him to base his argument around the body politic, at the expense of the individual, in a way that only a few contemporary politicians, like Dr Kissinger or Sir Keith Joseph, dare to do today. He allows nothing to obfuscate his central concern: the good of the State.

I consider the drinking of tea as LUXURY in the clearest sense of the word. There are differnt kinds of luxury, some are excesses on the virtuous side, and become vicious; others are vicious throughout, and have no appearance of virtue. The drinking tea is in the MEDIUM, rather inclining to the worst side, for it hurts health, and shortens life; but yet it is not so IMMORAL as some excesses are: but, POLITICALLY considered, it is not equalled by any ONE debauchery we are guilty of, unless we except the use of GIN.

Hanway's final trump is a truism which has been repeated as litany down the years, and, with the rise of the zealots who came to power in 1979, has recently been uttered with a rapidly rising frequency and pitch: that we must not live beyond our means. Not only are we threatened by alien invasion – China tea, French troops – but we are imperilled by the loss of our national substance. This, in the eighteenth century, took a very material form, in the shape of bullion. Hanway estimated that £200,000 went each year from Britain to China, and £150,000 of this was used to buy tea. The rest bought silk, silk and cotton manufactured goods, and porcelain. China imported some cloth, and some lead, but above all had an appetite for silver bullion. The sapping of national bullion reserves would lead to impoverishment, an inability to fight, and hence the 'GALLIC yoke'.

The consequences of the bullion drain are a matter for argument, but as far as the facts were concerned, Hanway was right. Nor was he the only person to have noted the China trade imbalance with alarm. The immensity of China, and the majestic obduracy of its rulers and their bureaucrats, made it as tantalizing and baffling a prize for the rest of the world as it is today. Although willing enough to take silver, China did not particularly need anything that Europe had to offer, so the enthusiasm with which the British took to tea put their country at an instant disadvantage. Worse, tea was not like iron, for instance, a raw material to be fashioned by manufacture and thereby gain in value. A commodity had to be found to turn the tables of trade. It duly was, and it was opium.

Although opium was probably first brought to China by the Arabs around AD 700, the Chinese requirement for it remained small-scale and only medicinal until the seventeenth century. The idea of smoking it seems to have arisen in the East Indies, with the example set by tobacco, and to have been transmitted to China via Formosa by the Dutch.[5] Peking seems to have perceived the drug in familiar terms. An imperial edict of 1815 spoke of 'opium flowing into the interior of this country, where vagabonds clandestinely purchase and eat it, and continually become sunk into the most stupid and besotted state, so as to cut down the powers of nature, and destroy life'. This was the first manifestation of an opiate as a social problem, and cast the die for modern drug controls.

Though the metaphor of 'flowing' may have been gained in the translation, it seems but a short step to the rising tides and floods of the British press of the 1980s. The Chinese expression for the rising tide was 'foreign mud'. There is an unpleasing symmetry between the two nations, each with their obsolete glory, their inability to change, and their assiduous efforts to preserve a myth of their essential superiority over other nations. Even the continual British complaint about allowing the fruits of innovation to moulder or be plundered has its counterpart in what Maurice Collis calls 'the first clash in the first war ever waged between China and the West'. A contemporary military analyst was confident that the Chinese military machine had not made any significant strides since its invention of gunpowder in the late thirteenth century. When the pride of China's fortifications, the shore batteries guarding the approach to Canton, opened up on the out-gunned British frigates *Imogene* and *Andromache* in 1834, many of those balls that managed to span the short distance to the ships just bounced off their timbers. Shoddy work by the powder-making subcontractor was blamed, but it may have actually protected the Chinese defenders – under the force of decent powder, their gun barrels tended to explode.

The Manchu dynasty had brought the energy flowing from insecure revolutionaries to the ancient Chinese civilization and made trade with Europe one of the foundations of its hegemony, but its dynamism stagnated towards the end of its first one hundred years. The opium trade blighted an already difficult relationship with Europe still further. In 1729, an Imperial decree banned the importation of the drug, except under license for medical use. The deterrent for those who broke the law was up to a hundred strokes of the bamboo cane, and the yoke of the cangue, a wooden collar which acted as an unanchored pillory.

Losing the legitimate channels for opium supply was not immediately a matter of great concern for the British. The cost of tea was still at the stage where it horrified only eccentrics like Jonas Hanway. In fact, the illicit opium traffic was fostered in its early stages by the internal problems of running the Indian colonies.

After Robert Clive defeated Suraja Dowlah at Plassey in 1757, the back of the Mogul Empire was broken, and Bengal fell under the sway of the East India Company. If the British Empire had collapsed at that point, there would have been precious little on which to build the sentimental legend of enlightened, benevolent administration. The colonists' *modus operandi* amounted to little more than inland piracy. Extremely high mortality rates for Britons carried off by India's most effective resistance, climate and disease, encouraged young men to make staggering fortunes and get home quickly.[6] Clive himself appears to have picked up something fatal out East. His family ascribed his death in 1774 to a laudanum overdose, the conclusion of years of opium addiction.

Inevitably, the colonists' greed caused turbulence. In 1763, all 200 Britons in the settlement of Patna were massacred. Coincidentally, Patna was the centre of the opium industry. The revolt was crushed, the puppet ruler removed, and Clive was recalled from England to take his place. The Nawab's effects were handed over, including a monopoly over opium. Clive's main task was to put a stop to the corrupt free-for-all that had built up the tension which culminated in the massacre. He realized that the British administration had to operate on an orderly foundation, and proper salaries would have to be paid to check corruption. Salt, tobacco and betel presented themselves as commodities suited to the extraction of revenue from the people, and a tax on land was also levied. This was to fund the East India Company administration. The profits would have to come from opium.

Those profits did not exactly tumble into the shareholders' laps. Famine struck Bengal in 1769, and three years later the British government had to bail the East India Company out. A governing council was established to oversee British India for the Company, and it was headed by Warren Hastings. He found himself compromised by the opium issue. He needed the money it raised, but his theoretical sympathies inclined towards free trade. 'I abhor monopolies,' he declared, 'especially those founded in violence.' A free trader would maintain that monopolies inhibited production. 'But was not this, in relation to opium, an argument in monopoly's favour? It may be argued that the increase of any production not necessary to life is not an advantage, if some other commodity equally valuable must be given up to make room for it; that it is not a necessary of life but a pernicious article of luxury, which ought not to be permitted but for the purpose of foreign commerce only, and which the wisdom of government should carefully restrain from internal consumption.'

This statement outlined a policy which was, if nothing else, to be impressively long-lived, as the conclusions of the Americans' Opium Investigation Committee testified in 1906. They summarized the British approach to opium in the Orient concisely: 'As carefully drawn laws protecting trade interests they are above criticism, barring their failure to quench the practice of smuggling. They do not pretend to be laws for the protection of a people against a vice, but rather commercial regulations guarding a branch of commerce.'[7] By this time, laws had been elaborated to protect the British population back home from the vice. The principle of 'External Use Only' operated, to enforce the isolation of outposts of the Empire within, such as the pockets of Chinese in Poplar and Stepney.

British policy, judging by the American report, seemed to be inherently directed towards smuggling. The East India Company combined a semblance of rectitude with a jealous grasp on advantage, a position which might strike modern critics of a secretive and ossified Establishment as typical. While guarding its opium monopoly, the East India Company managed to keep its hands clean, unloading the goods on to the black market by selling the opium to the smugglers' vessels (known as 'country ships') which it licensed. These ran their illicit cargo to China.

Meanwhile, another drug was being smuggled into Britain from the Continent: tea. The black market exhibited some of its classic symptoms, like the adulteration of supplies. The *London Chronicle* reported that one consignment of black market vegetable matter contained thirty lb. of smuggled tea and 1,030 lb. ash, elder and sloe leaves. A parliamentary committee estimated in 1784 that a third of the total annual 'tea' consumption, some four million lb., was not the genuine article.[8] Consumption had risen more than tenfold since the 1730s, and half of it was smuggled in. When William Pitt became Prime Minister, also in 1784, he was faced with a real tea problem. The illicit traffic was reduced by halving the excise duty, but this action also had the effect of doubling consumption: Britain got through twenty million lb. of it in 1789. The annual outlay on tea was £3 million, and her total state revenue amounted to only £16 million.

As the Crown's involvement with opium deepened from expediency to dependence, the prospect of violence became inescapable. Eventually war broke out in 1840 and was concluded in 1842 with the Peace of Nanking. Britain got both Hong Kong and an indelible stain on her national reputation. Balzac commented in *An Inventor's Tale* that the widely held image of the 'noble-hearted' Englishman was gone. After the Opium War, 'the English flaunt their perfidiousness in the face of the whole world'.

The consensus of history is that war was inevitable, and opium simply one of many possible triggers for it. Such a rich prize, such hubris in Britain's dealings with the rest of the world, and such an archaic and brittle state as China; all these pointed to a clash with an expanding and muscular Western civilization. China was destined to be opened up, and the Opium War was the grand opening. Karl Marx commented in a letter to the *New York Herald Tribune* that 'Isolation having come to a violent end by the medium of England, dissolution must follow as surely as that of any mummy carefully preserved in a hermetically sealed coffin whenever it is brought into the light of day.'

One of the strangest notions hovering around today's panic is the idea that drugs can present a threat to the nation itself. This view, as expressed by the group of MPs who went to America to be frightened and who came back warning that Britain was faced with the 'greatest peacetime threat' to her national well-being,[9] crowns a remarkable accumulation of similarly hasty statements. The implication is that crime and the sum of individual distress will somehow lay the body politic low from within. Drug-taking, particularly in the form of heavy alcohol consumption, may cause untold misery and impairment of production. Yet there is little historical evidence of whole societies being destroyed by drugs. In fact, societies seem to display an extraordinary resilience in the face of mass intoxication: it is individuals who do not. Opium and China may be close to being an exception. After the Peace of Nanking, China came under increasing cultural and economic pressure from outside. Among the many effects of that barbarian shockwave was an opiate problem which seems to have no parallel in scale before or since. But it is interesting to note that as one of the critical events leading to the grand opening of the Chinese market, opium played its part not so much directly but as a focal point upon which wider tensions and drives converged.

For Britain, the Opium War has a special significance. In the great debriefing that has accompanied the dismantling of the British Empire, the accounts remain contentious. A rosy-tinged story is being woven which attempts to reconcile the admission that exploitation and subjugation are inseparable from Empire with a claim to the comfortable traditional view of a civilizing mission in the world. It is probably the only episode in imperial history that is generally seen as unambiguously wicked. There will never be a 'Jewel in the Crown' for the Chinese adventures. However, the existence of one such occasion, for which Raj apologists do not have to labour to revise history, is a most useful channel for guilt.

The legacy of guilt is fear, and perhaps the Yellow Peril that haunted popular literature in the early part of the twentieth century was in some small measure the return of the repressed guilt. The idea of the Orient proved a rich and fertile ground in which to plant the exotica of a xenophobic imagination. Dr Fu Manchu, with his Limehouse satraps and his infernal genius, seeks revenge:

'There can be no human progress without selection; and already I have chosen the nucleus of my new state. The East has grown in spirit, whilst the West has been building machinery . . .

'My new state will embody the soul of the East . . .'

'Your Western progress, Alan Sterling,' he said, 'has resulted in the folly of women finding a place in the Councils of State. The myth you call Chivalry has tied your hands and stricken you mute. In the China to which I belong – a China which is not dead but only sleeping – we use older, simpler methods . . . We have *whips* . . .'[10]

The gargantuan brain of this Oriental Nietzsche[11] only obtains rest through the agency of opium. His plan in this particular volume involves 'a fantastic epidemic . . . a sinister mixture of Sleeping Sickness and Bubonic Plague'. It is transmitted by laboratory-engineered insects, and its key symptom is a purple discoloration of the skin. Half a century after its first publication, the association of opiates, plagues and epidemics continues. Purple patches have become known as the stigmata of the most terrifying 'plague' of all, and Lyndon Larouche, whose political theories are just as imaginative as Rohmer's novels, has asserted that AIDS is transmitted by insects.[12] Today these images, which had been wrapped by Sax Rohmer into an Oriental package, demonstrate a connection with horror that even he could never have imagined.

Notes

1   James Stephen Taylor, *Jonas Hanway, Founder of The Marine Society* (London, Scolar Press, 1985).

2   Jonas Hanway, 'An Essay On Tea, considered as pernicious to HEALTH, obstructing INDUSTRY and impoverishing the NATION', in *A Journal of Eight Days' Journey from Portsmouth to Kingston Upon Thames* (1756).

3   See Michel Foucault, *Madness and Civilisation* (London, Tavistock, 1971).

4   Unable to resist the temptation to do some rudimentary calculating of my own, I estimate that British per capita annual tea consumption was around 1 kg in 1790. Tea Council figures (published in the *Guardian*, 15 March 1986) put the current rate at 3.13 kg.

5   Maurice Collis, *Foreign Mud* (London, Faber & Faber, 1946).

6 cf. Geoffrey Moorhouse, *India Britannica* (London, Paladin, 1984).

7 Report of the committee appointed by the Philippine Commission to investigate the use of opium and the traffic therein (Government Printing Office, Washington, DC, 1906).

8 Taylor, *Jonas Hanway*.

9 'We fear that unless immediate and effective action is taken, Britain and Europe stand to inherit the American drug problem in less than five years. We see this as the most serious peacetime threat to our national well-being. Western society is faced by a warlike threat from the hard drugs industry.' From 'Misuse Of Hard Drugs, Interim Report', Fifth Report of the Home Affairs Committee, House of Commons, 1985.

10 Sax Rohmer, *The Bride of Fu Manchu* (World Distributors, 1961).

11 cf. 'Are you visiting women? Do not forget your whip!' Friedrich Nietzsche, in 'Of Old And Young Women', *Thus Spoke Zarathustra* (London, Penguin, 1961), p. 93.

12 *New Statesman*, 7 November 1986. In the same interview, the far-right American politician also makes some guarded comments, touching in the course of them upon Britain's historical involvement in opium trafficking, on his reported belief that the Royal Family is involved in the drug trade today.

THREE

The Orient Within

My mind feels as if it ached to behold and know something *great* – something *one and indivisible*, and it is only in the faith of this that rocks or waterfalls, mountains or caverns give me the sense of sublimity or majesty! But in this faith *all things* counterfeit infinity! ... It is but seldom that I raise and spiritualize my intellect to this height – and at other times I adopt the Brahman Creed, and say – It is better to sit than to stand, it is better to lie than to sit, it is better to sleep than to wake – but Death is the best of all! – I should much wish, like the Indian Vishna, to float along an infinite ocean cradled in the flower of the Lotus, and wake once in a million years for a few minutes – just to know that I was going to sleep a million years more.[1]

Something had come upon Samuel Taylor Coleridge from the East. At the close of the eighteenth century, not only solids and fluids but also spirit were emanating from India. Coleridge's choice of an Oriental religion to organize these currents of thought heralds a new and, in Western terms, awful undertow. This is not Christianity. It is an alien blasphemy. The ache for the universal – the something *great*, something *one and indivisible* – found its answer in the illusions of opium. 'Sleep' in Coleridge's letters is a euphemism for and partial description of the effects of the drug with which the poet was to have a relationship lasting the best part of forty years.[2] The addict reader may well recognize the idea of manipulating deprivation the better to appreciate gratification. Users speak of the ritual of postponing another dose just long enough to appreciate it more without really suffering, or spinning out the ritual of preparing the pipe or works so as to heighten the sense of relief. To wake once in a million years just to know that another thousand millennia of sleep were to follow would be the supreme refinement of this game.

In thus courting death, Coleridge takes some steps down the road which led Freud (and still more his disciples and exegetists) into the most unchartable of waters. The idea of a death instinct occurs late in Freud's work. He attempted to cope with a world of indefinable sensations by linking them under the name of Death, and he also used an Oriental sign when he found, beyond the pleasure principle, the Nirvana principle.[3] There seems to be a seductiveness about the idea of death for the Western imagination which is compounded by its ineffability, a quality exacerbated by the Western religious scheme of things. It is possible to see, in Coleridge's desire to drift like a happy wreck, Death being used as a metaphor for something else. That something else will be discussed in Chapter 8, but here what is most noteworthy is the opiate-induced liquefaction that courts death. A dangerous thing had been brought back from India.

Frank Sulloway describes Freud's almighty cleavage of forces between Eros and Thanatos, into Life and Death instincts, as the 'culmination of a biogenetic romance'.[4] Elsewhere he cites Iago Galdston's identification of a complex of ideas associated with Freud, via Wilhelm Fliess, as part of a Romantic tradition in medicine and philosophy.[5] Here these ideas were in conflict with those tendencies in science to reduce phenomena to physical or chemical effects – to remove an excess. Coleridge, too, sought excess in Romanticism. This movement, which flourished in the second half of the eighteenth century, was condemned to perpetual pursuit of the unattainable; its goals ranged from the spiritual to the political, from Xanadu to Polish independence. It depended entirely on the counterfeiting of fictions, from the rewriting of ancient love stories, to the creation of 'national' mythologies which conjured up a clutch of previously non-existent nations.[6] Molly Lefebure argues that Coleridge's claims about the supernatural presentation of poem to poet disguise the meticulous work done on the original shards of inspiration. She concludes that such deceit was typical of the times; 'indeed,' she observes, 'the ultimate mood of the period was virtually a cult of the fake.'[7] For S. T. Coleridge, travellers' tales provided glimpses of elusive visions; especially those collected by Samuel Purchas in the early seventeenth century: *Purchas his Pilgrimage*, and *Purchas his Pilgrimes*.

In the autumn of 1797, Coleridge retreated to a 'lonely farmhouse' near Culbone Church, on the edge of Exmoor. The poet delicately negotiates his way through the account of the moment of creation. As he sat in the farmhouse parlour, with *Purchas his Pilgrimes* open at Article the First, in the Third Part:

> Cublai Chan began to reign, 1256 the greatest Prince in Peoples, Cities, and Kingdoms that ever was in the World . . .
> In Xanadu did Cublai Chan build a stately Palace, encompassing sixteene miles of plain ground with a wall, wherein are fertile Meddowes, pleasant Springs, delightful Streames, and all sorts of beasts of chase and game, and in the middest thereof a sumptuous house of pleasure, which may be removed from place to place.[8]

As he read these words, he says, an 'anodyne' prescribed 'in consequence of a slight indisposition' caused him to fall asleep.

To anyone familiar with the arousal levels of opiate users, this will immediately suggest the untroubled drifting in and out of consciousness that makes those used to more obviously sociable forms of drug-taking wonder where the attraction lies. But behind the closed lids, he

> continued for about three hours in a profound sleep, at least of the external senses, during which time he has the most vivid confidence, that he could not have composed less than two to three hundred lines: if that can be called composition in which all the images rose up before him as things, with a parallel production of the correspondent expressions, without any sensation or consciousness of effort. On awakening he appeared to himself to have a distinct recollection of the whole . . . and instantly and eagerly wrote down the lines that are here preserved. At this moment he was unfortunately called out by a person on business from Porlock, and detained by him above an hour, and on his return to his room, found . . . that though he still retained some vague and dim recollection of the general purport of the vision, yet, with the exception of some eight or ten lines and images, all the rest had passed away . . . Yet from the still surviving recollections in his

mind, the Author has frequently proposed to finish what had originally, as it were, been given to him . . .[9]

And thus he began:

> In Xanadu did Kubla Khan
> A stately pleasure-dome decree:
> Where Alph, the sacred river, ran
> Through caverns measureless to man
> Down to a sunless sea . . .

The tabloid summary that Kingsley Amis supplied to accompany a reprinting of the poem in the popular paper which had shortly before devoted a whole issue to the horrors of 'public enemy number one', heroin, left even more unsaid.

> Coleridge said he dreamt this as the first part of a longer poem which he was busy copying out when a caller at the door interrupted the flow and destroyed his memory of the remainder. A good story, impossible to disprove, and anyway what we have is a masterpiece, perhaps the most romantic poem in the language.[10]

And what could be more anodyne than that brief resumé? Coleridge had been taking opium for dysentery, not the most romantic of disorders. He may also have been using it to allay anxieties brought on by money troubles. At all events, he took pains to obscure the action of opium on any part of him higher than his twisted bowels or aching teeth. He felt unable to admit to taking pleasure in the 'flattering poison', and in his covert action took a course diametrically opposite to that of De Quincey, whose name was and remains solely bound to the *Confessions of an English Opium Eater*. When a letter written by Coleridge, published posthumously, accused De Quincey of indulging in opium solely for pleasure, the latter retaliated with a similar accusation. Though the drug was almost unavoidable in nineteenth-century Britain, its sensual or euphoric aspects were covered in shame. 'Kubla Khan' is almost simple in its ecstasy, with merely the formality of a hint of danger at the end.

> And all should cry, Beware! Beware!
> His flashing eyes, his floating hair!
> Weave a circle round him thrice

> And close your eyes with holy dread:
> For he on honey-dew hath fed,
> And drunk the milk of Paradise.

This is the conceit of a neophyte opiate-drinker, in which 'dread' is nearly as empty a cipher as the toy arrows of Cupid that might appear in some doggerel about love. But 'dread' is there none the less: it is acknowledged, albeit fleetingly, at the end of this honeymoon verse. More profound is the sense of loss that appears in the Author's third-person account of the poem's creation. The idea that this vision is itself only a fraction of a much larger landscape of elation is in essence the myth of the golden moment. It is the vision that impels the addict to chase backwards in pursuit of the first fix, the original pleasure. The most romantic aspect of 'Kubla Khan' is the idea that there was much more, but the prosaic world got in the way and lost it for ever.

The poet's relationship with the drug followed a classic course from honeymoon to guilt and endless relapse. 'The Rime of the Ancient Mariner' was written in the same year as 'Kubla Khan' and a group of the finest of his other poems. The long night of Coleridge's addiction and his attempts to shake it off lay in the future, but the poem reads like a song of such experience. There is nothing in a relationship with drugs, however, that is not experienced in other relationships, and so the poem's date is not evidence of some strange foresight. Both the poem and the attempts to throw off drug addiction let loose guilt and *dread*.

> Like one, that on a lonesome road
> Doth walk in fear and dread,
> And having once turned round walks on,
> And turned no more his head;
> Because he knows, a frightful fiend
> Doth close behind him tread.

The Mariner is guilty of killing the Albatross whose corpse is hung round his neck as symbol and punishment of the crime; not the same thing as a monkey on the back, but not completely unrelated either. His ship is visited by the 'Night-mare LIFE-IN-DEATH' 'who thicks man's blood with cold'. He contemplates a 'thousand thousand slimy things' with loathing. Something intervenes when he tries to pray. Then, watching the water-snakes, he perceives their beauty, 'blue, glossy green, and velvet black'. In a flash he is able to breathe a prayer, and the Albatross drops off into the sea.

That could stand alone as a complete story, the dialectic of its morality satisfactorily concluded. It would make a fine folk-tale. But it is set within an epic of relapse and confession, two of the most salient features of becoming free from a drug dependency. The tale is told to the Wedding Guest by the Mariner, whose travails are hardly begun when he sheds the bird. He is sentenced to confess eternally, like those devotees who believe that their drug dependency is a life sentence, in the manner of original sin; Narcotics for ever and Anonymous. For them, there is a ritual demand for regular testimony: 'My name is . . . and I am an alcoholic/narcotic addict/chemical dependent.' The compulsion to testify to addiction replaces the compulsion to act it out by taking the drug. Addiction is seen as a permanent component of the soul. This perspective combines the venerable religious concept of original sin with ideas derived from science: the 'disease' of addiction is like a viral infection which hijacks the organism's DNA chains and thus changes its fundamental genetic character.

> Forthwith this frame of mine was wrenched
> With a woful agony,
> Which forced me to begin my tale;
> And then it left me free.

The agony returns, 'and ever and anon throughout his future life an agony constraineth him . . .' to perpetual motion and the perpetual retelling of the tale.

The foundering of joy on guilt was not Coleridge's only experience of drug-taking. He fell in with the Beddoes circle, a group of enthusiastic drug experimenters gathered around Dr Thomas Beddoes of Bristol. The latter had translated and edited John Brown's *Elementa Medicinae*, in which the eccentric Scottish doctor expounded the theories that came to be known as Brunonianism. Well over a century later, in 1913, the medical historian Fielding Garrison could scarcely contain his indignation over this 'coarse man of low habits' who 'turned against his quiet teacher with the plebeian's usual tactics of reviling his intellectual betters in order to exalt himself'. 'Yet the Brunonian theory . . . actually held the attention of Europe for a quarter-century and, as late as 1802, a *rixa* or students' brawl between Brunonians and non-Brunonians at the University of Göttingen lasted two whole days and had finally to be put down by a troop of Hanoverian horse.'[11] Brown regarded tissue as 'excitable', and classified diseases as 'sthenic' or 'asthenic' (as in 'neurasthenia'), according to whether they increased or diminished the state of excitement of the tissues.

The idea of stimulation persisted long after it had, presumably, lost its grip on the scholars of Göttingen. The argument between Holmes and Watson at the beginning of *The Sign of Four*, which opens with a terse but curiously sensual description of Holmes injecting himself, illustrates the way in which medical theories that have been superseded then pass into popular understanding. While Holmes acknowledges Doctor Watson's medical strictures on the physical damage done by the drug, he considers it worth the price. ' "My mind," he said, "rebels at stagnation. Give me problems, give me work, give me the most abstruse cryptogram, or the most intricate analysis, and I am in my own proper atmosphere. I can dispense then with artificial stimulants. But I abhor the dull routine of existence. I crave for mental exaltation." '[12]

It is notable that, although on this occasion, the substance in the hypodermic is cocaine, Watson's inquiry, ' "Which is it to-day, morphine or cocaine?" ' suggests that the great detective's explanation for his vice applies to both drugs. Although the concept of 'narcotic' has enveloped the opiates, alcohol is still popularly spoken of as a 'stimulant'. 'To this end,' Garrison continues, with burgeoning irony, 'opium and, of course, alcohol were Brown's favourite agents. Hippocrates said that no knowledge of the brain can tell us how wine will act upon any particular individual, and Brown proceeded to apply this experimental idea *in propria persona* to elucidate his theory, using successive doses of five glasses of wine at a time. Abuse of opium eventually killed him.' Garrison concludes by citing the verdict of another authority. 'His therapeutic ideas, Baas asserts, destroyed more people than the French Revolution and the Napoleonic wars combined, nor will we dispute the same historian's pronouncement that he was "morally deserving of the severest condemnation".'

Around the turn of the nineteenth century, though, orthodoxy was not the power it is today. The medical profession had yet to establish itself by fighting the battles through which it would triumph over competing systems and traditions, and in some of which the opiates would serve as pawns. Down in Bristol, Beddoes gathered around himself a clique of enthusiasts, among them Sir Humphry Davy, discoverer of sodium and inventor of the miners' safety lamp, Tom Wedgwood, the photographer, Coleridge and De Quincey. Coleridge's first use of opium is said to have been on the strength of a recommendation in the Beddoes edition of *Elementa Medicinae*. Beddoes's Pneumatic Institution was devoted to the treatment of pulmonary ailments; it was in the Institution laboratory that Humphry Davy discovered nitrous oxide, or 'laughing gas'. A use for it was found in the treatment of melancholy. Coleridge and others also appreciated its entertainment value. Beddoes's curiosity led him into a rather troublesome search for *bhang* – cannabis – which he acquired as a result of Tom Wedgwood's keenness to try the drug. The tone of the letter he sent to Wedgwood in February 1803, with the glad tidings about the arrival of the long-awaited substance, says much about the Beddoes's circle's attitude towards non-medical drug use.

> We will have a fair trial of *Bang* – Do bring down some of the Hyoscyamine Pills – and I will give a fair trial of opium, Hensbane, and Nepenthe. Bye the bye, I always considered Homer's account of the *Nepenthe* as a *Banging* lie.[13]

Also on the shopping list were 'red Sulfat' and 'Compound Acid'. Although this was long before the synthesis of amphetamine sulphate and LSD, let alone their non-medical use, the allusions do have a familiar ring for the modern reader.

Despite the gleeful plotting, that suggests nothing so much as a pair of suburban teenagers planning a lost weekend of multiple drug abuse, Coleridge's letters show a concern for discretion. Although contemporary records do not reveal anything of the intensity of emotion that has been directed towards illicit drug use over the last hundred years or so, what was then known as 'luxurious use' – so much more elegant and suggestive a term than the modern 'recreational use' – was something that could attract sharp censure. It was not something to be flaunted, and the acceptable drugs formed a protective cloud into which its unacceptable face could shade.

Reaction to the first publication of De Quincey's *Confessions of an English Opium Eater* in the *London Magazine*, in 1821, was strong and intrigued. A debate ensued as to whether the *Confessions* encouraged experimentation with the drug, and a general feeling seemed to emerge that the initially anonymous Opium Eater had failed to counterbalance the 'pleasures' of opium adequately with a description of its 'pains'. But the work did not engender hatred or hysteria. Its Introduction establishes that the habit was acquired as a result of the use of opium for medicinal purposes. Like the imperilled teenagers of today, De Quincey was introduced to the drug by a friend, though the promise was simply that of relief from neuralgia. Critical acclaim for the *Confessions* was based mainly on appreciation of the quality of the writing; but, unlike Coleridge, De Quincey made opium into the focus of the text instead of its secret presence. The *Confessions* are both a singular man's memoirs and a singular piece of introspective psychological exploration. *Dread* is to be found here, and it is explicitly organized around phantasmagoric images of the Oriental. This text shows that the association between fear, drugs and the East are made not only by individuals and agencies hostile to some forms of drug use, but even by drug devotees themselves.

In one of his more bemusing passages, De Quincey describes how, around 1813, he is ensconced in a cottage in the middle of some unspecified mountains far from the city. A Malay turns up at his door, in full Malay apparel, and terrifies the serving girl. De Quincey, hazarding a guess that his visitor is on the way to a port some distance away, preserves his reputation with the neighbours by uttering a polyglot string of snatches of foreign tongues that he has picked up. He receives an apparently cordial reply in what he takes to be Malay. The visitor lies down on the floor for about an hour, and then goes on his way. De Quincey gives him a lump of opium for the road.

Five years later, this agreeable, if inconclusive, encounter between different races becomes the key to a nightmare:

> The Malay has been a fearful enemy for months. I have been every night, through his means, transported into Asiatic scenes ... The causes of my horror lie deep; and some of them must be common to others. Southern Asia, in general, is the seat of awful images and associations ... In China, over and above what it has in common with the rest of Southern Asia, I am terrified by the modes of life, by the manners, and the barrier of utter abhorrence, and want of sympathy, placed between us by feelings deeper than I can analyse. I could sooner live with lunatics, or brute animals.[14]

The modern Orient stretches, roughly speaking, from the port of Yokohama to the shores of Tripoli. It is not really defined by lines of longitude: Yokohama is now honorarily Western, although it remains Oriental in the menace its manufacturers are seen to pose to the West. Tripoli, on the other hand, has been defined as supremely Other, and therefore Oriental, by the president of the USA. The Orient is a belt which spans the greatest non-Western civilizations, and will therefore always represent danger for the West.[15] De Quincey's Orient encompassed the same regions.

> Under the connecting feeling of tropical heat and vertical sunlights, I brought together all creatures, birds, beasts, reptiles, all trees and plants, usages and appearances, that are found in all tropical regions, and assembled them together in China or Indostan. From kindred feelings, I soon brought Egypt and all her gods under the same law. I was stared at, hooted at, grinned at, chattered at, by monkeys, by paroquets, by cockatoos. I ran into pagodas: and was fixed, for centuries, at the summit, or in secret rooms; I was the idol; I was the priest; I was worshipped; I was sacrificed. I fled from the wrath of Brama through all the forests of Asia: Vishnu hated me: Seeva laid wait for me. I came suddenly upon Isis and Osiris: I had done a deed, they said, which the ibis and the crocodile trembled at. I was buried, for a thousand years,

in stone coffins, with mummies and sphinxes, in narrow chambers at the heart of eternal pyramids. I was kissed, with cancerous kisses, by crocodiles; and laid, confounded with all unutterable slimy things, amongst reeds and Nilotic mud.[16]

The hapless Opium Eater is entangled in webs which bring him under the aegis of a welter of deities and systems of divine law. Guilt and retribution await him; and Nirvana, immobility lasting a thousand years, has turned into a sentence of living death by entombment. The Opium Eater's vision of the East seems to owe more to Luther than to the Buddha. The dread is not only of the Orient, but of the infinite surrounding it. 'Over every form, and threat, and punishment, and dim sightless incarceration, brooded a sense of eternity and infinity that drove me into an oppression as of madness.' And there he ended up, like the Ancient Mariner, among the slimy things.

Others among the educated classes also had close relationships with opiates. Many were writers, though none elected, like the Opium Eater, to make the drug the 'true hero' of their tales. Bramwell Brontë imitated De Quincey, but no doubt he did not originally intend to follow his forebear's example to the extent of developing a wretched dependency. Keats, Byron and Shelley resorted to laudanum on occasion. Wilkie Collins and Elizabeth Barrett Browning depended upon it. Despite the sinister light in which Dickens casts the drug and its devotees in *The Mystery of Edwin Drood*, he found it helpful at times during his last years. Sir Walter Scott wrote *The Bride of Lammermoor* while receiving opium and laudanum as treatment for a painful illness.

Many of these case histories illustrate how attempts to distinguish drug use as either moral or medical – 'luxurious', 'stimulant' or 'therapeutic' – tend to the spurious. Shelley 'would actually go about with a laudanum bottle in his hand, supping thence as the need might be.' At the time, he was suffering from physical pain, and had just separated from his wife. It would not have been easy to separate the effect of each of these upon him, not would it be possible for anyone to measure just which caused the greater suffering. But the relative slimness of the contemporary pharmaco-poeias meant that opiates were likely to be indicated for so many ailments, major and minor, that large sections of the population were exposed to the 'secondary' effects of the drug upon the mind. More sickness and the availability, compared to today, of fewer drugs, created a receptive environment for opium. The substrate of physical illness legitimized a greater degree of incidental relief, just as the concept of physical dependency would later legitimize the treatment of the opiate addict as a sick person rather than as a criminal.

It would appear that the acceptable use of opiates against physical disorder blended gracefully into the acceptable use of the drug as a general tonic. While the Duke of Wellington claimed that George IV drank spirits 'morning, noon, and night', and had to take laudanum to 'calm the irritation' thus induced, others found more dignified uses for opium preparations. The action of opium upon language was not restricted to the written word. William Wilber-force, tending towards Holy Orders under the influence of evangelical Christianity, was instead persuaded to use his oratorical powers in the Commons, in the cause of the abolition of slavery. He would take opium before addressing the House. Gladstone was wont to add laudanum to his coffee for the same purpose. The drug was evidently considered to be a useful reinforcement for the social skills. Horace Walpole recalled Lady Stafford remarking to her sister, 'Well, child, I have come out without my wit today', on an occasion when she had not composed herself with a dose of opium. It was scarcely a dependable aid to public speaking, though. One doctor, elected President of the prestigious Hunterian Society, overdosed slightly as a result of pre-speech anxiety and passed out. By contrast, it caused another member to become so incoherent that he was laughed out of the room. A third, highly regarded and tipped for the Presidency, passed an eve-of-election meeting apparently deep in thought. He regained consciousness to find the other candidates' speeches concluded, the meeting over, and his Presidential prospects vanished.

Opium was able to take the individual and set him or her aside from the rest of the world for a while. It took no account of class. In 1863, Dr Henry Julian Hunter described how 'a man may be seen occasionally asleep in a field leaning on his hoe. He starts when approached, and works vigorously for a while. A man who is setting about a hard job takes his pill as a preliminary, and many never take their beer without dropping a piece of opium into it. To meet the popular taste, but to the extreme inconvenience of strangers, narcotic agents are put into the beer by the brewers or sellers.'[17]

Hunter was writing about the Fens, an area which, despite being what Thomas Hood called 'dreary, foggy, cloggy, boggy wastes', is elegant in its illustration of the dynamics of drug use. Dutch assistance had not prevented these wetlands, which extended across Norfolk, Huntingdonshire, Cambridgeshire and Lincolnshire, from being subjected to perennial flooding. The interior of the region was dank and isolated; populated by the small, dark folk known as 'Fen tigers'. Because of the perpetual dampness, ague, a sort of malaria, was endemic. The traditions of herbal medicine persisted in such rural areas, and, as a local doctor testified, a specific for the local complaint was known. 'A patch of white poppies was usually found in most of the Fen gardens. Poppy-head tea was in frequent use, and was taken as a remedy for ague.'[18]

Popular use of drugs in the nineteenth century cannot be understood outside the context of the contemporary medicine as a whole. Although orthodox medicine had abandoned the theories based on the ancient notion of humours in the previous century, orthodox doctors continued to practise the 'heroic' treatments that the old order prescribed. The medical concept to which Dreser apparently referred when he gave diacetylmorphine its common name dictated such remedies as blistering, bleeding, and the adminstration of large doses of unpleasant drugs. The prospects of such treatment drove the burgeoning affluent classes into the care of the mesmerists, homoeopaths, hydropaths and galvanic healers who presented themselves as more palatable alternatives. These enjoyed considerable success during the 1830s and 1840s, forcing the orthodox practitioners into frenetic activity and not a few contortions in order to establish themselves. As for the lower classes, the consultation fee was a much more direct disincentive to medical care. Even at the end of the nineteenth century, a visit to the doctor would take 2s. 6d. (a half-price rate for the poor) out of a labourer's weekly wage of between 18 and 25 shillings.

43

The masses, then, looked after themselves. In the countryside, herbal lore and the practice of growing and gathering herbs carried on. But by the middle of the century, most of the population had been urbanized. For the city proletariat, the hedgerows and meadows might as well have been on the moon. What they had was chemists' shops.

These came to play an important role in Fenland self-medication as well. The herbal tradition in other parts of the country acknowledged the opium poppy in passing, but did not accord it any special weight. In the Fens, specific local conditions had given it a special status and, with the increasing influence of the pharmacies, this status was transferred to commercial opium preparations. On market days, the East Anglian chemists would do a roaring trade as people bought in the week's supplies for themselves, their children, and even their livestock. The commodity permeated Fenland life to the extent that, it was said, it needed no name: a penny set down in silence on the chemist's counter got a box of opium pills in exchange. 'There was not a labourer's house,' another writer could claim, '. . . without its pennystick of opium, and not a child that did not have it in some form.'[9] It was the 'tigers' deep in the Fens who were at the core of the practice, rather than the town-dwellers among whom it was sold. The centre of the trade was what the *Morning Chronicle* called 'the opium-eating city of Ely', where 'the sale of laudanum . . . was as common as the sale of butter and cheese.' The higher ground that bordered the region also marked the limits of the grand opium zone. In 1867, the British Medical Association estimated that half of the opium imported into the country was used in Norfolk and Lincolnshire.

Fenland opium consumption seems to have peaked about this time. Ague had reached epidemic proportions in 1858 and 1859, but the region was changing. Attempts at drainage were meeting with greater success and, as a result, more land was available for farming. Travelling gangs of both men and women formed themselves to work the new acres, and this in itself led to an increase in one particular form of popular opiate use: as women went out in the gangs, child-minding became more common, and many minders used opiates to dope their charges into manageability. But the overall effect of the area's transformation was to dissolve the foundations of its opiate culture. A pharmacist working there during the first years of the twentieth century described the historical scourges of the Fens' as 'ague, poverty and rheumatism'. Opium was a palliative for all three. Even in its most strictly medical aspect, it was an appropriate medicine for a malarial area full of poor people. Quinine was available at the time of the ague epidemic, but the price of an ounce of it would buy about a pound of 'opic'. The fever was waning as early as the 1860s, however, when the malarial attacks were observed to be weaker. By the turn of the century, they were rare altogether.

Legal restrictions also contributed to the decline in opiate use. The 1868 Pharmacy Act made it a little more difficult to sell the drug without a licence – though the protests of Fenland pharmacists excluded it from Part One of the Act. In 1924, the Senior Medical Officer at the newly established Ministry of Health told the energetic Sir Malcolm Delevingne of the Home Office, Under-Secretary with responsibility for operating the new drugs legislation, that Fenland opium use had persisted until curtailed by regulations passed during the First World War. Adult use in these latter years was largely a relic of bygone times, as were the users, but traces of the tradition could still be found. Children and animals were its remaining objects. The former were given opium pills in the 1920s and, a few years after the passage of the Dangerous Drugs Act of 1920, East Anglian farmers alarmed the Home Office with the number of applications they made for veterinary laudanum. Whitehall let them be: it was considered that these requests were no more than a matter of custom among people who would never dream of putting the medicine to any other use.

The Fenland opium era, obscured as it has been by history, provides an example from within Britain itself to suggest that, under some circumstances, it is possible for a popular culture to learn for itself how to manage opiates. It also emphasizes that a society which comes to use opiates on a large scale is not doomed, like the Ancient Mariner, to everlasting bondage. Many Fen people did become addicted, but they did not undergo criminalization and the commitment to a mono-economy that is the lot of the modern addict, caught between the pincers of high cost and the continual search for a scarce drug. There were many deaths from overdose, too, but the price of opium seemed an acceptable one to many observers, as well as to the population of the region itself. They were able to reach conclusions concerning opiate use in this particular population which would be unthinkable in milieux ridden with political *Angst*, like Britain in the 1980s; or the cities of Victorian England, haunted by the spectre of a mysterious and threatening proletariat. But, at the time, Dr Elliott of Whittlesey was able to sum up the position thus:

> It is ridiculous to compare opium with alcohol, which, when taken in anything like excess, ruins the health and fills our jails and workhouses. We should be inclined rather to class opium with tobacco in its ill-effects as regards the body . . . it is proved beyond all doubt: 1) that the habit is extremely prevalent; 2) that the quantity consumed is very great; 3) that, after all, it does very little harm.[20]

Opium came in a kaleidoscope of preparations. There were opium pills, raw opium, the alcoholic solution known as laudanum, the camphorated tincture called paregoric, the powdered mixture of ipecacuanha and opium named after its inventor, Thomas Dover, opiate lozenges, opium enemas, soap and opium, lead and opium, and plenty more. They were sold in markets, grocers' shops, and, most importantly, in chemists' shops. Replacing the herbal traditions among the city proletariat, and eventually doing the same for the rural populace as well, the chemists came to occupy a vital stratum in medicine. Doctors would sell their diagnostic skills and advice to the better-off, and would nearly always dispense the drugs they prescribed themselves. The chemist would, less formally, provide the same service for his humbler customers. He would advise on the condition, and sell the customer-patient the drug he recommended. In the 1830s and 1840s, he was also ahead of the doctors in his leaning towards drug-based therapy. And of the drugs in the pharmacopoeias of the times, there was just one without which the whole therapeutic movement of the period would have foundered. Jonathan Pereira, author of a textbook of

therapeutics, testified that 'opium is undoubtedly the most important and valuable remedy of the whole Materia Medica. We have,
for other medicines, one or more substitutes, but for opium we have
none.'[21]

Opium in its array of forms was used for the widest range of
conditions which did not demand the attentions of doctors.
Laudanum seems to have been the most popular opium preparation
among the poorer classes. It was used for coughs, diarrhoea,
rheumatism, toothache, period pains, hangovers and all the other
day-to-day ills that exercised themselves with particular cruelty
upon the poor. Medical practitioners used it in cases of cancer,
rabies, ulcers, gangrene, neuralgia, sciatica, respiratory illnesses,
dysentery and gout. Particularly important among its many other
applications was the treatment – probably introduced into Britain
by doctors with experience in India – of cholera, the apocalyptic
diarrhoea. It remained a standard therapy until the last major
epidemic in 1866. It was used for a host of specific ills, and it
permeated a world in which poverty, the universal chronic
condition, cried out for the solace which opium excelled at
providing. The editor of the *Practitioner*, Dr Francis E. Anstie, saw
the poor people who took opium as 'persons who would never think
of narcotizing themselves, any more than they would be getting
drunk; but who simply desire a relief from the pains of fatigue
endured by an ill-fed, ill-housed body, and a harassed mind.'[22]

Opium in its 'stimulant' aspect was never embraced by respectable society. It was always feared as a medium for the dissemination
of vice. But its use in ways which went well beyond the strictly
medical was received with tolerance and even a degree of approval
– if, that is, the opiate users were not members of those classes
perceived by the dominant classes as 'dangerous'. Certain ideas
about chronic users – addicts – began to sort themselves into fixed
patterns. In 1873, round about the beginning of that era in which
heroin and the figure of the drug fiend were born, the *Medical Times
& Gazette* was able to describe chronic opium eaters as 'dirty,
slovenly, lazy, lying, and sanctimonious'. This briefly sketched
stereotype has proved extraordinarily durable. But there is a crucial
difference between this definition and its present-day variants,

47

which lies in the additional characteristics which could be identified in the subject. Nowadays, if one were to extend the indictment, it would continue in the same vein – prone to stealing, self-deceiving, and so on. Despite the value given by modern public opinion to the notion of 'balance', it was the Victorian observers who felt more able to interleave such familiar characterizations with observations in a more positive vein. The *Medical Times & Gazette*'s account continues:

> There are none of the deeds of brutal violence that are inspired by beer, and none of the foul language. Where others say 'damn', they say 'bless'; and, in fact, you may almost know an opium-eater by his use of the word 'blessed'. 'Law, mum,' said an old woman, 'what a beautiful dog of yourn, and what a blessed tail he've got!' 'Our Tom have been stealing, and deserve to be hanged, he dew, bless him!'[23]

Were it not for what came before, one might almost suspect that author of doting upon the drug-takers.

Notes

1   In Molly Lefebure, *Samuel Taylor Coleridge: A Bondage of Opium* (London, Quartet, 1977), pp. 252–3.
2   See Berridge, *Opium and the People*, ch. 5; and Lefebure, *Samuel Taylor Coleridge*.
3   See Frank J. Sulloway, *Freud: Biologist of the Mind* and Jean Laplanche: *Life & Death in Psychoanalysis* (Johns Hopkins University Press, 1985).
4   Sulloway, *Freud*, p. 393.
5   Sulloway, *Freud*, p. 146.
6   cf. Neal Ascherson (*Observer*, 9 June 1985): 'I am always fascinated when people talk about "the forging of a nation!". Most nations are forgeries, perpetrated in the last century or so.'
7   Lefebure, *Samuel Taylor Coleridge*, p. 258.
8   cf. Lefebure, *Samuel Taylor Coleridge*, p. 251.
9   Lefebure, *Samuel Taylor Coleridge*; also in *Coleridge: Poems & Prose* (London, Penguin, 1957), p. 87.
10 Kingsley Amis in the *Daily Mirror*, 1 March 1985.
11 Fielding H. Garrison, *Introduction to the History of Medicine* (4th

edition) (Philadelphia, W. B. Saunders Company, 1929), pp. 314–15.

12 Sir Arthur Conan Doyle, 'The Sign of Four', in *The Penguin Complete Sherlock Holmes* (London, 1985), p. 89.

13 Lefebure, *Samuel Taylor Coleridge*, p. 63.

14 Thomas De Quincey, *Confessions of an English Opium Eater* (London, Penguin, 1971), pp. 108–9.

15 cf. Edward Said, *Orientalism* (London, Penguin, 1985).

16 De Quincey, *Confessions*.

17 See Berridge, *Opium and the People*, ch. 4, and the same author's 'Opium in the Fens in the Nineteenth Century', *Journal of the History of Medicine* (July, 1979), pp. 293–313.

18 Charles Lucas in Berridge, *Opium and the People*, p. 39.

19 Berridge, *Opium and the People*, pp. 38–9.

20 Berridge, 'Opium in the Fens', p. 312.

21 In Parssinen, *Secret Passions, Secret Remedies*, p. 22.

22 Berridge, *Opium and the People*, p. 36.

23 Parssinen, *Secret Passions, Secret Remedies*, p. 51.
The latter portions of this chapter are based mainly on the relevant chapters of Berridge, *Opium and the People*.

FOUR

Morbid Varieties

A sense of *action* is at the heart of the concept of law. The law punishes wrongdoing; it commands acts of justice which vanquish acts of injustice. Law as it is most widely understood is Newtonian. A measured reaction will be the result of any given action. You do something wrong, you break the law, you will be punished. Ask a schoolchild, an embryonic citizen, what the law is, and the answer will be to do with the *doing*. Yet law, and the larger entity of power in general, is to do with *having* and *being*. Western social systems tend to recoil from the idea of prosecuting someone for being what they are. The notion of policing someone for 'being a subversive' arouses alarm. It is acknowledged to be necessary, but it frightens because it conjures up the spectre of a brutal and sinister logic underneath, and at odds with, the principles of justice. It is felt to be wrong, and therefore the policing of individuals must operate at the rudimentary level of what they do.

There were no homosexuals in the eighteenth century. There were simply acts which waged war on nature. A man convicted of sodomy (in the modern sense of the term: the burden of unnatural vice it carries has only recently been refined down to a specific act) was simply a man who was guilty of a crime. That guilt did not establish him as any particular kind of person, other than as a lawbreaking one:

The nineteenth-century homosexual became a personage, a past, a case history, and a childhood, in addition to being a type of life, a life form, and a morphology, with an indiscreet anatomy and possibly a mysterious physiology. Nothing that went into his total composition was unaffected by his sexuality. It was everywhere present in him: at the root of all his actions because it was their insidious and indefinitely active principle; written immodestly on his face and body because it was a secret that always gave itself away. It was consubstantial with him, less as a habitual sin than as a singular nature.[1]

So the nineteenth century produced a network of policing that was far too complex to be delegated to codified law and its enforcers alone. It was scientific and intimate. It policed the homosexual, for example, by its meticulous definition of what he was. However many of his unnatural criminal acts escaped detection, the science of classification caught *him* without even needing to touch him. Foucault felt able to give the homosexual a date of birth, 1870, taking it from the date of publication of an article instrumental in constituting the new species. Among his cousins was the addict.

The flux of ideas does not generally lend itself so readily to a chronology of years and days. It is the other major means of control, that of the law itself, which supplies a backbone of dates and places for the modern era of drug history. That history is in small part a history of the relationship between drugs and society, and in large part the history of class struggles.

The date at the head of the list is 1868. It can be said to mark the inauguration of an era in which, as drugs were progressively limited in and excluded from acceptable social roles, they came to acquire the magic aura of forbidden substances. But the immediate significance of the 1868 Pharmacy Act lay in the fact that the law and the two rival young professions of medicine and pharmacy had managed to agree a treaty. Among the articles of the Act were restrictions on who might sell opium, and how they might do it. The idea that the law might punish *having*, that it could declare a substance anathema and prosecute people for possessing it, was a long way off.

The prize at stake was the creation of an élite. With corner shops

51

selling drugs to the poor and cult practitioners attracting an affluent clientele away from orthodox physicians, it became vital to gain a class advantage that was enshrined in law. Descriptions were to be turned into titles. The Pharmaceutical Society formed itself in 1841, with the intention of reserving the term 'chemist' for those who could muster sufficient education to pass the Society's own examinations. Twenty years later, some of those excluded from the Pharmaceutical Society organized themselves into the United Society of Chemists and Druggists. It was unable to mount a successful counteroffensive, eventually admitting defeat and dissolving itself, but competition between the two Societies killed the respective Bills each introduced to establish their status.

A more fundamental antagonism was that between pharmaceutical and medical interests. An emerging profession has invested far less in the status quo, and elements within that profession may feel that it will only make room for itself by rearranging the established order. The public health movement provided a conduit for both altruistic and professional aspirations. It also instigated an alliance between professionals in medicine and those in the nascent administrative departments of government. Figures brought them together; the establishment of the Registrar-General's office in 1837 (three years after its freelance equivalent, the Statistical Society) created a focus for the organization of public affairs around statistics; it was the dawn of numerically controlled government. In a very broad sense, the trend was towards technocracy. The validity of any given socio-political position was increasingly subjected to tests of a scientific kind. Opium was considered not as a moral temptation or a magical substance, but as one among several prosaic poisons whose effects were recorded in mortality statistics. Dependency on the drug came to be known as 'chronic poisoning'.

Although the public health campaigner Edwin Chadwick and his ally in the Registrar-General's office, William Farr, pioneered the use of statistics as the cutting edge of social engineering, it was not until much later that today's machine-readable technical specifications evolved. These early efforts were more like essays in every sense; texts resulting from a strategic alliance between the impassioned description of human misery and the confident voice of science: the language of progress. Statistics were not the prolific figures that nowadays operate by swamping and bewildering. Farr and Chadwick's weapons were 'vital statistics'. Their arithmetic was effective by virtue of its simplicity. Before its debasement in the tabloid press, the term 'vital statistics' meant, simply, matters of life and death.

In the 1860s, a third of the deaths ascribed to poisoning involved opiates. Between 1863 and 1867, the Registrar-General's office recorded 631 fatalities caused by opiate poisoning. In fifty-six of these cases, the victim was a child aged between one and four. A further 235 were infants. The collation of mortality statistics, about as clear and unambiguous as it is possible for figures to be, provided a foundation of fact for what had hitherto been the suspicion of a public health problem.

The public health movement itself was an attempt on the part of the affluent classes to understand and influence the tide of history. There they were, extracting profit from the engines of the industrial revolution, building the cities which they themselves had to hack their way into, like jungles. They were corralling the poor masses, organizing them into streets, mills and factories. Yet inside those alleys and workshops, a class was taking shape which its masters could not understand. Its way of life, its conditions of existence, and above all its morals were therefore objects of fervid investigation. The political power of the proletariat was an area which would become theoretically clarified as the century went on. The potential of the new class to damage the social order was perceived in many ways that were not explicitly political. One of these was concern about the working class doping itself for pleasure. The superior classes could view with equanimity the prospect of the rural poor; traditionally quiescent, respectful and manageable, deriving a little self-indulgent pleasure from opiates to make life less wearisome and painful. The disturbing bulk of the urban working class, *terra incognita*, was another matter. However, neither contemporary nor subsequent investigations turned up much evidence of opiate-crazed urban masses. The nearest thing to widespread 'stimulant' use of opiates among the urban proletarians seems to have been the habit of using laudanum or some other opium preparation to dispose of the after-effects of a different stimulant, alcohol. As Wellington's report on George IV indicates, this was a practice that united king and commoner.

The infant mortality statistics were the public health campaigners' strongest suit. They underpinned the efforts made by would-be controllers from the middle classes to influence the working class in that most emotionally difficult field: motherhood. The Ladies' Sanitary Association proselytized through its penny tracts ('The Massacre Of Innocents', 'Why Do Not Women Swim?', 'The Evils Of Perambulators') and in the *Englishwoman's Journal*. 'Few but those who have been much among the poor,' it opined, 'know how fearfully mismanaged their little ones are – how the infant shares his mother's dram and all her food, from red herring to cucumber – how he takes medicine sufficient homoeopathically to treat the whole community – and how finally, an incautiously large dose of laudanum wraps him in the sleep that knows no waking.'[2]

Working-class mothers were damned however they raised their children. If they stayed with their infants, they were accused of crimes of diet from red herring to laudanum. If they went out to work, they were assumed to have consigned their brood to a childminder who would simplify her job with liberal dosages of opiates. In fact, only a minority of working-class women had work which separated them from their children. A plethora of opium preparations specifically marketed for use on children was available. Their names ranged from the cosy (Mrs Winslow's Soothing Syrup) and the sweetly innocuous (Godfrey's Cordial) to the dubious (Atkinson's Infants' Preservative) and the slightly chilling (Street's Infant Quietness). There might well be some truth behind the implication of the name of Atkinson's product: widespread dosing of infants with opiates may have had some effect against the diarrhoeal illnesses which were the main cause of infant death.What was unquestionably false was the Manchester manufacturer's claim that the medicine contained no 'pernicious stupefactives, whose basis is laudanum and other opiates'. Laudanum and chalk proved a simple but lucrative formula for Atkinson's, who claimed to be selling 70,000 bottles a year during the 1840s.

The poor certainly had little else to help them hang on to some sort of health. There was a genuine and widespread belief that opium was good for a baby. It was supposed to make the child grow – quietly. The hardships of one young Nottingham lace-worker whose child was illegitimate summarize the dynamics of infant-doping among the poor.

> She could not afford to pay for the nursing of the child, and so gave it Godfrey's to keep it quiet, that she might not be interrupted at the lace piece; she gradually increased the quantity by a drop or two at a time until it reached a teaspoonful; when the infant was four months old it was so 'wankle' and thin that folks persuaded her to give it laudanum to bring it on, as it did other children.[3]

As the Registrar-General was able to show, infants were killed by opiates in disturbing numbers. Opiates were also the preferred poison for suicides until the 1890s, when they were overtaken by carbolic acid. These mortality figures provided the main basis for the medical profession's support, on public health grounds, for the restriction of the availability of opiates. The 1868 Pharmacy Act was primarily a vehicle for executing the Pharmaceutical Society's strategic design to establish pharmacy as a profession. Creating legal and bureaucratic difficulties for chemists, and sapping their profits, was no part of that design. The first draft of the Bill included opium among the list of the poisons whose sale was to be controlled. The drug then vanished from the proposals altogether. It later transpired that this had been at the behest of chemists from the Fenland area.

Medical interest, represented by the British Medical Association (which had been founded in 1832) and the ten-year-old General Medical Council, thought it was time for the system of opiate use, until then in the control of chemists and their plebeian customers, to be transferred into its own hands. It took a dim view of its pharmaceutical rival's machinations. The GMC's Pharmacy Bill Committee 'were of the opinion that the statement that regulations as to the sale of opium would interfere with the trade profits of druggists in certain parts of England, constituted the strongest ground for inserting opium in the list of poisons'. For the government, Robert Lowe, a future Chancellor and Home Secretary, agreed with the doctors. He put opium back in the Bill, in Part Two of the schedule. The Pharmaceutical Society got what it wanted: the 'barbers, booksellers, chandlers, confectioners, drapers, general dealers, grocers, hairdressers, herbalists, ironmongers, marine-store dealers, oilmen, printers, publicans, stationers, storekeepers, tailors, tobacconists, toydealers, wine merchants' in its President's inventory were prohibited from selling poisons.[4] Chemists became the sole vendors. A chemist could only sell a Part One poison like potassium cyanide to someone he knew, and he had to record details of the sale. Its container had to be labelled with specified information, including the legend 'poison'. The labelling of Part Two poisons was controlled in the same way; the other particulars of their sale were not.

Despite the apparent superficiality of these controls, they had some effect on the mortality figures. There was a slight overall decline in deaths, and a more definite reduction in infant mortality. In the years preceding the Act, the latter rate ran at around 20.5 per million: it fell immediately and was down to about a third of the pre-Act level by the 1880s. The campaign against infant drugging continued, however. It was part of the pressure exerted upon unlicensed child-minders: another attempt to create a profession from which the wrong sort could be excluded.

Non-professional groups also sought to extend the policing of opiates. Attempts to build up a domestic lobby against Britain's role as a Far East opium pusher remained sporadic until the 1870s, when the Anglo-Oriental Society, formed in 1874, enjoyed a few influential years. It was a pressure group which would not be entirely unfamiliar to the better-behaved and better-heeled activists of, say, today's environmental movement. While it mobilized liberal middle-class opinion on moral and humanitarian positions, it differed from its twentieth-century successors in its religious substructure. The core of its inspiration, and of its funding, came from the Quakers; and, as its initial momentum waned, missionaries and other Christians came to replace the Society's secular flock.

56

As is common among such organizations, it devoted much of its energies to influencing parliamentarians. The stance it adopted was a call for a Royal Commission on the opium question. The demand was granted, but the tactic rebounded on the campaign. In 1893, the Commissioners went East and, like so many of their compatriots, were induced by the mass of the Indian subcontinent and its population to come to an understanding. Despite a dissenting minority report, the Commission in general was at ease with opium. It took its cue from those like the hundred-odd doctors canvassed by the British Medical Journal, which reported that 'Everyone seems assured that a change from opium to alcohol would be a change to the infinitely worse.'[5] The Commission found in favour of the opium pundits with whom the Anglo-Oriental Society had been skirmishing for years. Those who had been out East were able to bring personal observations to the subject. 'As regards opium-smoking,' Sir George Birdwood wrote to *The Times*, 'I can from experience testify that it is, of itself, absolutely harmless.' He continued with a testimonial to the Empire's subjects: 'There are few finer people in the world than those of Goojerat, Kattywar, Cutch, and Central India,' proclaimed the knight, 'and they are all addicted to the habitual use of opium.'[6]

The Commission's view of opium use in India was a benign outlook in which opium was taken, unexceptionally, as a medicine, and, discreetly, as an intoxicant. The drug was in equilibrium with the culture of the region, whose inhabitants understood how to use it judiciously. A Parliamentary body thus condoned a modest degree of 'luxurious' drug-taking. Since English law, in so far as opium came under its control, had labelled it – literally – a poison, the Royal Commission's opinion of the drug meant a significant shift in thinking. The movement against the drug had been able to use the 'poison' label as a pivot on which to turn a most significant new concept: a model of addiction based on its resemblance to disease. Several forces shaped the disease model, and many forces have kept it alive into the 1980s.

The anti-opium movement was an expeditionary force sent out by the anti-alcohol movement, a much larger and more significant current in the flux of nineteenth-century discourse. It says much about the perception of the place of opiates in British life that the forces which opposed alcohol so firmly were only mildly aroused by opium – and that response was chiefly directed, in the time-honoured fashion of the concerned liberal, at the plight of foreign people far away. The temperance and abstinence movements were able to make great play of alcohol's toxic qualities: the tales of the temperance ladies who would prove the absolute evil of alcohol by dropping worms into it and drawing a lesson from their sacrifice are crude, if striking, examples of the tactic. On a more sophisticated plane, the campaigners were able to forge a profitable alliance with science. They were able to support what was essentially a moral proposition by pointing to a scientific *non sequitur*. While their primary concerns revolved around behaviour – intoxication, violence, debauchery, the neglect of children and of work – they sought to lay a medico-scientific foundation on which these preoccupations might rest. The task of science in this campaign was to say, whatever your attitude to the behavioural effects of alcohol, you must accept the pathological evidence that shows how the toxin ravages animal tissue. Then it goes on to whisper the suggestion that, since the action of the drug at the cellular level is harmful, its action at higher levels is probably also pathological. Science is prone to lend itself to unscientific innuendo.

On the alcohol front, science and medicine surged ahead. There was little difficulty in establishing the existence of physical damage associated with alcohol: the process of mapping the havoc wreaked by alcohol upon the body continues fruitfully to this day. The anti-opium agitators pursued the idea of poison, seeking to demonstrate that, in addition to their effects upon moral character, opiates damaged the physical organism. But the anti-opium forces could find very little comfort in pathology. There was no firm evidence of a process comparable to that involving alcohol. One of the most remarkable aspects of the opiate issue is that, despite the passing of a century in which every incentive has been present for the critical study of this class of drugs, such evidence remains extremely scanty. For a group of chemicals which can have such an impact upon the psyches and fortunes of the individuals who take them, their physical effects seem to be extraordinarily benign.

The anti-intoxication movement's principal think-tank was the Society for the Study of Inebriety. Formed in 1884 (some fourteen years after its US counterpart, the American Association for the Study and Cure of Inebriety), it deployed a morally driven science. It combined a temperance heritage with powerful state connections. Dr Norman Kerr, its first President, was one of many SSI members who were involved in the temperance movement.[7] His experience extended beyond just the wealthy: in 1874 he had started a general practice in St John's Wood and Marylebone, an area which included the blue-black slums across the Edgware Road from Paddington.[8] The concept of inebriety was established, but its nature was undetermined. Was it, Kerr wondered, 'a sin, a vice, a crime, or a disease'?

The Society for the Study of Inebriety answered his question unequivocally. It existed to 'investigate the various causes of inebriety and to educate the professional and public mind to a recognition of the physical aspect of habitual intemperance'; and inebriety was 'a diseased state of the brain and nerve centres, characterized by an irresistible impulse to indulge in intoxicating liquors or other narcotics, for the relief these afford, at any peril.' As the century aged and left its 'golden' 1850s and 1860s behind, policing proliferated. The question was not whether inebriates merited closer control than they hitherto had done. It was a question of which system of power should take responsibility for them. Kerr argued that the condition was a disease akin to insanity and therefore belonged in the realm of medicine. Such arguments, of course, generally sweep off humanitarian sentiment in their wake: the underlying issue of policing tends to be ignored or passed *nem. con.* Kerr was not simply trying to redefine the character of inebriates. Not content with diminishing their status as responsible subjects, he sought their compulsory detention.

The hostilities between the medical and pharmaceutical professions during the progress of the Pharmacy Bill would be described today by government spokesmen as an 'incident' rather than a 'war'. Medicine staged a raid into Pharmacy's territory; opium was the tactical objective. In other areas, medicine was challenging fundamental constructs of the social order. The law depends on the idea of the rational being who possesses free will. Medicine weakened this axiomatic principle of legal responsibility when it developed its concept of madness by inserting the insanity plea between 'guilty' and 'not guilty'.

Inebriety was not only thought of as related to insanity; it was also believed to be capable of inducing the latter. In his Annual Report for 1874, a Lancashire asylum attendant bemoaned 'the fact that among the labouring class insanity has of late years increased by a reckless course of inebriety, favoured in great measure by a plethora of money and an abundance of leisure.'[9] The rot had set in earlier than had been realized.

The idea that habitual drunkenness was also a disease went back a long way; to the late eighteenth century. In 1819, Carl von Bruhl-Cramer coined the name 'dipsomania' for a compulsion to drink. Medicine gradually took over the understanding of madness that had previously lain in the care of philosophers. Two currents of thought had passed down to it from the eighteenth century. One was that owing to Hobbes, who believed that madness resulted from an excess of passion. It would arise if the intellect were insufficient to control and direct the passions. The other was propounded by Locke, who saw madness as a failure of the reasoning faculty.[10] These two concepts crossed in the notion of a monomania. This was a one-dimensional madness, which afflicted just one aspect of an individual's thought. In a Hobbesian light, it could be a flaw in the shell of intellect through which one single jet of passion could flare; in its Lockeian aspect, it was a localized breakdown in the faculty of reason which gave rise to delusions on one particular subject. Various species of monomania were discovered: dipsomania and nymphomania have survived to be belittled in popular speech. In the 1830s the asylum-reformer Jean-Etienne-Dominique Esquirol declared the inability to abstain from alcohol to be a monomania. In 1833, James Prichard defined 'moral insanity', a relative of monomania which took after its Hobbesian side:

This form of mental disease has been said ... to consist of a morbid perversion of the feelings, affections, habits, without any

hallucination or erroneous conviction impressed upon the understanding; it sometimes co-exists with an apparently unimpaired
state of the intellectual faculties.[11]

Promiscuity was a central feature of the Victorian age; a promiscuity
of theory and an orgy of classification, in which chimeras beyond
number were conceived. Prichard's combination of the ancient
dynasty of morals and the parvenu discipline of psychiatry was a
relatively simple operation. When medicine, 'the founding science
of all the sciences of man',[12] reasserted itself with the disease
theory, three sciences had to find a common language.

As the modern age constituted itself, madness figured increasingly in that process. It became the outside of civilization, being the
antithesis of the reason on which that civilization was founded.
Classical thought, the predecessor and foundation of the nineteenth
century's romanticism, 'brought together, in a single field, individuals and values between which the preceding cultures had seen
no resemblance; imperceptibly it moved them in the direction of
madness, thus paving the way for an experience – our own
experience – in which they will already appear as belonging to
mental alienation'.[13] These individuals and values had in common
their lack of social usefulness; their lack of work. Madness was also
seen as a consequence of civilization, the unnatural strains of which
were causing an increase in the proportion of insane members of
the population. The idea of nervous systems exhausted by their
exertions within the maelstrom of capitalism persisted in the
concept of neurasthenia, which helped keep Brunonianism going
into the twentieth century. Those unfortunates who inherited
'nervous diathesis' – an inadequate nervous system – were liable to
develop neurasthenia. Its discoverer, George Miller Beard,
described the condition in 1869. He identified 'brain-workers' as
those most likely to succumb. Thomas Crothers saw how, if opiates
were stimulants in the Brunonian sense, they might attract
neurasthenics and cerebrasthenics who needed a nerve tonic. This
made 'active brain-workers, professional and businessmen,
teachers and persons having large responsibilities' particularly
vulnerable to drug addiction. Conversely, one of his contemporaries
hypothesized, blacks were less likely to become dependent on drugs

than whites because they lacked the 'delicate nervous organization' which had evolved in the most sophisticated and pale-skinned specimens of humanity.

Crothers understood addiction as a condition in which an external agent, the drug, interacted catastrophically with an internal flaw. Opiates, he suggested, left a pathological impression on the nervous systems through which they coursed. On the inadequate neurology of the neurasthenic, or someone with the kind of inherited neurotic tendency which might incline them to seek relief from every discomfort, the impression might never wear off. This trace would be the germ of addiction. He cited a case in which an American Civil War combatant became addicted to the opium that he had taken to relieve the pain of a war wound. Although he kept his affliction a secret, his daughter became addicted to morphine after pregnancy. His son acquired a habit too, after a drinking bout.

This example combines the idea of neurasthenia with another important nineteenth-century current of thought: degeneration. It originated with Benedict Augustin Morel, who published his version of the theory in 1857. Again, environment and heredity combined to wreak the damage. A flaw could not only be inherited, but would worsen down the generations: where the first generation was nervous, the second might be neurotic, the third psychotic, and the fourth idiotic. The congenital predisposition could be brought out and worsened by external factors, including opium and alcohol.

Vieda Skultans sees the progress of psychiatric thought in the nineteenth century as a sort of romance, starting out in the glow of idealistic optimism and ageing into a fearful defensiveness. She uses the term 'psychiatric romanticism' to describe the prevailing mood of psychiatry in the earlier part of the century; a humanism with faith in the power of the individual's will to overcome mental disorder. It gave way to a dark vision of untranscendable inner constraints on the powers of the individual. It was almost as though the increasing complexity of classification moulded the individual into an immobile set of itemized characteristics. Such was the fate of the fluid individual who entered the century with unmapped capacities and untrammelled willpower. The new pessimism congealed during the final quarter of a century, with the idea of 'character'. Humans could be classified into psychological (not to mention racial) paraspecies, just as Linnaeus had classified the kingdoms of nature into animal and plant species. Indeed, Linnaeus himself applied his taxonomic principles to the classification of mental illness.

The loss of national and imperial momentum evident during that period had an influence upon psychology. So did the stagnation which stymied social mobility. Self-help, as advocated in Samuel Smiles' famous tract, lost its appeal when the economic environment for its practice became more hostile. Sales of Smiles's work dropped off after the 1870s. The belief in social mobility through individual enterprise gave way to a perception of a static social order determined by inheritance – biological, not economic, inheritance. An explanation had to be found for what Skultans ironically calls the great Victorian social evil: 'the failure of the working classes to acquire the essential virtues of thrift, temperance, industry and family responsibility.' It clearly lay in an adaptation of the theories which Darwin had unleashed. What united the proletariat was its inferior biological endowment; one that was getting worse. This was of vital interest to a nation beginning to realize that it did not reign indisputably supreme in a turbulent imperialist world. The condition of the young men recruited to fight the Boers gave such anxieties a specific focus.

Evolution's final triumph was the endowment of a moral sense, and it was the first thing to go when a race started to degenerate. It was not the only thing, though. Henry Maudsley outlined the views of a Mr Thompson, surgeon to the General Prison of Scotland, who held that 'there is among criminals a distinct and incurable *criminal class*, marked by peculiar low physical and mental characteristics; that crime is hereditary in the families of criminals belonging to this class; and that this hereditary crime is a disorder of mind, having close relations of nature and descent to epilepsy, dipsomania, insanity, and other forms of degeneracy. Such criminals are really *morbid varieties*, and often exhibit marks of physical degeneration – spinal deformities, stammering, imperfect organs of speech, club-foot, cleft palate, harelip, deafness, paralysis, epilepsy, and scrofula.'[14]

The title of the work in which Thomas Crothers presented his

63

theory of narcotic addiction was *Morphinism and Narcomanias from Other Drugs*. It was morphine which delivered the opiate issue into the hands of medicine. Originally isolated from opium in 1804, it was being manufactured in the 1820s. Techniques by which substances could be introduced into the body through the skin had been practised – morphine and opium were sometimes applied to the flesh, the skin having been removed by blistering – but it took the development of the hypodermic syringe in the 1850s to make full use of the potential of transcutaneous administration. Physicians took to the device with enthusiasm. By 1869, a doctor was able to assert that 'there are probably few medical men now to be found who cannot bear testimony to the marvellous power of narcotics introduced beneath the skin.'[15]

The new technique introduced a precision into opiate administration which pointed it further in the direction of medicine. Because the technique arose in medicine it was easier to keep it there. In their delight, the physicians saw no hints of trouble. 'Of *danger*,' emphasized Francis Anstie, 'there is *absolutely none*.' The wife of Dr Alexander Wood, one of the pioneers of the hypodermic, is the first person known to have died from an injected overdose.

The doctors thus, inevitably, created a disease of their own. A new variety of drug habituée was detected: the morphine dependent. She was the casualty of a medical service which ministered to the wealthy; she was middle class, but 'she' was by no means always female. Records suggest that the proportion of women among Victorian morphine addicts was not unduly high, yet medical wisdom held that the morphine addict was typically female. Such women were understood to be weak and sensitive creatures, delicate products of a sophisticated society whose delicate nervous organization was especially susceptible to the seduction of invading opiates. Morphine, born of medicine, was treated as a medical problem. Opium-related problems must have been more numerous, since its use extended far beyond the middle classes whose doctors introduced them to morphine. But medicine did not explore the effects of industrial civilization on those whose toil produced it with the same diligence that it brought to the infirmity of the bourgeoisie. Nowadays, it is sometimes remarked, middle-class children who flounder on the nursery slopes of education are found to be 'dyslexic'; working-class children with such difficulties are just plain thick. Middle-class Victorian drug addicts were neurasthenic; working-class ones were merely degenerate.

The presence of morphine within medicine placed it close to disease. The consequent classification of its disorders as disease brought opiates, and drugs as a whole, under closer medical supervision. The process was launched in 1877 with the publication of Eduard Levinstein's *Die Morphiumsucht*, which appeared in English translation as *Morbid Craving for Morphia*. Levinstein was the first to align the lust for morphine with dipsomania, but he claimed it for the physician rather than the psychiatrist: he considered it a 'human passion', not a form of 'mental alienation'. The 1870s had seen a burst of medical interest in morphine. In the following decade this had turned to concern about 'morphinism', which was said, with little apparent justification, to be increasing catastrophically. The nomenclature raised itself to a higher pitch, the -ism being augmented by 'morphinomania'. The latter term became more popular. The morphinist was the co-operative patient; the one who genuinely wanted to be cured. This patient was not a genuine specimen of dependency, but an anomaly (probably caused inadvertently by a course of medical treatment) who disguised the true nature of the drug habituée. The morphinomaniacs were those with the secret inner weakness that led them to their vice. They were to be treated as lunatics. Across the Atlantic, they were coming to be known informally as 'drug fiends'.

The medical descriptions of drug dependency are full of sentences like two-headed monsters, awkwardly trying to reconcile languages of science and morality. The 'vicious habit', a Northampton doctor warned in 1884, was 'undoubtedly a growing disease'. 'It is not merely because physical necessity required a larger quantity of narcotic to be taken, that the confirmed debauchee increases his dose,' Anstie considered, 'but it is because his debased moral nature loves the delights which can only now be obtained by such increases.'[16]

Levinstein's remedy for the 'morphia-evil' was clearly defined, though, and – according to him – reliable. The patient was to be confined for up to a fortnight in a barred room, attended by strong nurses and denied any means of committing suicide. Relief would be provided by warm baths, bicarbonate of soda, the sedative chloral, and unlimited amounts of champagne and brandy. Levinstein looked forward confidently to the day, not far off, when such heroic treatment would have freed Germany from *die Morphiumsucht*. Kerr was less sanguine. 'The opium inebriate does not destroy his furniture, beat his wife, dash his child's head against the wall, or use his narcotic career dealing with his hand death and desolation all around,' he allowed. 'Nor does he, as the tippler of alcohol, so degenerate his tissues, injure the structure of his vital organs, or originate organic disease, by the direct poisoning action of the stupefying agent which consigns him to an early grave.' But opiates were likely to be a life sentence: 'opium transcends alcohol in the generation of a more irreclaimable and incurable diseased condition. Cured alcohol inebriates are not uncommon . . . cured opium inebriates are comparatively few in number.'[7]

In such passages medicine had expounded the horrors of withdrawal and the overwhelming difficulty of kicking the habit. It had also characterized those who took the drug, who were, in the not untypical opinion of T. Clifford Allbutt and W. E. Dixon, neurotics who 'scent intoxicants from afar with a retriever-like instinct, and curious in their sensations, play in and out with all kinds of them'. These authors favoured iced champagne, nutritive enemas and turtle soup to alleviate the rigours of withdrawal. Thus medicine and opiates entered the twentieth century.

Notes

1   Michel Foucault, *The History of Sexuality*: Volume 1: An Introduction (London, Penguin, 1981), p. 43.
2   In Berridge, *Opium and the People*, p. 100.
3   In Berridge, *Opium and the People*, p. 100; Parssinen, *Secret Passions, Secret Remedies*, p. 44.
4   In Parssinen, *Secret Passions, Secret Remedies*, p. 71.
5   See Dolores Peters, 'The British Medical Response to Opiate Addiction in the Nineteenth Century', *Journal of the History of Medicine* XXXVI (October 1981), pp. 455–88.

6   In Parssinen, *Secret Passions, Secret Remedies*, p. 90.

7   See *Morbid Cravings: The Emergence of Addiction*; catalogue of an
    exhibition held in conjunction with the Centenary Meeting of the
    Society for the Study of Inebriety, Wellcome Institute for the
    History of Medicine, 1984; also Sir Humphry Rolleston, *British
    Journal of Inebriety* XXXII (July 1934); and *British Journal of
    Addiction* (Centenary Edition) 79 (1984).

    One of these temperance activists, George Sims, coined the
    memorable and profoundly ambiguous slogan 'Out of the Dram
    Shop, Back to the Breast'.

8   Sir Humphry Rolleston, *British Journal of Inebriety* XXXII (July
    1934), p. 1.

9   P. McCandless, 'Curses of Civilisation: Insanity and
    Drunkenness in Victorian Britain', *British Journal of Addiction* 79
    (1984), p. 52.

10 Skultans, *Madness and Morals*.

11 ibid., p. 183.

12 Alan Sheridan, *Michel Foucault: The Will to Truth* (London,
    Tavistock, 1980), p. 43.

13 Foucault, *Madness and Civilisation*, p. 58. Foucault is speaking of
    the seventeenth century; arguing that the division between labour
    and idleness in the Classical age replaced the exclusion of lepers
    from society in the Middle Ages. The asylum replaced the lazar
    house, and into it were driven the useless, among whom were the
    mad. 'In the Classical age, for the first time, madness was
    perceived through a condemnation of idleness and in a social
    immanence guaranteed by the community of labour. This
    community acquired an ethical power of segregation, which
    permitted it to eject, as into another world, all forms of social
    uselessness. It was in this *other world*, encircled by the sacred
    powers of labour, that madness would assume the status we now
    attribute to it.'

14 Henry Maudsley, *Body and Mind* (London, Macmillan, 1873),
    pp. 66–7.

15 Dr Edward Wilson, quoted in Parssinen, p. 80.

16 Peters, 'British Medical Response', ibid.

17 Parssinen, *Secret Passions, Secret Remedies*, pp. 88–9: much of the
    material dealing with morphine here also comes from Chapter 7 of
    this work.

FIVE

Dora

> Absolute dullness and dreariness seem to prevail everywhere. As these two demons drive the Caucasian to drink, so they drive the Chinese to opium. As an individual may by habitual toil and attention to business become incapable of amusement, so a race of almost incredible antiquity, which has toiled for milleniums, may likewise reach a point in its development where the faculty of being amused may have atrophied and disappeared, so that all that remains of that desire is to spend leisure in placidity. And nothing contributes to this so much as opium.[1]

Thus youth pronounces its verdict upon the ancient. Though one would not expect to find such visionary speculations in a modern official report, the circumstances did, perhaps, merit something beyond bureaucracy. America had at last marched into the imperial arena. It was fitting for voices of the youngest and most vigorous imperialist power, in this case those of the Philippine Commission's Opium Investigation Committee, published in 1906, to muse upon the fate of an empire in its dotage.

It would be agreeable to imagine that the Committee's testimony reminded its members that their country was also mortal. They themselves had recent experience of deceleration, if not decline. As the United States filled up the territory within its borders, the explosive growth which had carried it towards the twentieth century began to lose its momentum. America had entered the highest stage of capitalism. At first it bought its way in, snapping up Alaska for seven million dollars. Then the time came for it to shed blood, taking upon itself the task of finishing off the decrepit Spanish empire. One outcome of the Spanish–American War was that in

68

1898, the year that Bayer launched heroin as a cough mixture, the United States annexed the Philippines. Dollar imperialism had given way to a more traditional mode of domination, and among America's new responsibilities was the Philippine opium problem.

The problem was not actually Filipino; it was Chinese, and, previously, the Spanish had policed it on racial lines. The people who supplied opium to the minority Chinese community were those who had bid most at auction for the contracts to do so. The Spanish raised a substantial amount of revenue in this way, and, by forbidding the sale of opium for smoking to Filipinos, prevented the substance from crossing ethnic lines. They contained a practice within the culture of which it was a part, and made money out of it.

The Americans were also very concerned with keeping opium smoking to the Chinese, but their motivation was symbolism rather than the convenience of colonial administration. Opium in the bloodstreams of elements of the white lower classes in Chinese dens was too symbolically close to yellow blood in white veins and the pollution of the Anglo-American ascendancy by an underworld. But there was no model for investing drug controls with the requisite magical properties. In the Philippines, the new rulers adopted a combination of the commercial-bureaucratic policing pioneered in Britain by the 1868 Act, and a touch of the simple repression for which various US statutes like that passed against opium smoking by San Francisco in 1875 had set precedents. They taxed opium and banned the dens. Consumption went up, and spread among the Filipinos.

Governor Taft and the Philippine Commission soon came to the conclusion that the Spanish contract system should be restored, but they faced opposition from the missionaries. The latter considered the taking of opium, and the taking of profit from it by the state, to be morally wrong. The Opium Investigation Committee, formed in response to the controversy, recommended a phased prohibition. Sale of opiates for nonmedical purposes to Filipinos was banned, as was, subsequently, its importation for such purposes.

Having imposed a system of control upon its new piece of empire, America now proceeded to set about organizing a global system of narcotics policing. Bishop Brent, the Episcopalian missionary who had been prominent in the opposition to initial US policy on opium in the Philippines, and had sat upon the Opium Investigation Committee, pressed Theodore Roosevelt to embark on this course. The first meeting of the international Opium Commission was held in Shanghai in 1909: Roosevelt hoped his initiative might repair the damage done to Chinese–American relations by a ban enacted in 1887 on the importation of opium into the United States by 'any subject of the Emperor of China'. Importation had continued; but the only traders allowed to practise it were now white. America had one major credibility problem as far as its bid to preside over the world's narcotics policing system was concerned: the disorder in its own house. A national statute banning the importation of opium for smoking by citizens of any state was hastily passed by Congress. Possession of the drug was to be sufficient evidence of importation, unless a defendant could persuade a jury otherwise. The law thus technically punished the act of importing opium, but effectively rendered possession illegal. It brought legal controls to the verge of declaring that *to have* a substance was criminal, and thereby giving a drug the magical property of being forbidden.

The effect was to put the price of smoking opium up, to thin out the dens, and to make cheaper drugs more attractive. White smokers, far less culturally rooted in the dens, soon abandoned opium for morphine and heroin. The Chinese smokers became fewer in number as well, mainly because the Chinese population itself was diminishing. By 1920 there were a mere 50,000 Chinese people in the United States, half the total of thirty years before. One group was able to carry on smoking – the wealthy. People in the entertainment world and their camp-followers continued with the habit if they could afford it, looking down on their poorer fellows who had to make do with cheap pleasures and drugs that came as powders. 'White stuff' was held in contempt.

The third group of opiate users were the morphine addicts; older, of higher social status, and addicted as a result of medical treatment. Around the turn of the century, another class of morphinists had rapidly declined in numbers. These were men unfortunate enough to be of an age for military service at the time of the Civil War, and who had become addicted to the opiates they had originally received to alleviate the pain of their wounds. Many died in the years around 1900, just as opiate use in the *demi-monde* was increasing. While opiate addiction in America meant middle-class ladies and war veterans dependent on morphine, there was no question of opiate drugs being magically invested with wickedness. As drug demography changed during the latter part of the nineteenth century and the early part of the twentieth, the law transformed itself accordingly.

The 1909 Smoking Opium Exclusion Act concentrated together the two most significant factors in drug legislation. It managed to introduce the notion of a forbidden substance as part of an offensive against pollution. By banning the importation of opium, America brought the most fundamental principle of defence against social pollution into operation. The essence of a social entity is what separates it from other social entities, thus bestowing the profoundest significance upon its political border. America decreed that opium was a foreign substance which must not cross the line.[2] It was given the status of a foreign invader.

The horror of Otherness which haunts America has found expression in every field of discourse from Federal law to popular movies. In *Invasion of the Body Snatchers*, the extraterrestrial enemy is last seen being transported down the highway on the back of a truck in its plant-like pod form, as though it were a legitimate consignment of Californian farm produce. Narcotic contraband itself is often concealed in shipments of fruit. In *Rambo*, post-Vietnam fear of the rest of the world grows into a fantasy of taking the fight to the enemy in his lair. In *Red Dawn*, Americans are allowed to be heroes more appropriate to an age in which the resistance fighter and the anti-imperialist guerrilla are on the moral offensive: they take to the hills to resist the Russian, Cuban and Nicaraguan invaders. And in the TV series *Miami Vice*, a multiracial force of police officers defend America's southern peninsular outpost against a constant bombardment of drugs and foreign crime. Sometimes the villains are traitors; foolish yuppies who are drawn into the vice trap through their ill-advised penchant for cocaine, or, more often, business people whose desire for profit

71

puts them among capitalism's renegades. These are the collaborators, but the real enemy is the mêlée in which the superstitious Haitian, the voodoo ritual and the beautiful female assassin from an unnamed left-wing Central American republic can all be brought to an American city. Drugs are the medium through which the unAmerican criminal conspiracies can cross the line. In the real Latin America, the 'war' against drugs puts US soldiers into the heart of the continent, and helps legitimize the presence in Central America of military forces whose purposes range far beyond the objectives of the Drug Enforcement Agency.[3]

In the early years of the century, though, drugs did not yet rouse such fears. Hamilton Wright, one of the US delegates to the Shanghai Commission, understood the need for domestic legislation to assist the deployment of American power via the international legal system. The 1909 Act was not enough, and the Hague Conference was looming. Wright drafted an Antinarcotic Bill whose comprehensive bureaucratic regulations slammed straight into the drug industry's obdurate resistance. He fought dirty. In his official report to the Senate on the Shanghai discussions, he wrote what was effectively a pulp shocker. Cocaine had been taken up around the beginning of the 1890s by black New Orleans dockers, who may have heard about the use of coca leaves by peasants in South America to increase stamina artificially. The workers' drug became popular among black people, and was indeed used recreationally. In Wright's account, it was a detonator for the sexual menace of the negro. White women were now even less safe in their beds.

Naturally, statistics were as important a weapon as racism in Wright's arsenal. His figures, he proclaimed, spoke louder than words. They said that the previous half-century had seen an increase in the importation of opium of 351 per cent, but a population increase of only 133 per cent. However any progressive Senators looking at early twentieth-century trends would have discovered a per capita decline in the consumption of opium for both medical and other purposes. Scientific, journalistic, and even White House authors embraced the Wright ratio as an off-the-peg statistical aid in which accuracy was much less important than the flavour. One historian judged that the figures 'provided the conceptual basis for remedial legislation regarding the problem in the first two decades of the twentieth century'.[4] Wright's work also heralded the new voice in which the new century would be prone to speak of drugs: a very shrill one. He was a pioneer beyond the field of imperialism. His consciously constructed drug hysteria was wasted on Senators and Congressmen, but the popular papers were years behind him.

The Bill itself failed to be passed by Congress, but Wright succeeded in setting up the Hague Conference with the power actually to draft a treaty. This conference eventually convened late in 1911, and had produced an international Convention by the end of the following January. An act basically similar to Wright's ill-fated 1910 proposal was eventually passed in the USA late in 1914. Its passage was induced by the need to comply with the Hague Convention's stipulation that signatory states must control the manufacture and sale of opium, morphine, heroin and cocaine, and ban the consumption of those drugs for nonmedical purposes. The essence of the legislation, known after its Congressional sponsor as the Harrison Narcotic Act, was traditionally bureaucratic, ordaining that sales of narcotics be recorded and that the pharmacists who sold them register with the Internal Revenue Bureau. The first narcotics squads were thus born of the tax authorities.

While the principle had been established that opiates were to be used only for medicinal purposes, it was not clear whether this included all administration of opiates by medical practitioners. Was a doctor who prescribed morphine in order to keep an addict's withdrawal symptoms at bay practising medicine? On the face of it, the prevention of physical malaise was obviously within the physician's brief. But was it right to treat symptoms in a way which perpetuated the underlying condition? If drug dependency was a disease, then it was the doctor's duty to cure it. If it was a vice, the doctor had no business feeding it. This conundrum is still a factor which, along with the class of person with whom the practitioner has to deal, lowers the professional status of the doctor who chooses to work with drug dependents. The issue was argued through several court cases in which the government tried to have

73

maintenance prescription declared illegal. The United States eventually succeeded in this aim in the 1919 action known after the principal defendant as the Webb case. The dependency clinics which had sprung up in response to the mushrooming street opiate culture were run out of business. Voyeuristic tourists were deprived of the spectacle of addicts queuing outside the New York City Clinic. The sightseeing trips and megaphone commentaries could not pursue the dope fiends underground.

New York City was the central zone of the new heroin sub-culture. Firms manufacturing the drug had premises there, conveniently close to the delinquent city dwellers who were bringing the drug directly into their way of life without attaching themselves to any exotic foreign matrix like the opium den. The youthful street gangs with which the city is still identified had been formed, and peer pressure spread the 'decks' of heroin among them. Either through the machismatic urge to find new ways of giving drug-taking the quality of an initiation rite, or for the sake of a more intense sensation, sniffing the drug yielded fairly swiftly to injection. The word 'addiction' came into favour just before the First World War. It remains the name which presides over both authoritative and lay discourse upon the subject, despite more recent attempts to dilute and calm the concept by calling it 'dependency', or simply talking about 'drug abuse'. The dominant colloquial term, which dispenses with any semblance of sympathy or courtesy, was coined in the early 1920s, roughly a decade into the street heroin era. A gang of New York addicts raised cash to support their habits by selling scrap metal they scavenged from junkyards. They became known as 'junkies'.

Whatever their name, they posed problems. What was it that drove them to narcotics? What was to be done with them? And just how many of them were there anyway? More than a million, said Richmond P. Hobson, taking his cue from a highly imaginative Treasury Department report prepared by Andrew DuMez in 1918, a period during which the temperature of the drugs debate was raised in a successful effort to toughen up the Harrison Act. Hobson was a veteran of American boundary rearrangements, a hero of both the Spanish–American War and the temperance

74

campaign. Prohibition left him high and dry, until he discovered the narcotics menace. In his new crusade, he wielded a pseudo-science of his own devising which flaunted a breathtaking familiarity with the neurological basis of morality:

The entire brain is immediately affected when narcotics are taken into the system. The upper cerebral regions, whose more delicate tissues, apparently the most recently developed and containing the shrine of the spirit, all those attributes of the man which raise him above the level of the beast, are at first tremendously stimulated and then – quite soon – destroyed . . . At the same time the tissue of the lower brain, where reside all the selfish instincts and impulses, receive the same powerful stimulation. With the restraining forces of the higher nature gone, the addict feels no compunction whatever in committing any act that will contribute to a perverted supposition of his own comfort and welfare.[5]

Hobson also made extravagant use of the Treasury Department's pseudo-statistics. The Department was privately embarrassed, but could not muster the nerve to denounce its own handiwork. No doubt the scientific community would have been keen for Hobson to share with it his evidence of cerebral lesions resulting from acute exposure to opiates, such data having eluded their accumulated investigations to this day. Contemporary neuroscientists must have envied his untroubled approach to the problem of mind-brain dualism. His effect on the public seems to have been less equivocal. The state, supported by a public opinion constructed with the dubious specification Hobson had obtained in large part from government suppliers, was closing inexorably upon the junkies.

Events in Britain were taking a similar course, but the scale was smaller and the passions less florid. A Liberal government pledged to end the infamous Chinese trade had been elected in 1906, and had reached agreement with China on a phased termination the following year. Britain had finally faced up to this shameful aspect of its imperial history, it was felt, and was perfectly capable of tackling it without being policed by a cabal of rival imperial powers. The United Kingdom was thus a less than enthusiastic participant in the Shanghai Commission. But then a new factor presented itself. Reports from India and the colonies of the Far East indicated a worrying increase in the smuggling of morphine and cocaine. Britain took the opportunity provided by the 1911 Hague Conference to insist that these drugs be internationally controlled. Germany saw in this a potential threat to its pharmaceutical industry, and accordingly insisted that the agreement would only be binding if ratified by all the signatories. These were not moves calculated to speed up the proceedings.

The situation in China was transformed by events outside the Hague Conference jurisdiction. The process started with the Opium War which finally forced the Manchu dynasty to bow out in 1912. The empire next door was waiting, and Japan exerted its leverage upon its massive neighbour mainly through the ancestral home of the outgoing dynasty, Manchuria. Part of the tribute exacted by Japan at the end of the Russo–Japanese War in 1905 was the Port Arthur–Changchun railway. With its ownership came a string of economic and administrative rights in the north-western province. The new nationalist Chinese regime had galvanized the torpid anti-opium policies into life (the British-organized trade was finally brought to an abrupt end in 1913). However China still suffered a foreign-imposed opiate problem which its Japanese adversary deliberately exploited. A British businessman reported to his Consul in 1917 that 'the distribution of morphine was either winked at or encouraged by those in authority as part of the policy for the peaceful penetration of Manchuria by the Japanese'.[6]

Japan was, however, an Allied Power, playing its part in the war effort by seizing German possessions in China and the Far East and building up its military might the while. British concern about opiates was put in its place by a Foreign Office staff officer: 'The prohibition of morphia exports would preclude a considerable number of Japanese from earning their living by poisoning the inhabitants of Manchuria and would add fuel to the fire of Japanese irritation. In fact it seems essentially a question to be postponed until the end of the war.'

Almost all Japan's supplies for this chemical warfare came from Britain. Morphine use had been spreading in China since the

1880s, having been introduced by Westerners offering a cure for opium addiction. By the time the Manchus retired from the scene, Chinese morphine addicts knew what brands they preferred, and the labels were British. An import ban in 1909 brought the familiar rigmaroles of smuggling to China's newer opiate menace.

An explosive increase in British morphine manufacture around 1914 and 1915 hardly seems surprising. But a closer look at the graph shows that the boom started around 1913, and ended with about a year of the Great War still to run. Import figures from Japan indicate that around this time, Japanese demand multiplied to about thirty times the level of a few years earlier. It would appear from an analysis of the figures[7] that British morphine production was governed by demand from the Far East rather than the Western Front. The Japanese were enabling Britain to carry on profiting from Chinese addiction. Pressure from the anti-opium lobby overruled the Foreign Office mandarins, and an end-user certificate system was introduced. Applicants for morphine export licences had to produce Japanese government certificates confirming that the drug was for medical use in Japan or its territories only. The legitimate traffic came to a halt.

Some time in the early years of the century, Arthur Ward and his wife were later to relate, they consulted an ouija board to find out how Mr Ward should earn his living. 'C–H–I–N–A–M–A–N' replied the board obligingly. Scouring Limehouse for relevant information, Ward came to hear about the Chinaman who was to provide the key to his future. 'Mr King', it was rumoured, was involved in gambling and drug rackets. Then Ward set eyes on the mysterious Oriental, whose face 'was the living embodiment of Satan'. Though this gentleman was, as like as not, a perfectly respectable member of the community, he had the distinction of providing a vital seed for the imagination of the writer who would make his name as Sax Rohmer – 'I knew that I had seen Dr Fu-Manchu!'[8] The Doctor made his début in 1913, shortly after his eponymous imperial family had made their exit. *The Mystery of Dr Fu-Manchu* introduced him to a thrilled public:

Imagine a person, tall, lean and feline, high-shouldered, with a brow like Shakespeare and a face like Satan, a close-shaven skull, and long, magnetic eyes of the true cat-green. Invest him with all the cruel cunning of an entire Eastern race, accumulated in one giant intellect, with all the resources of science past and present. Imagine that awful being, and you have a mental picture of Dr Fu-Manchu, the yellow peril incarnate in one man.

The menace was a conspiratorial and organized one. 'I knew that the enormous wealth of the political group backing Dr Fu-Manchu rendered him a menace to Europe and to America greater than that of the plague ... His mission was to remove all obstacles – human obstacles – from the path of that secret movement which was progressing in the Far East.' In a thoughtful digression, Dr Petrie, the narrator, subsequently speculates about the nature of this organization:

> What group can we isolate and label as responsible for the overthrow of the Manchus? The casual student of modern Chinese history will reply: 'Young China'. This is unsatisfactory. What do you mean by Young China? In my own hearing Fu-Manchu had disclaimed, with scorn, association with the whole of that movement; and assuming that the name were not an assumed one, he clearly can have been no anti-Manchu, no Republican.
>
> The Chinese republican is of the mandarin class, but of a new generation which veneers its Confucianism with Western polish. These youthful and unbalanced reformers, in conjunction with older but no less ill-balanced provincial politicians, may be said to represent Young China. Amid such turmoils as this we invariably look for, and invariably find, a Third Party. In my opinion, Dr Fu-Manchu was one of the leaders of such a party.

Such a shadowy and powerful Third Party might have been able to prevent China's descent into political chaos, which by the 1920s had reduced to a shambles attempts to interdict morphine. The period which saw the replacement of one British opiate offensive against China by a more modern variety – morphine, with its dreadful welter of miseries caused by unsterile injections – was the one in which popular writing projected its most lurid visions of the 'great yellow hand ... stretched out over London'. Rohmer sent frissons of excitement through his readers' sensitive European nervous systems with his fantasy of a conspiracy to turn 'the balance which a wise providence had adjusted between the white and yellow races', and 'place, it might be, the whole of Europe and America beneath an Eastern rule'. From among the 'most mysterious and most cunning people in the world' had emerged 'the most ghastly menace to our present civilization which has appeared since Attila the Hun'. Drugs were used by Fu Manchu (he lost his hyphen after the earliest novels) to immobilize individual adversaries in the heat of the chase, and to extend his penetration of the West through its seamy underbelly. They also introduced a flaw into his edifice of power: he himself was a slave to opium. Rohmer's creation was a popular success, and a model for those writers whose feats of inventive imagination could never receive due acknowledgement, owing to the conventions of journalism. In the role-reversing spirit of *Red Dawn*, they described the Chinese drug menace to Britain. In the spirit of *Miami Vice*, they realized a basic principle of popular writing about drugs: a drug story is usually a sex story. The opium dens evolved into 'dancedope dens', where a 'sickening crowd of undersized aliens' preyed on 'pretty, underdressed' young English women.[9]

Sex was fundamental to the affair which led to the enactment of the forerunner of modern British drug legislation. In February 1916, an ex-convict and prostitute were convicted under DORA 40 – Regulation 40 of the Defence of the Realm Act – of supplying cocaine to Canadian troops stationed in Folkestone. Some forty soldiers in the unit were said to be addicted to the drug. The idea that prostitutes might pose threats to the soldiery beyond the traditional moral and medical ones aroused alarm, and provided the press with a new configuration for the sexy drugs story. Drug use among troops was not, however, the automatic headline trigger that it is today. Savory & Moore, the old-established Mayfair retailing chemists, advertised small packets of drugs in *The Times* as a 'useful present for friends at the front'. Police investigations in the West End of London uncovered a thriving market for cocaine among prostitutes on Shaftesbury Avenue and Charing Cross Road. Boxes containing the drug were found on a man detained after being seen to approach women in the area. He was not actually seen selling any of it, though, and the judge therefore ruled that no offence had been committed. There was nothing unlawful about simply possessing cocaine. The law had been more successful when, in 1913, no less an institution than Harrods had been fined for breaching the regulations on sales of cocaine and morphia.[10]

DORA 40 made it an offence to threaten the defence of the realm by getting soldiers intoxicated – the actual intoxicant was not specified. The prohibition was made more explicit by the enactment of DORA 40B, which forbade the supply of narcotic drugs (among which cocaine was included) to any member of the armed forces, except by pharmacists dispensing doctors' prescriptions. Meanwhile, larger drug issues remained unaddressed. It had transpired that much of the smuggling in the eastern parts of the Empire that had prompted the British to take a more active part in the Hague Conferences was, in fact, organized and supplied from Britain itself. The United Kingdom had yet to produce the domestic legislation to which the Hague Convention had bound it.

Just as America had passed a crude statute with an international gathering in mind, and supplanted it later with a fuller package of legislation, Britain put together a makeshift package with what was at hand. On 28 July 1916, an order-in-council extended DORA 40B to civilians. Its main target was cocaine, which was henceforth to be available on a doctor's prescription only. Possession of the drug without such authorization was declared illegal.[11] Smoking opium was also banned, and medicinal opium subjected to the same restrictions as cocaine. The pharmaceutical profession was cool in its reaction; the medical profession, granted new powers over narcotic drugs, welcomed the measure.

Victory in 1918 meant peace, and the expiry of DORA. It also apparently precipitated the demise of Billie Carleton, a twenty-two-year-old actress, who was found dead after attending a Victory Ball at the Albert Hall. A cocaine overdose was thought to be responsible, though this was never proved. Suspicion, and a considerable amount of attention from hyperventilating popular press, focused upon Reginald de Veulle, a dress designer with a questionable background and an unquestionably foreign name. Testimony at the inquest told of how the pair, who were rumoured to be linked by both carnal and narcotic vice, would pass nights at parties where the guests gathered to smoke opium, dressed as if for bed. Such luxurious pyjama parties also feature in contemporary accounts of transatlantic fast living; the tabloids' pulses raced then as much as they do today for the equivalent accounts of hedonism behind closed doors.

The Carleton case provided a focus around which the press could construct a formation that described narcotics and the world in which they were to be found. This world turned on an axis that ran between Limehouse and the West End, linking foreignness with an indigenous *demi-monde* deeply implicated in immorality and criminality. This story hung on a framework of titillation, exciting the readers with glimpses of a way of life that was attractive, immoral and demonstrated to be self-destructive. In other words, it was the standard self-contained, non-subversive sensational press story of which the twentieth-century tabloid is made. As such stories are wont, it carried in its train a string of ideas that made drugs what they were. In 1918 they were still vicious. Opium addiction was beginning to be spoken of in superlatives, bestowing upon the newly illegal drugs a senior rank in the hierarchy of social evil. According to the *Daily Express*, it was 'perhaps the most expensive of vices', beside which 'moral forces and even family ties count as nothing.' The *Daily Mail*, perched uncomfortably between ancient and modern concepts of morality and psychiatry, described the habit as 'a vice of the neurotic, not a habit of the normal'.[12]

The idea that drug addiction was the result of a meeting between a chemical and a flawed constitution was reasserting itself in a modified guise. The old theories of degeneration and neurasthenia had fallen into disuse. 'Moral insanity' made a comeback, combined with a more recent innovation of German origin called *psychopathische Persönlichkeit*. Just what constituted the concept that became known as the 'psychopathic personality' remained vague, but the phenomenon seemed particularly prevalent on the fringes of respectable society and beyond.

The psychopathy school of thought was competing with a body of theory which considered drug dependency to be simply a physical disorder. In America, Ernest S. Bishop hypothesized that addiction was a disorder of the immune system. The invasion of the body by morphine caused the organism to produce antitoxins, just as it would in response to intruding microbes. These antitoxins would, however, inconveniently become toxic themselves in the absence of morphine, causing withdrawal symptoms and the need to take more of the drug. George Pettey, working on similar lines, suggested that opiates stimulated the intestine to secrete poisons which it then took increased doses of opiates to neutralize. Either way, drug dependency was a somatic calamity rather than a psychological one.

This did not lead the physical theoreticians to a tolerant view of delinquent addiction. They restricted their brief to the physical core of medicine, and delegated the response to the associated disciplines of morality, psychiatry and the law. The American Public Health Association's 1920 report of the Committee on Habit Forming Drugs, to which Bishop contributed, concluded that 'vicious, degenerate and criminal types should be handled on a basis of vice, degeneracy or criminality and treated for their addiction-disease in places suitable to their personal or class characteristics.' Bishop considered delinquent drug dependency to be 'a job for underworld control, and not for medical handling at all'. More important to Bishop and his colleagues were the 'genuine' addicts, who were like the previous century's class of 'deserving poor' – except that the medically addicted morphinist to whose benefit such a categorization worked was unlikely to be of the same class as the vicious, criminal and degenerate types who spoiled things for the reputable unfortunates. Some practitioners were inclined to label classes by the drugs they preferred. 'The morphinist has guts, while the heroinist has only bowels,' remarked one.

The psychopathy camp saw things the other way round. The wicked were the true addicts, and the blameless patients were anomalies which clouded a vivid concept. As nature and enlightened medical practice reduced the number of 'iatrogenic' addicts – those whose condition was the result of medical treatment – and opiate use spread within the criminal classes, the balance of numbers within the addict population shifted towards the undesirables. So, therefore, did the relative quantities of empirical data presenting themselves to the theorists. During the 1920s and

1930s, psychopathy theories of addiction won out over the physicalist ideas which had arisen earlier. That did not render such ideas extinct, however:

> When biochemical abnormalities are discovered in addicts (as I am sure they will be someday), a new era of clinical research will open. Will these abnormalities appear in all persons exposed to narcotics, or only in some? Can they be replicated in animals? Can treatment restore the change to normal? Can addiction be considered a metabolic disorder, like diabetes, and its progress followed with a chemical index? These are exciting questions, and are the ones that investigators will be asking in the future.[13]

The author was Dr Vincent Dole, writing in 1978. Archaic ideas thus survive in scientific discourses on drug dependency, as well as in popular ones.

The man who drew the map of pathological psychology among drug addicts was Lawrence Kolb, a psychiatrist. In 1923, he concluded from his surveys that addicts fell into six classes. One of these consisted of normal people addicted by medical accident. The others were examples of 'psychopathic diathesis', ranging from the irresponsible to the criminal. There were the carefree pleasure-seekers, the crystallized neurotics, the habitual criminals, and there were the inebriates. Kolb thought that psychopaths might crave the relief from feelings of inadequacy which narcotics afforded; as though, despite their moral blindness, these deviants were intuitively aware of their objectively inferior condition. But the essential element in their disorder was the way that they felt pleasure when they took narcotics. Normal people only experienced relief from pain. To derive pleasure from drugs was no longer immoral: it was scientifically abnormal.

Kolb's conceptual policing, operating as it did within only one domain of ideas, was more comprehensive and coherent than Bishop's. He even took the fight to the physical theorists' own ground, conducting experiments (in collaboration with Andrew DuMez) in which serum from human addicts was injected into white mice. It did not render the animals less susceptible to opiate overdoses: the antitoxin theory was dealt a powerful empirical blow. On the question of what actually to do with addicts, Kolb's views were liberal. He felt that they should be 'supervised rather than repressed'. When he arrived at Lexington Hospital, the first national centre for drug dependants, he was dismayed to find that the architect had derived his ideas from the penal domain: it was designed like a prison. Kolb did what he could to house the inmates outside the cell blocks.

He also stood against the swelling current of opinion which favoured the compulsory detention of addicts. One interdisciplinary-minded professional who was prepared to take the language of medicine into the territory of the prison was Dr S. Adolphus Knopf. While granting that 'higher types of unfortunates' might be cured, he held that 'chronic criminals and chronic narcotic addicts . . . should be chronically confined where they can no longer be a menace to society'. Those less qualified to bandy medical jargon around felt no inhibition about doing so. In a tract written to whip up support for moves to establish farms on which addicts would be concentrated, Winifred Black argued that 'a dope addict is a disease-carrier – and the disease he carries is worse than smallpox, and more terrible than leprosy. Why not isolate him, as you would a leper?' Her pamphlet, which had the backing of publisher William Randolph Hearst, was entitled *Dope: The Story Of The Living Dead*. In other quarters, actual death was being propounded as the final solution to the junkie problem. Against this were raised the voices of Dr and Mrs Curtiss, founders of the Order of Christian Mystics. The policy would be harmful, because 'we simply send them out into the astral world where they can prey upon humanity, ten, a hundred, yes a thousand times more viciously than if they were set free while still in the flesh.'

The popular press notwithstanding, Britain was dull by comparison to America. The illicit use of drugs was highly restricted. It became more so after the passage in 1920 of the Dangerous Drugs Act (DDA), which was essentially DORA 40B elaborated. A flurry of prosecutions ensued in the first few years of its operation, and then settled down to a few per year. Medical support for the measures turned to indignant opposition when an amendment proposed in 1923 attempted to ban doctors from prescribing themselves narcotics. The suggestion that the scale of medical corruption was such that legal action was necessary was taken as an insult. The proposed amendment was duly withdrawn.

Drugs were the responsibility of the Home Office, which, under Sir Malcolm Delevingne, had seen off the new Ministry of Health's bid to take control of the issue. Both Delevingne and the government had an international perspective, though. Britain was bound by an article inserted into the Versailles settlement at its own insistence to implement the pre-war Hague decisions. The Foreign Office was relaying international pressure, generally of American origin, for harsher legislation that the domestic situation hardly seemed to merit. Delevingne had a vision of the issue that readers of the Fu Manchu thrillers would appreciate. He allowed a universal quality to some opiates: while considering many forms of drug-taking to be attractive to particular races and unattractive to others, he thought dependency on morphine, heroin and cocaine to be 'universal forms of addiction'. And he had a modern sense of demonology: 'It has often been remarked that drug addicts – at any rate those of the vicious type – seek to make converts (or perverts) of others, and it is common enough, I suppose, in the experience of the authorities of most Western countries to find groups or coteries of persons – usually of the degenerate type – where the practice prevails. In this way the habit easily tends to spread from country to country. The most potent cause of all, however, has been the propagation of the habit by drug traffickers for the purposes of gain . . .'[14]

Under Delevingne, the Home Office was inclined to a penal policy along American lines. The Ministry of Health had different interests to consider. Illegal drug-taking in the pursuit of pleasure was basically confined to two groups. Opium smoking was the almost exclusive preserve of the Chinese. The white hedonist fringe was after cocaine. There was little apparent interest in heroin, though the drug was not unknown. The opiate question thus revolved around the respectable medical morphine addicts. While the DDA had dealt effectively with the groups deemed to merit only judicial handling, it left the issue of the maintenance prescription unresolved. It also left a loophole through which 'degenerate' users could obtain controlled drugs legally: the rogue doctor.

After the 1923 defeat of the amendment, Delevingne tried to tidy up the legislation with Health Ministry assistance. This department was unenthusiastic about limiting the medical professionals' right to prescribe. The conflict was resolved in classic fashion, by appointing a committee. Officially entitled the Departmental Committee on Morphine and Heroin Addiction, it came to be known by the name of its chairman, Sir Humphry Rolleston. It was loaded with representatives of medical interests, and the evidence it heard came in large measure from doctors. Heroin received an emphatic endorsement when the Committee addressed a League of Nations inquiry as to whether it could be banned without removing an essential drug from the pharmacopoeia. British doctors were unimpressed by the American witch-hunt that had led Congress, acting with an eye to setting an international example, to pass legislation in 1924 intended to expunge all traces of heroin from American blood and soil. They decided against banning it.

When it published its findings in 1926, the Rolleston Committee shaped British attitudes to opiate addiction that have persisted into the latter part of the century. It pronounced that 'the condition must be regarded as a manifestation of disease, and not a mere form of vicious indulgence. In other words, the drug is taken not for the purpose of obtaining positive pleasure, but in order to relieve a morbid and overpowering craving.'

Notes

1 Report of the committee appointed by the Philippine
  Commission to investigate the use of opium and the traffic
  therein (Government Printing Office, Washington, DC, 1906),
  pp. 28–9.
2 See Mary Douglas, *Purity & Danger* (London, Ark, 1984).
  Douglas discusses the definition of pollution as matter which is
  in the wrong place. Thus mud in a field is not pollution, but
  becomes so when it is trailed into the house on a pair of boots.
  Heroin in a hospital (where it is usually labelled diamorphine) is
  in its proper place, but it becomes pollution when it is illicitly
  taken across the hospital's boundaries into the outside world.
  Douglas distinguishes four kinds of social pollution:'The first is

danger pressing on external boundaries; the second is danger from transgressing the internal lines of the system; the third, danger in the margins of the lines; the fourth is danger from internal contradiction, when some of the basic postulates are denied by other basic postulates, so that at certain points the system seems to be at war with itself.' (p. 122) The phenomenon of drug smuggling illustrates the first variety, while the distinction between medical and nonmedical use around which the example above turns would seem to be a case of the second.

3   In July 1986, US troops, transported in Black Hawk helicopters, participated along with local forces in raids on cocaine-processing laboratories in north-eastern Bolivia. The Americans were deployed from the Panama base which previously attracted attention for its role in President Reagan's campaign against Nicaragua. (See *Guardian*, 17 July 1986.)

4   Arnold H. Taylor, quoted in Courtwright, *Dark Paradise*, p. 30. The account of American drug policy in this text relies very heavily on Courtwright's work.

5   In J. Epstein, *Agency of Fear* (New York, G. P. Puttnam & Sons, 1977); quoted by Tony Borzoni in his unpublished 1984 Cambridge M.Phil. thesis, *The Mythology of Heroin and the Press*.

6   See Parssinen, *Secret Passions, Secret Remedies*, p. 150. The subsequent quotation appears on p. 151. This work plays a similar role to Courtwright's for the material on Britain in this chapter.

7   Such an analysis is to be found in Parssinen, *Secret Passions, Secret Remedies*, ch. 10.

8   See D. J. Enright's Introduction to *The Mystery of Dr Fu Manchu* (London, J. M. Dent, 1985).

9   See Parssinen, *Secret Passions, Secret Remedies*, p. 168.

10 Virginia Berridge, 'Drugs and Social Policy: The Establishment of Drug Control in Britain, 1900–1930', *British Journal Of Addiction* (Centenary Edition) 79 (1984), pp. 17–29.

11 Virginia Berridge, 'War Conditions and Narcotics Control: The Passing of Defence of the Realm Act Regulation 40B', *Journal of Social Policy* 7 (July 1978), pp. 285–304.

12 Berridge, reviewing Parssinen in *Medical History* 29, pp. 210–17. The *Daily Express* quotation was originally published on 9 December 1918, and that from the *Daily Mail* on 12 December 1918.

13 Berridge, *Opium and the People*, p. 246. The example is given in the final chapter in which present-day drug issues are compared

with the nineteenth-century ones with which the bulk of the book is concerned.

14   The 15th Norman Kerr Memorial Lecture: 'Some International Aspects of the Problem of Drug Addiction', *British Journal of Inebriety* 32 (3) (January 1935), pp. 125–51.

SIX

The Post-War Boom

A Number 15 bus took me to Paddington Station. I walked along Praed Street, then down several side turnings. I soon found the right road. It was narrow, and dirty, and decayed. At the corner a man in an off-white jacket was selling ices from a barrow. He asked me for a light and I noticed his dirty hands . . .

It was Sunday afternoon. A hot afternoon that made you want to be anywhere in the world but in a Paddington backwash. Everyone was sleeping, or reading at open windows, or leaving home for the park. Everyone, that is, but the kids playing on dark area steps . . . and the drunk lurching homewards swearing to himself . . . and a man called Raymond Thorp waiting for me in one of the houses that stretched depressingly into the distance.

I counted the numbers to the right house. It was quieter at this end of the street. Just a radio crackling from an open first-floor window, and a baby crying somewhere in the shadows. A woman sat on the steps reading the *News of the World*. She looked up and smiled. 'It's hot. Really hot.'

'Yes,' I said. 'It's real hot.'

There were six bell pushes on the door jamb. Two of them had fading name tags. The others were blank.

I pressed the one marked 'Housekeeper'. Far off I could hear a train whistling its way from the station. I pressed the bell again. The third time I tried a woman came to the door. 'Mr Thorp?' I asked. She wiped sticky hands down her skirt. 'Room 3, first landing. But 'e won't answer the door. A rum 'un that bloke. Be glad when e's gorn.'

There was no carpet on the stairs. They groaned at each step. Halfway up I became conscious of the smell. It was stale and vegetable. And it was hot. Outside room 3 I knocked on the door with my knuckles. Then louder . . . and louder. There was no reply. Gently I tried the handle. It turned and I stepped into the room.

It was like a thousand other Paddington bedsitters. A wardrobe of sorts, a bed, a chest of drawers, and a yellowed mirror. The room smelt. But at least it was cool. The curtains were drawn against the sun. An insect of some kind buzzed leisurely above my head – and a man lay outstretched on the bed staring at the ceiling. He turned his head to look at me. An empty, almost stupid look. He seemed to be about thirty.

'You're the writer, aren't you?' he said. 'Sit down.' His voice was high and trembling. I sat on the edge of the bed and lit a cigarette. 'Bunny sent me. He says you want to write your story. He says you want it all on paper.'

The tone of the story is firmly set by that introduction. *Viper: The Confessions of a Drug Addict* purport to be Raymond Thorp's own story, but they bear the indelible stamp of newspapers like the *News of the World*, from which ghost-writer Derek Agnew is at pains to dissociate himself. Despite brackets provided by an introduction and an afterword with Agnew's own signature on it, it is difficult to read *Viper* as anything other than a disreputable fictional cousin of something by Colin MacInnes.

Viper opens with Agnew tracking twenty-four-year-old Raymond Thorp down in the bedsit badlands of Paddington. Agnew's gift for making the most mundane details of inner-city scenes seem redolent of unimaginable squalor marks him out as a fine specimen of the breed of metropolitan-colonial hack whose work nowadays regularly portrays 'black' districts for readers in leafier zones. It stands him in good stead when it comes to redrawing Thorp's map of Soho and the jazz scene in the austerity years after the Second World War.

Thorp's world starts with an axis; not the old West End – Limehouse one, but a more mundane commuting run between the centre of town and some anonymous suburb south of the river. Of lower middle-class origins, he gets a job befitting his station, as a junior clerk. It is 1948, and he is seventeen. He comes to life in between knocking-off time and the late train home, hanging around in a Soho basement listening to jazz. There are strange sights –

'coloured' GIs, women dressed from head to toe in black – and the strange smell of cannabis. Peer pressure, above all in the form of the boy's self-image, and the fear of being a suburban 'square', nudges him past his fears into a flirtation with the exotic substance. Thorp is in on the absolute beginnings of the modern British drug culture.

It is easy to forget that this is not explicitly a work of fiction, and it comes as an exciting surprise to find Thorp in real places like Feldman's jazz club, still on Oxford Street today, trading as the 100 Club. This is only a passing phase for Thorp, though, for he hears from a 'young Negro' about a place where the music 'really gets the joint a' jumping'. 'Within weeks everyone was discussing the new club. At Feldman's people who had been to the Club Eleven were pointed out to you. Whispers went around that it had all the atmosphere of Basin Street and Dixieland days. But few among us seemed prepared to make the jump from Oxford Street to Soho. Because there were other whispers, ugly whispers . . .'

In his biography of club proprietor and sax player Ronnie Scott,[2] John Fordham describes the foreign vision that held Club Eleven's habituées in thrall. The Windmill Street basement was a crucible for the new 'bebop' style of jazz, a sound for those whose dissent was expressed in a way of life rather than articulated by an ideology. Behind its doors could be found styles of behaviour and dress which must have seemed especially bizarre and provocative compared to the post-war austerity outside. Partisans of the 'trad' jazz style, mustering in the genteel regions of the south-east, derided the hipsters, 'fruit-salad' ties and all. Club Eleven was colourful: the most significant colours, however, were those of the people themselves.

Government reports to the United Nations on drugs in the first few years after the war smack of that quality which the English conceive of as modesty and with hindsight might well regard as complacency. The drug problem was divided between two groups: the medical profession, from whose ranks came a quarter of registered addicts, and the 'alien' populations of big cities. The authorities were satisfied that narcotic use was contained by the professional and ethnic boundaries surrounding these groups.

Among the 'aliens', pockets of opium use were still reported among the Chinese. This was not the only alien drug scene, though. Indian hemp – cannabis – was now being smoked by the newer arrivals from the West Indies and Africa.[3]

Fordham identifies wartime London as the incubator for the embryonic jazz subculture. The music was played in Soho shebeens which attracted black American servicemen, and Britishers who found palliatives for the bombing in a more exotic range of preparations than were to be found in the public houses. Cannabis was one of these. The recently developed amphetamines were also popular, as were other drugs which approximated their stimulant effect. The shebeens evolved into more conventional clubs revolving around jazz. These were the latest incarnation of an underground matrix where races mixed, and drugs spread into white majority society through its treacherous margins.

Drug use was a silent or coded phenomenon even before the clubs began to be targeted as centres of vice. Thorp recounts how graduation from Feldmans's to Club Eleven opened his eyes: 'These were *professional* layabouts as distinct from the kids from the suburbs who went to Oxford Street. I found that spades and musicians I had known for months were regular hemp smokers, some of them even injecting or sniffing cocaine or heroin. Now that I knew this I could understand the references I heard to "tea" – the slang term for a hemp cigarette then in use.' When his involvement with what subsequently becomes known as 'charge' grows to the point of dealing in it, Thorp starts to mix with black people outside the jazz dives. His first port of call is a pub near Warren Street tube station, 'a meeting place for many of London's coloured drug addicts'. 'A number wore coloured shirts outside their trousers. Others, elaborately tailored drape suits with broad rimmed hats and startling ties. I felt at home among these people. Their loud voices and unexpected outbursts of childish pleasure worried a lot of folk. But those I had met around the jazz clubs I found kindly, simple, and anxious to please.'

The complacent voice of mid-fifties English racism acquires a different tone when Thorp hits the Dorian Gray trail eastwards to buy hashish. 'We had to go straight away, so go straight away we did, bumping down the Mile End Road, further and further East, in his springless pre-war car. We left the car a few roads from Cable Street – it was risking it to take it right into the area. The spades down East were so poverty-stricken they were likely to take the tyres if they couldn't take the whole vehicle. We went to Cable Street and found the right number. Spade women, fat and ugly, leant out of windows and stared down curiously at us . . . Although I felt at home with the spades up West they seemed to be bred differently in the East End. I didn't like the glances we were getting from men sitting in their shirt sleeves on doorsteps or standing in little groups without talking.'

The scene is cool at first. 'Although there were occasional articles in the press about the growth of drug addiction in post-war London, the law never seemed to take it seriously.' For a while the Soho 'vipers' – cannabis smokers – amuse themselves bothering rookie policemen for lights. The smell is still unfamiliar. But the viper's downhill slide is inexorable. He meets a junkie who, in Ancient Mariner fashion, detains him with a monologue upon the degradation of the needle. And the police are beginning to close in. Club Eleven itself was fingered as a hemp marketplace when a ship's steward was arrested in possession of the drug at Southampton. Detective-Sergeant George Lyle, addressing a meeting of the Society for the Study of Addiction later that year, confirmed the pariah status that already attached to drug users even among the criminal classes. 'We often get information about drugs from people who would not normally tell us the state of the weather if asked, such as thieves and prostitutes,' he told his attentive audience.[4]

Lyle gets a walk-on part in *The Confessions*. Thorp has let his viper's tongue wag at work. In due course, two men call to see him: 'Big men with calm, self-assured faces. The sort of men you like to have on your side . . . Their faces were kind, but their eyes were hard and questioning . . .' After being charged and bailed at Marylebone Magistrate's Court, Thorp heads for Club Eleven and a smoke. He is told of the events of 15 April 1950.[5] Thorp's arresting officers, Lyle and Carpenter, had been among the vice-squad force who raided the joint. The official account describes how the squad found between 200 and 250 people on the premises at 50 Carnaby Street, to which the club had moved a few days before. The crowd was mixed in sex and race; most of the individuals were aged between seventeen and thirty. All but one of the eleven men arrested were white. Ten were charged with possessing hemp, and two were also caught in possession of cocaine. Three of the accused were American seamen. Many others jettisoned the goods in time. ' "There must have been a small fortune lying around the floor. A lot of cats were arrested and the cloakroom was full of unwanted coats, pockets bulging with hemp. But here's the real giggle. Someone had unloaded a slab of hashish on a shelf in the kitchen. The law picked it up and looked at it but thought it must be some kind of meat extract. So the man got his hash back." ' Ronnie Scott was less fortunate. Playing a Charlie Parker tune with his eyes shut, he received a rude shock on opening them to find his field of vision almost blocked by a large uniformed sergeant. He had to leave it to the law to remove the cocaine from his wallet. From the floor the officers collected twenty-three packets of hemp, one of cocaine, and some hemp cigarettes. They also found a small amount of opium and an empty morphine ampoule. The Government duly reported this notable occasion to the United Nations.[6]

The law does not deter Thorp from his career in degradation, and his friend Jed's terminal junkie testimony does not dissuade him from the first injection. Needle aversion and nausea give way to a high. 'After this the charge could never be the same again.' However, the charge remains the biggest monkey on his back. He muses with curiosity about how 'spades' seem to be able to smoke it 'with none of the suffering that the white cats endure'. The idea of racial drug immunity recalls the theories of a bygone age about whites being more susceptible than blacks to opiate addiction because of their more 'delicate nervous organization'.

The Soho scene deteriorates along with the viper. At last, he realizes he wants to die. He goes straight out into the street and wanders the city, 'seeing nothing, hearing nothing'. 'Then I got my bearings. I was in Praed Street. In Paddington, shuffling along that depressing dirty street. I went into a chemist's. With the last piece

94

of silver I had in the world I bought two bottles of aspirin tablets. They'd got the answer. Then I walked into Paddington Station, down the sloping drive into the station and along past the platforms. I found a water tap and a luggage trolley and I sat down and I got ready to die.'

He changes his mind. He leaves the terminus and wanders out. On passing a church, he pauses to con the parson, but stays to talk instead . . .

Agnew completes the account. The reader will be glad to know that Thorp has kicked cocaine and heroin on his own, and with medical treatment may beat the hemp. Interestingly, the most melodramatic passages in the book are the descriptions of needle-using 'white drug' addicts. They are portrayed, authentically enough, as the addicts most physically and mentally ravaged by their habit. Yet cannabis is continually thrust to the foreground. The devastation it causes seems to be moral, rather than medical. Although the text illustrates the idea of progression from cannabis to heroin, the idea of 'soft' drugs which are dangerous because they lead to 'hard' ones is absent. Cannabis is presented as a serious menace on its own. Is this simply sensationalism, or plain ignorance? Almost the very last of Agnew's afterwords suggests a different explanation:

> Let's face another unpalatable factor, too. That like it or not it is the black races who are responsible for the post-war spread of hemp smoking in Britain. The men who hold this view are not anti-colour. They are not conducting a witch-hunt against West Africans and Africans (*sic*). They are stating a simple fact. Thousands of these immigrants are pouring into Britain every year. A majority of them smoke hemp. They do not leave their vice at home – they bring it with them. And the blunt truth is that numbers of them take perverted satisfaction from 'lighting up' a white girl. I know. I have watched it happen. And it is a horrible sight!
>
> We cannot stop them entering Britain. We can at least put them out of society's way for a long, long time, once they have been convicted of drug offences. The law must be strengthened all round. Until it is, we are fighting a tiger with a bamboo cane.

To put it another way, we can't stop blacks coming over here, but we can use the drug laws to criminalize them, lock them up and keep them out of our society. Prophetic words. *Viper* is less a drug text than that of a society alarmed about racial pollution, and the consequent eruption of deviant subcultures; the drug that dissolves barriers between the races is the one that instils the most terror. The objective, individual misery of heroin or cocaine addiction is a side-issue. That can be beaten on its own, *Viper* allows. But the race-mixing will take more than medical treatment.[7]

In the late 1930s, the police had been able to pinpoint the heroin subculture within a small group of Londoners who tended to be of 'good social standing'. Three principal figures with continental connections were identified. Home Office Drug Branch officials in the early fifties were likewise on virtually first-name terms with the objects of their surveillance. One of these was Kevin Saunders, who worked as a porter at All Saints' Hospital, Chatham, from which 3,120 heroin tablets, 5 ounces of morphine and 2 ounces of cocaine were stolen in April 1951. The crackdown on the jazz clubs was said to have caused a cannabis shortage, and the diverted medical supplies filled the gap. About a dozen new addicts who became known to the Home Office were thought to have been introduced to opiates by Saunders, who was known to his customers in Soho as 'Mark'. The Drugs Branch compiled a dossier of individuals known to them within the circles in which 'Mark' moved. Ten of the original twenty-six listed were dead by the time Bing Spear published his follow-up study in 1969. Seven of these were addicted at the time of their deaths, three actually dying of heroin overdoses. Two of the survivors were also addicted, though one would have undergone enforced detoxification on imprisonment in 1967.[8]

Twelve of the group were classified as musicians. One contemporary doctor went so far as to claim that 'the addicts we have in this country ... are nearly all instrumentalists in jazz bands'. He observed that 'Nearly all these addicts I see are unstable people, many of them psychopathic, but many psychopaths and unstable people are not yet drug addicts, and pedlars are quite adept at seeing the potential psychopaths who could become future customers.' The pedlars, however, were addicts selling drugs to support their habit, rather than the professional pushers of tabloid mythology.[9]

In 1954, the Home Office began to record heroin addicts as a separate category within the addiction statistics. There were fifty-seven of them. Among the new additions to the next year's tally was a twenty-one-year-old man who had assured himself of a minor footnote in the annals of British drug culture three years earlier by becoming the first teenager to be caught in possession of hemp. His career was a paradigm for the school of thought that regards cannabis as an induction course for heroin addiction: he was still dependent on the latter when he died in 1965.

During the mid-fifties, heroin was a side-issue. Thanks to the 'British system' established by Rolleston, it had remained in medical use, and had thus avoided the magical properties acquired by being declared anathema. From the commendations it received in the *British Journal of Addiction*, one would be more likely to get the impression that heroin was the toast of the medical profession rather than its deadly foe. The testimonials were prompted by government moves to bow to American pressure (articulated through the World Health Organization) to ban heroin completely. Doctors leapt to its defence, insisting, as had their predecessors in the 1920s, that heroin had unique properties which made it superior to other opiates in certain circumstances. Dr Arthur Douthwaite praised its 'stimulant' effects, and the way in which 'it is possible, therefore, to have pain controlled by heroin and yet carry out intellectual pursuits which may be important to somebody, even if he is doomed to die.' Though Douthwaite may have been using the word 'intellectual' in a broad, scientific sense, the turn of phrase perhaps indicates the class of terminal patient that he had in mind. He also recommended it as a substitute cough suppressant for patients upon whom codeine was ineffective, and argued that illicit drug use was a quite separate matter. 'It does not come from doctors but from Marseilles and the Middle East. No Government ban here can possibly prevent its importation and distribution. It is a social problem. People become addicts because of the social conditions under which they live.'

In another contribution to the debate, a surgeon pointed out the differing standards that applied to opiate-using members of differing social groups. 'How many women would you find in Oxford Street or in High Street, Geneva, without a box or bottle of Veganin or codeine tablets in their handbags?' he asked. 'I think you would find far more than those addicted to heroin. Consider chlorodyne. A four-ounce bottle of chlorodyne for 3s. 9d. contains a third of a grain of morphine, equal to several doses of heroin in its effect, and there are women in towns and country who drink a bottle of chlorodyne a day and nobody says anything about them.'[10]

British medical opinion found plenty to disagree with in the work of the WHO. The *British Journal of Addiction* gave a very tart review to a WHO document on addiction which laid heavy emphasis on the disease model.[11] The Sixth World Health Assembly had argued in 1953 that heroin was not irreplaceable in medical practice, and that a ban would combat illicit use. In Britain, heroin was considered to have particular advantages over morphine in the control of chronic pain, and it was felt that a ban would encourage the growth of a black market for illegally manufactured supplies. Moreover, a ban would violate the British doctor's prescription rights. Marshall Aid, NATO and America's global thermonuclear status were one thing. The status of British doctors was another. The Special Relationship may have secured British compliance to American wishes for over forty years, but even the United States could not beat the collective will of the British medical profession. The plans to ban heroin were scrapped.

One significant group seemed to be vanishing from the addict population. The blameless victims of medical misfortune, who had helped preserve an acceptable face for drug dependency, were a dwindling band. Ellis Stungo, a psychiatrist, discounted this form of addiction altogether. 'It is common knowledge and experience,' he averred,

> that heroin can be discontinued without serious difficulty once the painful condition for which it has been administered has cleared up. The only exceptions tend to occur in cases of medical men and dentists who, of course, under existing regulations, can readily obtain supplies of the drug.

Cases of addiction arise almost exclusively from the illegitimate use of heroin by sensation-seeking psychopaths, hysterics in search of happiness and solace, and other unstable characters, for strictly non-therapeutic purposes.[12]

It is possible that Stungo considered that the medical men and dentists with discontinuation difficulties were psychopaths or hysterics who had slipped past the profession's exhaustive selection procedures. But the separation by paragraph and tone of the medical domain and the illegitimate one suggests that he does not bracket the medics with the sensation-seekers; and that he would agree that if physicians prescribed drugs to provide hysterics with solace, this would be a legitimate therapeutic practice. He links two often-opposed concepts of the origins of addiction. There is the view that the mentally unstable are drawn to narcotics as if predestined to do so. The other is that availability causes addiction. It is an opinion which brings together such superficially disparate figures as Sir Malcolm Delevingne and that arch-collaborator from the drug underworld, the frustrated pathologist William Burroughs. The former declared in 1935 that 'drug addiction is, at bottom, a matter of drug supply.'[13] 'Addiction is an illness of exposure,' said the latter thirty-odd years later. 'By and large those who have access to junk become addicts . . . There is no pre-addict personality any more than there is a pre-malarial personality, all the hogwash of psychiatry to the contrary.'[14]

Whatever the cause, heroin use increased steadily. Seven new heroin addicts were notified to the Home Office in 1957, and another eleven in 1958. Another committee was clearly required. The Interdepartmental Committee on Drug Addiction was convened by the Ministry of Health in 1958, to update Rolleston. In the chair was the neurologist Sir Russell Brain, who acquired the ultimate personalized style of address for one of his vocation when he was awarded a peerage and became Lord Brain. The Committee's first report, published in 1961, reaffirmed Rolleston, saying that addiction was 'an expression of mental disorder rather than a form of criminal behaviour'. The Rolleston system worked when given a small, socially conformist addict population. With effective law enforcement applied to a small underworld scene to reduce drug-taking among the undesirables, maintaining and treating a few hundred co-operative patients caused little trouble. It also allowed doctors to take care of their own, concealing the embarrassingly high proportion of drug-takers from the medical profession in its own collective bosom. But with the growth of the drug subculture in the fifties and sixties, and the cultural gap that widened between generations, the system began to fail. A mere forty-seven of the total number of addicts – not just heroin addicts – known to the Home Office in 1959, owed their habits to illegitimate sources. By 1964, 329 out of 753 fell into this category. Only 15 of the 342 heroin dependents were medically addicted. In the early sixties, the numbers were roughly doubling every two years. Those mesmerized by threats of thousands of addicts in the 1980s heroin panic might reflect that, at early-sixties rates, one million new addicts would have been notified in 1984.[15]

The system broke down in large part because of a few maverick doctors – and the publicity they attracted. The eccentric Lady Isabella Frankau genuinely believed that she was preventing the development of a black market, never realizing that she was its main supplier. She treated her patients with mixture of imperiousness and generosity. One of her patients, Barry Ellis, appeared in a 1984 television documentary fondly reminiscing about the old private prescription system. He might well do so: Lady Frankau once gave him a car. Her generosity, however, was not restricted to providing her patients with personal mobility. In 1962, she prescribed some six kilograms of heroin. On one occasion, she prescribed nine grams to one patient, who got another six grams from her three days later 'to replace pills lost in an accident'. 'Your problem, gentlemen, can be summed up in two words – Lady Frankau,' Lord Brain told the men from the Home Office.[16]

A woman who was still attending a drug treatment clinic in the late 1970s described how she made her way to Lady Frankau's Wimpole Street practice seeking psychiatric help, on the recommendation of friends: 'So I went in and she said, "Sit down, oh yes, you are Miss Wrighton. I don't usually take girls on, they are usually prostitutes, but I've been over your case." She said "I do hope you are not injecting cocaine. I do hope you are sniffing it, because you'll get an orgasm if you inject it." My goodness I was only very young. I didn't know what she was talking about.' Sent away with a prescription for four grains each of heroin and cocaine, Louise Wrighton got a taste for drugs in general and a passion for cocaine in particular.[17]

Following the second Brain Report, published in 1965, ordinary doctors were banned from prescribing heroin. Licences exempting physicians from the ban were issued mainly to senior hospital staff and doctors working in the new Drug Treatment Centres. Professional resistance to the restrictions was sapped by embarrassment at the damage being done by the profligate practitioners. Lady Frankau died before the Brain recommendations were implemented by a new Dangerous Drugs Act. Other doctors bridged the gap until the centres started operating; the most notorious of them being John Petro. The first physician to administer penicillin, Petro wrecked his career through personal failures, in particular his gambling losses. Left without a surgery, he wrote prescriptions for heroin in the teashop at Baker Street Underground station. He attracted the attention of the media, the law, and his professional peers. At one point he was holed up practising from a Vauxhall Viva parked in Victoria Street, E15. After the heroin ban came into force, he prescribed methamphetamine until finally being struck off the medical register.

The Rolleston Report had placed addiction in the realm of disease. The first Brain Report refined this concept to the psychiatric realm of 'mental disorder'. Faced with what was now coming to be understood as a social problem, the Brain Committee then reconsidered the idea of disease, and used it to define a strategy for the public good rather than the treatment of the individual. Explaining why it was recommending that the Home Office should in future be formally notified of addicts coming to the notice of doctors, it compared its proposals to the existing system of notification for specified communicable diseases:

> We think the analogy to addiction is apt, for addiction is after all a socially infectious condition and its notification may offer a means for epidemiological assessment and control. We use the term deliberately to reflect certain principles which we regard as

important, viz., that the addict is a sick person and that addiction is a disease which (if allowed to spread unchecked) will become a menace to the community.[18]

The analogy is treated virtually as equivalence: disease is not a model for addiction, but becomes a definition of it. This provides a basis for the venture into policing by introducing the idea of 'social infection'. The irrational language of social pollution is just a step away.

Other agencies rose to the task of pronouncing upon drugs. Social scientists, operating in an atmosphere of estrangement between authority and youth, addressed the issue within the framework of theory about social deviancy. The conflicts of the time are revealed in occasional phrases amid the jargon. One researcher surveyed the personalities of addicted adolescent males and found that 'In all series the personality deviated from the norm with oral fixation, maternal dependency, introverted schizoid and *non-aggressive* traits.' The inadequately aggressive males also suffered from 'ego pathology with poor reality testing, inability to delay gratification, low frustration tolerance and a marked tendency to retreat into passivity in frustrating situations. In addition they report low self-esteem, depression and pessimism, difficulty in relating except on a manipulative level together with disturbances in sexual identification and rejection of the *conventional American male role*.'[19]

A similarly distressing unAmericanism was denounced in an exposition of the hardline Phoenix House programme of treatment for addiction:

> Addictive or character disorders suffer from a lack of identity, which can be considered a deficiency syndrome ... In Phoenix House the teaching of socialization and its consequent morality is made both explicit and emphatic ... We regard antisocial, *antimilitary*, amoral and acting-out behaviour as 'stupid'.[20] [my italics]

Many young American men became anti-military after serving in Vietnam. Many also became dependent on heroin. However, a follow-up study suggested that this was not the death sentence with which the public was liable to associate almost any illicit drug use. Lee Robins found that eighty-five per cent of the American service personnel in his sample who went to Vietnam were offered heroin. Of the thirty-five per cent who accepted the offers, nineteen per cent became addicted. Three years after their return, only eight per cent of the original total had used the drug in the past two years. Less than half of these used it more than once a week for a month or more, and a quarter took it daily. It seemed as though, like hospital patients suffering pain, the troops' need for heroin largely vanished when they were removed from the conditions that prompted it.[21] Charles Winick evolved the idea that addicts may simply mature out of their dependency, which is essentially a condition of early adulthood. It had been assumed that the scarcity of addicts over the age of forty was due to junkie mortality, but follow-up studies like Winick's suggested that addicts found it easier to kick the habit as they approached middle age.

In mid-sixties America, anyone who used heroin more than six times became an addict – and that was official. The word came from Henry M. Giordano, head of the Federal Bureau of Narcotics. He drew this conclusion from a survey carried out under the auspices of the National Institute of Mental Health, in which 28 young black men out of a sample of 235 admitted to having used heroin. All but six had become addicted, and of the exceptions, none had used the drug more than six times. A little scientific knowledge was obviously a dangerous thing in the hands of a representative of the state. The relationship between taking heroin and becoming addicted to it remains mysterious, but evidence accumulated that the link was by no means automatic. Some researchers came to the conclusion that at any given time, there were as many, and perhaps more, people taking heroin in a controlled manner than were addicted to it. Others reported the existence of 'weekend' users who took the drug on occasion in a controlled manner, without accidentally lapsing into dependency (and thus contradicting the idea so forcefully conveyed by the British government publicity campaign of a decade later: that the idea of controlled use is a tragically vain illusion). Among these were some veterans of both addiction and Vietnam.[22]

One project which fragmented and dissipated itself in a jungle of non-compatible schools of jargon was the attempt to pin a personality on the addicts. Julius Merry summarized the state of opinion in 1972 thus: 'Most addicts to heroin suffer from disorders of personality. Attempts to identify a specific type of personality disorder in relation to drug addiction have not been successful and some reports indicate that the personality disorders preceded the onset of addiction.

'The present addiction problem in the Western world is being seen more and more as a response to social conditions than simply a result of disordered personality.'[23]

Despite the increasing complexity of the patterns of theory and data in the scientific and clinical fields, certain simple beliefs came to be taken as self-evident elsewhere. As late as 1980, an unnamed source could say on behalf of the Home Office that 'All we can do is support these people for a time. But once they're hooked, they have effectively passed a death sentence on themselves.'[24] And that was the voice of an official.

Notes

1   Derek Agnew, Introduction to *Viper: The Confessions of a Drug Addict* (London, Robert Hale, 1956), authorship attributed to Raymond Thorp.

2   John Fordham, *Let's Join Hands and Contact the Living* (London, Elm Tree, 1986).

3   Annual British Government Report to the United Nations on the traffic in opium and other dangerous drugs. See *British Journal of Addiction* 46 (1) (1949).

4   *British Journal of Addiction* 50 (1) (1950).

5   Belatedly, since by his account this visit takes place on the eve of his own court appearance, the date of which he gives as 10 September 1951. No wonder his friend exclaims, 'Brother, haven't you been around here lately?' In fact Club Eleven had shut its doors for good within a few months of the raid the previous summer.

6   H. B. Spear, 'The growth of heroin addiction in the United Kingdom', *British Journal of Addiction* 64 (1969), pp. 245–56.

7   cf. Colin MacInnes's *City of Spades* in *The Colin MacInnes Omnibus* (London, Allison & Busby, 1985, p. 59): 'You see, between you and me, this colour problem's becoming quite a problem for us, too. Particularly in the matter of dope. Of

course, these boys, it doesn't do them much harm, I don't suppose, they're used to it, even though it's not within the law. But the girls, Mr Pew, the younger girls they give it to! It's corrupting them. Yes, corrupting them and making them serve these black men's evil ends.' Linking the ideas of racial drug immunity and the corruption of vulnerable white females makes the black men's ends seem all the more evil. The speaker is a police officer.

8   Spear, 'The growth of heroin addiction', ibid.

9   Dr J. A. Hobson, *British Journal of Addiction* 53 (1) (1956).

10 Dr Arthur Henry Douthwaite; Arthur Lawrence Abel, *British Journal of Addiction 53 (1) (1956)*.

11 *British Journal of Addiction* 54 (2) (1956).

12 *British Journal of Addiction* 53 (1) (1956).

13 *British Journal of Inebriety* 32 (3), pp. 125–51 (1935).

14 William S. Burroughs, *Kicking Drugs: A Very Personal Story*, *Harpers* 235 (July 1967), pp. 39–42; quoted in Courtwright, *Dark Paradise*, p. 5.

15 Gerry V. Stimson and Edna Oppenheimer, *Heroin Addiction: Treatment and Control in Britain* (London, Tavistock, 1982). This excellent study contains a wealth of information about British drug policy and its results. Also Julius Merry, 'Social History of Heroin Addiction', *British Journal of Addiction* 70 (1975).

16 Brian Freemantle, *The Fix* (London, Corgi, 1986).

17 Stimson and Oppenheimer, *Heroin Addiction*, pp. 76–7.

18 Interdepartmental Committee on Drug Addiction, Second Report (London, HMSO, 1965, p. 8); Stimson and Oppenheimer, *Heroin Addiction*, p. 53.

19 See Joy Mott, 'The Psychological Basis of Drug Dependence: The Intellectual and Personality Characteristics of Opiate Users', *British Journal of Addiction* 67 (1972), pp. 88–99.

20 Dr Mitchell Rosenthal, quoted in Berridge, *Opium and the People*, pp. 257–8.

21 Lee Robins *et al.*, 'Vietnam Veterans Three Years after Vietnam', in *The Handbook of Substance Abuse* 11 (Human Science Press, 1980; quoted in Borzoni); John Kaplan, *The Hardest Drug: Heroin and Public Policy* (Chicago, University of Chicago Press, 1983), especially pp. 32–80.

22 ibid.

23 *British Journal of Addiction* 67 (1972), pp. 322–5.

24 *Sunday Times*, 24 February 1980, quoted in Stimson and Oppenheimer, *Heroin Addiction*, p. 225.

SEVEN

A Siamese Cat in the Council Flat

'I Baked Dog In My Oven', barked the *Sun*'s front-page banner for 8 January 1986. *Sun*-watchers considered it among the summits of that publication's headline excesses, though it was outshone by the celebrated effort for 13 March, 'Freddie Starr Ate My Hamster'. There was a drug angle to the dog story, in that the teenager who was sentenced to three months' detention for the crime claimed to have been suffering the after-effects of LSD taken the night before. (Freddie Starr later appeared as a reformed tabloid junkie, citing his misfortunes as a warning to readers. It was not suggested, however, that the eccentric comedian's appetite for hard drugs led to his appetite for small mammals.)[1]

The *Sun*'s rivals, however, were concerned with a drug story of a more classic kind. Daphne Guinness, of the brewing family, described the central character as 'my own Blenheim spaniel',[2] but that was all there was to the canine angle.

The *Daily Mirror*'s description was more informative. 'MARQUIS OF BLANDFORD, heir to a £66 million fortune, great nephew of Sir Winston Churchill', was how it built up its subject, in order to slam him with the banner 'YOU COMMON CRIMINAL'.[3] The words were those of the magistrate who jailed him for three months for breaking the terms of a probation order by not notifying the authorities of a change of address. This infraction came to light when the heir to Blenheim Palace was found living beneath a clothes shop on the Edgware Road in what a police officer described as a 'cocaine smoking den'.[4] Blandford had originally been sentenced for possession of heroin and kicking in a chemist's window while looking for more. 'Lord Blandford,' the magistrate said, 'through the illegal taking of drugs, you, one of the richest and most powerful men in the land, have become a common criminal.' When the original order was imposed, the bench had drawn a general lesson from the case: 'The highest in the land can fall to the lowest when drugs are taken.'

The media and the magistrates both latched on to the way in which heroin dissolved the class barriers that had survived satire, social democracy and the sixties. Those concerned with the maintenance of social order must have deplored this form of downward mobility. The tabloids dwelt with relish upon the contrast between Blenheim Palace and the surroundings in which the 'Marquis of Porridge'[5] now found himself. Readers from humbler stations in life were encouraged to take pleasure in the aristocrat's downfall, a streak of disguised malice being one of the few vestiges of the movement to transform the country's class structure which was permitted to surface in the media of the 1980s.

The attention lavished on Jamie Blandford tends to support the premise that rich people are considered more newsworthy than ordinary ones. But the heroin story of the 1980s has a much more significant class dimension. Heroin emerged as a focus for media attention during 1984, a year in which Britain resembled a country whose forces were at war abroad. Every night the conflict between the miners and the Government dominated the news, exciting and tormenting the viewers. The casualties were negligible by the standards of war, but the struggle constantly evoked military imagery. The deadlock between the two sides, and the inflexible tactics of the miners' leadership, prompted comparisons with the First World War. The media emphasis on violence and the increasingly military appearance of the police also helped to make the dispute look like a war. Above all, there was Margaret Thatcher's notorious allusions to 'the enemy within',[6] widely construed as an attempt to class the miners as enemies of the nation – enemies comparable to the Argentinians over whose military defeat she had presided two years before. The rolling shock of the year-long strike threw subterranean national anxieties into stark relief.

The social-democratic era had been founded on compromise, expediency, and the hope that these political principles would lead painlessly to equality and social justice. The electorate knew that it had ended that era when it opted for Victoriana; regulation in the home and deregulation in the marketplace. On accession to the highest office, Margaret Thatcher recited the prayer of St Francis of Assisi (incidentally introducing one of her royal affectations): 'Where there is discord may we bring harmony.' Discord was to be the keynote of her years of power. The populace had admitted the degeneracy and shallowness of the post-war consensus, but it liked the idea of everybody agreeing on the basics. Britons wanted a solution to the national malaise as well, though, and at last enough of them plucked up the nerve to opt for radicalism – in the trappings of a return to a Victorian golden age. They got riots, the decimation of the nation's industrial base, and a numbing rise in unemployment. Whatever else might be happening to the nation, it was not getting more united.

As it became clearer that the miners were being beaten, consensus discovered a profound sympathy for them. Their heroism and dignity were recognized. Another Britain was to be seen in the pit communities, a precious heritage of honourable labour and mutual solidarity, in one of the traditional industries upon which Britain's greatness was founded. Yet it was clear that this was a class struggle. However deep the sympathy for the miners might run, the issue was still divisive. The strike helped turn the tide of opinion against the Thatcher experiment, but it deepened the social divisions.

One of the many aspects of the Government's tactics which backfired upon it was the attempt to drum up support by casting the dispute as a rerun of the Falklands war. There was still too much solidarity within the working class, and respect for it from the middle classes, for a body of workers at the very heart of the labour tradition to be declared Other and treated as enemies. The Prime Minister was seen to be deliberately dividing the nation still further. With the country in such a condition, issues upon which there was general agreement were at a premium. It was the moment for heroin to make its greatest contribution to national morale.

Heroin is the consensus issue *par excellence*. Everybody is against it. Even most junkies are against it. It was clearly a problem that was increasing in magnitude as the decade wore on. It was therefore newsworthy, and gave the nation a chance to simulate going to war. Martial imagery is the norm in descriptions of the implementation of drug-control policy. The use of the word 'war' to describe drug control is routine in headlines and accompanying newspaper columns. An alternative which gives special emphasis to its moral dimension and the alien nature of the enemy is 'crusade'.[7] On the borders of America, actual skirmishing takes place. Both sides have automatic weapons, and the good guys have spy planes, counter-insurgency aircraft and attack helicopters too.[8]

There is one essential difference between the way in which illegal drugs were represented from the fifties and the seventies and the meaning given to them – especially to heroin – in the 1980s. During the earlier decades, illegal drugs were seen as the preserve of a deviant subculture, which menaced both itself and society at large. The hipsters of the fifties, lurking in their shady locales with their alien associates, evolved into a whole intercontinental youth movement proclaiming the dawn of a new age. Cult or mass movement, this was a matter for deviancy theory. When a teenage boy in the sixties grew his hair, turned against and renounced his parents, he joined the mass of the deviant movement and became the legitimate target of the relevant authorities. When a youth falls into heroin dependency in the 1980s, there is no body of people for him to join. A family torn apart by a habit remains an isolated tragedy. Heroin is no longer seen as being contained within a limited group of people. It has become universal again.

By bombing Buckingham Palace during the Second World War, the *Luftwaffe*'s fliers probably raised Londoners' morale more than they damaged it. It was not, of course, that the East Enders wanted the Royal Family's home to be levelled as so many of theirs had been. It was because the highest were seen to be suffering along with the lowest. Now they had more in common than ever before. The nation was united by the menace that threatened king and loyal subjects alike. Forty years later, people would sigh wistfully for the spirit of the Blitz. It was in meagre supply, as were enemies upon whose hostile nature the nation could agree.

Reports of the Marquis of Blandford's fall were like newsreel footage of rubble in the Palace grounds. Blandford became an example of the principle that heroin was a menace to all sections of society. The sixties had swung along on shallow assertions that a touch of affluence for the workers and stardom for the odd Cockney photographer would break down the class system. Something known as a 'classless accent' was taken as evidence of progress towards a 'classless society'. The discovery of fundamentalist Marxism by militant students and young workers at the end of the decade seems a most understandable reaction to such vapid substitutes for political thought. There is little left of the idea of classlessness in the papers nowadays; except for the idea of the extent of heroin's menace. That is one way of illustrating the difference between the 1960s and the 1980s.

Concealed in the baggage of the class message, and in the ambivalence with which ordinary people regard the rich and famous, is the mean pleasure taken in the spectacle of the privileged getting themselves in a state. 'The British Aristocracy Really Screws It Up' was the punchline to a sketch in the satirical *Spitting Image* television programme which featured a Blandford puppet in a parody of one of the TV anti-heroin 'advertisements'. When Olivia Channon, the twenty-two-year-old daughter of Trade and Industry Secretary Paul Channon, was found dead after an end-of-exams party at Oxford, the press enthusiastically 'peeled away the posh façade of Oxford's Hooray set to reveal a sad world of waste and decadence'.[9] As usual, the *Sun* was the least mealy-mouthed of the popular papers in its incitement to envy. 'For most undergraduates, the three years at university are spent scrimping and saving in the struggle for a degree. But for the Hooray Henrys and Henriettas – upper-crust sons and daughters of rich businessmen, bankers, MPs and industrialists – it's one long binge.' Alcoholic and sexual indulgence were 'passed off as young people sowing their wild oats'. Now the new indulgence in drugs was bringing the idle rich their comeuppance. 'Wealth means worry,' the *Sun* reassured its proletarian readership, totting up Henry and Henrietta's annual bills ('College fees . . . paid on the rates. Casual designer clothes . . . £4,500'). No estimate was provided for drugs overheads, but Henry's lifestyle was costed at £48,385 a year. Henrietta managed on a mere £22,000.

The case demonstrated a feature of drug stories which make them so valuable for the popular press: a combination of sensation, titillation, voyeurism, and a built-in moral. The dead woman's 'secret diaries' – how many diaries are public? – were a major focus of interest, being said to reveal the 'amazing double life' of the Oxford 'Smart Set', and to 'lift the lid off the sordid world of the upper-crust drug addicts who spend fortunes feeding their habits'.[10]

The whole episode was a festival of *Schadenfreude*. Each paper was able to pick an angle to suit its own particular preferences. The *People*, the Sunday paper that had most resisted the general tabloid reorientation towards showbiz glamour, found a good traditional suburban witchcraft story in some undergraduate games played by the Channon household. Neighbour Bill Bowell described how the students set up crosses in the garden, lit candles, and 'bayed at the moon like wolves'. 'We always called the German chap Count Dracula after that,' he said.[11] The German chap must have made Fleet Street editors think Christmas had come early. Count Gottfried von Bismarck was none other than the great-great-grandson of the Iron Chancellor. Channon's exotic friend simply radiated sinister Teutonic perversion. The *Sun* printed a photograph of the prematurely-aged roué looking even more foreign in eyeliner and a Valentino turban.[12] The sheer quantity of gossip and fable amassed by the hacks unleashed among the dreaming spires made an editorial decision as to whether the Count was an evil degenerate or a wacky hedonist superfluous. On one page, both options were available. 'DRAG FUN AS A NUN' was the headline for the top half, affirming that 'nothing is sacrosanct when von Bismarck decides to have fun. He lives a bizarre life of comic debauchery – hosting the wildest parties, drinking to excess, and raising hell.' Down below was 'Blood on the Table', an account of a 'sick' party thrown by the Count, where pigs' heads were suspended above the dinner, and a guest was 'absolutely sickened by the sight of blood dripping on to plates of food'.[13]

The story would have been fantasy made flesh had von Bismarck turned out to be a heroin dealer like 'The Count' that Kenneth Anger describes preying on 1920s starlets in *Hollywood Babylon*. In fact, those charged with supplying heroin to Channon were her cousin Sebastian Guinness and her friend Rosie Johnston. The papers highlighted her lifestyle by describing what killed her as a 'cocktail' of drink and heroin.[14] Although much of the newsprint devoted to the affair dwelt on the debauched amusements of rich undergraduates, there was a current of commentary which sought to portray Olivia as a secretly unhappy person. This was fuelled initially by a 'suicide note' which turned up in a dustbin, speaking of rejection in love. The post-mortem pop psychology was necessary because of the strength of media conviction that drugs imply inner problems. One common account of the origins of a habit holds that evil pushers trick ordinary kids into trying the stuff, at which point their problems start. An article informing parents how to spot if their kids are on drugs, trailing in the wake of the Olivia story, described drugs as 'an evil that can hit anyone'.[15] But the idea of drugs singling out the inadequate personality remains strong. While it is perfectly in order to attribute alcoholic excesses to a straight-forward search for pleasure, drugs are deemed to be less simple. This is partly because of the strong media pressure against mentioning drugs and pleasure in the same breath. Censorship of pleasure, as though the mere scent of it will send children flocking to the pushers, produces a bizarrely distorted representation of why people take drugs. The insistence on denying the link between drugs and pleasure seems to make it difficult for some commentators to discuss drug abuse without invoking a flawed psychology.[16]

The Channon story had everything. There was even the traditional axis linking high society and low life. In this case it pivoted upon Paddington Station. There, presumably after the collector had punched her 'AWAYDAY TICKET TO HEROIN HELL', Olivia Channon would phone her pusher and, 'suitably dressed down', travel to rendezvous 'in sleazy Brixton'.[17] The light touch of derogatory racial association was continuing a tradition that began around the 1920s with the Billie Carleton case. Genealogy of a different sort was a vital ingredient in the story.

There were Royal connections. The élite circles in which the central characters moved were small. Junior Royal Lady Helen Windsor was identified as a friend of the deceased, but she was small fry. This one went to the top. 'DRUGS COUPLE TO MEET QUEEN?' wondered the *Star*, speculating on whether Rosie Johnston and Sebastian Guinness would cross the monarch's path at Her Majesty's Royal Ascot ball.[18] The idea of the Royal Family as Britain's most popular soap opera is common currency. The Channon affair crashed into the storyline like a Gothic-tinged melodrama – or simply one of those implausible disaster movies which have a habit of turning up when the ratings are flagging.

The Royal presence might bring one particular soap to mind. There was another dynasty involved, though. The Guinness story fell somewhere between American glamour-soap and Greek tragedy. Six other members of the 'doomed dynasty'[19] had met untimely deaths in the previous twenty years, one of them from a heroin overdose. The scandal surrounding the latest tragedy flushed Princess Diana's brother out on to breakfast television to appear pious. Identified as an acquaintance of the von Bismarck set, the young aristocrat denied that he had ever seen or been offered any drugs in three years at Oxford, despite having acquired the soubriquet 'Champagne Charlie' for the kind of alcohol-induced behaviour that gets proletarian youths packed off to detention centre. 'All students drink a lot,' he averred. 'I don't think there's anything wrong with that.' A touch of Gown snobbery crept into Viscount Althorp's testimony when he claimed that 'the people who take drugs are about three or four people, mostly not connected directly with the University, but affiliated colleges in Oxford and London.' Drawing on a piece of folklore usually related in connection with schoolchildren, he mentioned hearing stories about 'pushing' at college gates.[20] A few days later, the news of 'DI'S DRUG SHOCK' broke. According to the *News of the World*, Althorp had previously told Australian television viewers of his 'agony' at a party when 'someone slipped something' into his drink. This revelation of his sole drug experience, considered the reporters, was 'bound to stun the Princess of Wales, a leading campaigner against drug abuse'.[21]

It was all curiously similar to the brouhaha that enveloped Oxford in 1965 when former premier Harold Macmillan's twenty-year-old grandson Joshua died of a heroin overdose. The press descended, producing articles like the *Sunday Times*'s 'Confessions of an Oxford Drug-Taker'.[22] Richard Compton-Miller, later to find fame in Fleet Street, described how he and his colleagues on the student paper *Cherwell* found 'about two hundred people taking drugs in Oxford reasonably seriously, about a thousand taking it sort of on and off, intermittently, but only about five or six people taking heroin or cocaine . . . There must be about four or five people in Oxford who take cocaine and heroin now.'[23] On Althorp's evidence, the problem has actually diminished over the intervening twenty-odd years.

Once the titillation of a sensational drug story like the Channon affair has faded away, it is time for the concluding moral to be drawn. 'After Oxford, a lesson for all parents' was how the *People* introduced its how-to guide to home detection of drug abuse. 'From cossetted aristocrats to underprivileged kids, Britain's youth can be lured into the seedy world of heroin and cocaine,' it warned. 'Drug addiction respects neither riches nor rank.'[24] While the DHSS leaflets for parents are adorned with the kind of photos proudly displayed on mantelpieces, the demographic profile of addiction in the papers is definitely 'U' shaped. The twin peaks of the curve are at the top and bottom of the social scale, linking the people who live on big estates – country ones and council ones.

At the start of the 1980s heroin panic, the problem was originally painted in greys, as an expression and intensification of the plight of inner-city youth. The young had ceased to be a threat. The end of the baby boom and of the Youthquake saw to that. The traditional relationship between youth and its elders could be resumed: fear and rejection on the part of the old gave way to feelings of responsibility and protectiveness; and guilt. Youth was no longer seen as an enormous subversive gang, but as passive victims of the world their parents made for them. Above all, the political offensive launched by the Conservative administration meant that the prospect of youth growing up into a world without work weighed heavily upon the public conscience. The kids hadn't voted for it, after all. But they were in the front line.

Heroin draws much of its power to appal from its initial public appearance in the 1980s as a phenomenon connected with unemployment. It enables the issue of the dole to be kept alive. There are only so many television interviews to be done with scrap-heap kids before apathy and boredom spread from the kids to the production team and the audience. News and current affairs are like the visual systems of flies and frogs. They respond with surefire alacrity to movement, but are functionally blind to situations which do not change. Mass unemployment, afflicting the young disprop-ortionately, is a fixture of the 1980s landscape. It is understood that the unemployed are particularly vulnerable to medical and psychiat-ric disorders, and heroin was initially identified as an addition to the list of these ills. Whether or not heroin dependency is actually caused by unemployment,[25] it is understood by the public to be associated with it. Moreover, heroin is perceived to be something which displays the characteristics of worklessness. Addicts lie about, dangerously uncoupled from the rhythms and disciplines of work. They are unproductive, but spend vast sums on their habit: this is what the idle rich and the idle poor have in common. The addict is a symbol of a society at the very heart of whose problems is a decline in productivity. Around that core hovers allied anxieties about laziness and indiscipline in the national character, and about that cardinal sin of the Thatcher era, 'spending beyond one's means'. The addict is a human metaphor for the decaying nation.[26] As if this were not enough, there is the shameful possibility that the addict is also an actual result of that decay.

The economic aspect of heroin addiction also stirs a related group of anxieties. These are less to do with guilt and more to do with fear. The Victorian bourgeoisie were continually aware that the masses who had been concentrated into a proletariat to create wealth for their superiors were liable to coalesce spontaneously into a menacing concentration: the mob. In the 1980s, the mob gathered among those left over from the concentration who had remained behind, useless, in the inner cities. While youth as a whole has become an object of pity, the black youth has become a figure of terror. Heroin has never been associated with young blacks. It represents a sort of inverse violence, an incomprehensible campaign of self-directed disorder. It is, however, associated very strongly with the crime required to support a habit. The junkies can inflict plenty of damage on others in the course of their own self-destruction. Heroin not only accentuates public fears of crime, but also serves as an explanation for what in past years would have been attributed to 'mindless' anti-social tendencies.

Heroin also provides an answer to the latent question of what kind of misfortune would befall the young and workless. Inner emptiness poses that question: the emptiness of the industrial hearts of the abandoned inner cities; the emptiness of unoccupied young lives. The unwelcome squatter in both turns out to be heroin. There is an alien presence in the estates; a Siamese cat in the council flat, as the singer Ian Dury put it some years ago.[27] It is a punishment visited on those who are already victims. The craving for supplies of the drug does, however, give the unemployed something to get up for in the mornings.

The new addicts, perceived as victims, are not excommunicated from family and society as their predecessors have been. Perhaps the fact that the problem is perceived to exist only among the whites helps keep them part of the family. They are treated more like kidnap victims, and everybody has a part to play in the rescue operation. Although the inner-city Skag Kids are the symbol of national decline, they are not the only young people liable to find themselves unemployed. Something had to be found to occupy idle hands, and a series of state-subsidized temporary work schemes were provided. These were a source of cheap labour, thus helping to do what the Government had signally failed to do with adult skilled and middle-class employees: to force wages down. They were heavily publicized, in an attempt to counteract the strong popular impression that the Government was unconcerned about unemployment. And they provided limited instruction in the patterns of behaviour and discipline – patterns to which earlier generations had graduated straight from school. The job creation schemes gave youngsters a course in the virtues of obedience, honesty, application and punctuality; then sent them off to the dole wanting more of the same. The ones who got hooked the most might be lucky enough to realize their desires as members of the new service class, winning little plastic stars for especial subservience in the face of pitiful wages from their employers in fast-food chains.

But McDonalds and the Youth Training Scheme were not capable of taking care of the entire problem. For one thing, there is the world of 'leisure', in which the young consumers have dangerous stretches of independence. They can hardly be blamed for their tastes. They have never known their parents' (or, more likely, their grandparents') world, in which capitalism fed mainly on the profits from production. These are the children shaped by a capitalism which now, above all, needs them as consumers. It teases and seduces them from their earliest years, teaching them to want. Its urgency demands an urgency from the consumption force: instant gratification, credit to be arranged. It trades on sensuality in everything from home furnishings to holidays in the sun. It teaches that pleasure in itself is nothing to feel guilty about. And as consumers become jaded, it devises more luxurious, more intense pleasures.

Of course, consumer capitalism needs producer capitalism to keep the consumption disciplined. Consumers must learn to abide by the rules: no stealing, and no spending beyond one's means. Wage-earning teaches such lessons and provides these disciplines. There are contradictions, particularly in capitalism's need to get consumers to borrow. It has had a difficult job destroying traditional reservations about buying on the 'never-never'. Those unfortunates for whom money is rendered invisible by a credit card, and who run up huge debts without any hope of settling them, are often treated sympathetically. They are regarded as victims of a psychiatrically pathological compulsion – they are considered to be 'credit-card junkies'.[28] The similarity to drug addiction is acknowledged.

The young have been saturated in consumerism from infancy, but when they leave school and childhood, many of them are no longer channelled into the adult world of work. They see nothing morally wrong in consuming things solely for pleasure, and they feel no obligation to work for such pleasures. Drifting unshackled from workplace disciplines, the Thatcher Generation kids also drift away from respectability and legality. Yet competing traditional ideas, especially the one that says that the worth of an individual depends on them working, set up a conflict. Poverty and boredom add to the stress. All of this points in the direction of drugs, the skeleton in the cupboard of consumer capitalism.[29]

The trinkets and baubles of youth-seeking consumer capitalism have been placed on show in the name of the anti-drugs campaign. Television warnings produced in commercial format by the Scottish health authorities were nothing less than state-sponsored lifestyle marketing. Full of gaudy graphics and shiny teenagers dancing in discos, they looked for all the world like advertisements for a teen magazine or a range of make-up. The state was officially backing a formation of industries optimized for extracting money from teenagers, and recommending the products as accessories for an alternative lifestyle to drug addiction.

In the terms set by the anti-drugs campaign, the Scottish commercials were open to criticism that they missed the target. It might be the Benetton kids' idea of a good time, but it wasn't going to appeal to an alienated skid-row youth with an anti-social haircut and a taste for music that sounded like an ox being tortured in a thunderstorm. For any teenager with rebellious leanings, it was more likely to make a druggy lifestyle seem attractive in comparison. The equivalent television presentations for English and Welsh viewers are quite different. Directed by Ridley Scott, famous for the science-fiction films *Alien* and *Blade Runner*, they focus on the user. In the more celebrated of the two advertisements, a young man's initial cockiness ('I can handle it') about his heroin use declines in stages along with his health and his posture. 'I could give up tomorrow ... couldn't I?' is his querulous last word. The other features a young woman whose downhill progress is symbolized by her toppling over, like a dummy. The commentary – the young woman, unlike her male counterpart, has only the punchline to herself – chronicles the colonization of the various parts of her life by heroin.

The posters and television advertisements commissioned by the Central Office of Information and the Department of Health and Social Security have sought to intensify the image of heroin's toxicity by failing to point out that most of the physical miseries associated with its use are the effects of self-neglect and dirty 'street' supplies, rather than the essential properties of the drug itself. But by comparison with the Scottish campaign and most other attempts to mobilize youth against drugs *en masse*, the efforts of the Yellowhammer advertising agency have a certain ethical superiority.

The creative people at Yellowhammer themselves would probably not see things that way. The agency was awarded the account because of its successful work in the youth market for clients such as the HMV record shop chain and the New Musical Express – in other words, because it was hip. It thus took up a special position in the construction of the discourse on drugs. The preceding couple of years had seen a groundswell of articles in the press, and broadcasts on the subject, as well as passing allusions to the phenomenon in a variety of media. This outpouring of text and speech was essentially independent of responsible authority; of state, medicine or education. It was there mainly to serve the interests of the popular press, and was loaded with sensationalism, titillation and moral indignation. By the time that the *Daily Mirror* produced its Shock Issue devoted to the subject late in 1984,[30] the commercial media had convinced the public that the nation's youth was being threatened by a plague of heroin.

The Government was thus under pressure to do something. As it happened, heroin was just the kind of enemy it had been looking for. It responded to the media campaign in kind, with a media campaign of its own that would maximize the chance that the Government would be seen to be doing something. The phoney war on drugs is being fought almost entirely with propaganda leaflets. Because of the association with unemployment, the Government can be seen to be concerned about an effect of mass idleness – without admitting either its own responsibility for the dole statistics or any causal link between being out of work and being on heroin. And it provides the perfect issue around which the Conservative Party can vaunt its image as the party of law and order. It can also use the idea of a mushrooming drug menace as a justification for the pre-existing project of strengthening and enriching the police force.

Yellowhammer, however, is not the Government. Its brief from the Government was to put together a campaign with the intention of reducing the misuse of drugs, especially heroin, among young people. The emphasis on heroin is consistent with the way that the drug issue has been presented by the media, and with the agreement between papers such as the *News of the World* and Home Office minister David Mellor that the major illicit opiate is 'Public Enemy Number One'.[31] In the event, it became Yellowhammer's exclusive target. The research they commissioned indicated that the vast majority of young people were never going to take heroin anyway. The most resistant were those who had tried 'soft drugs' but had not taken to them, and those who regarded themselves as 'discerning' cannabis users. Girls, and young people of West Indian ancestry, were also 'heroin-resistant'. Yellowhammer, commendably, interpreted their assignment strictly, and did not attempt to influence the behaviour of the great heroin-resistant masses. They also decided that posters and TV advertisements were not going to get the monkeys off addicts' backs, and so they have targeted young people 'on the cusp' of experimenting with heroin. Their scripts and copy thus display an insight into the mentality of the adolescent and the dynamics of drug dependency that is of secondary importance to campaigns with ulterior motives. Whether the two million pounds of Government money which paid for the first year of official publicity would have been better spent on providing facilities for treatment, as many voluntary bodies have argued, was not for the advertising agency to say.

The BMA is not among the bodies keen to hop aboard the bandwagon. It had criticized the priorities indicated by the 'high profile' given to a WHO-sponsored international meeting on drug abuse which was called by Britain, and held at Lancaster Gate in March 1986. In a statement made jointly with the Action on Alcohol Abuse charity, it said: 'The Government's emphasis on illicit drugs is misplaced. By lavishing attention on a relatively minor problem, the Government diverts public attention from the far greater damage and misery caused by alcohol and tobacco.'[32] It went on to estimate that 100,000 people die prematurely from smoking each year, and a further 6,500 deaths could be attributed to alcohol abuse. The most recent year's tally of deaths caused by illegal drugs was 235. Against this mortality rate, the Government was pitting £411 million a year, compared to £6 million spent on curbing alcohol and tobacco abuse. That, calculated the two organizations, worked out at £35 for each tobacco death, £344 per head for alcohol-related fatalities, and £1.7 million for each death caused by illegal drugs. But then, the Government was engaged in a weightier project than that of improving public health. The Prime Minister herself spelled it out: 'Britain – like the rest of Europe – is up against a determined effort to flood the country with hard drugs to corrupt our youth – to undermine the stability of our country.'[33]

For Mrs Thatcher, the idea of a foreign conspiracy destabilizing the country and flooding the beleaguered island has obvious political attractions – especially since so many people, asked what was responsible for the state of the nation's youth, would consider the two words 'Margaret Thatcher' sufficient answer. But heroin provides assistance in the construction of other sorts of discourses about the condition of British society. It has become a vital ingredient in lists: whenever criminal menaces or social blights are enumerated, drugs are prominent among them. It has also become an optional ingredient to be added, like monosodium glutamate, to spice up perennial tabloid stories.[34] And it is strongly defined as acting against the fundamental unit of society: the family.

The British drug panic of the 1980s largely excludes the idea of the dope fiend, in the interest of national unity. This leaves all the more vitriol for the pushers, and above them, the drug barons. (One might almost yearn for the return to the tabloids of the vanquished band of union barons, bogeys from pre-Thatcher days.) Their prey is the innocent, who are still the responsibility of their parents. One source of drug-related strife was identified by Liberal Party leader David Steel: 'Alcohol used to be a major source of family violence. Now drugs are quickly catching up. More and more children are being neglected, their parents hooked on hard drugs.'[35] It is not an especially potent argument, as the *non sequitur* caused by the association of 'hard drugs' with neglect rather than violence underlines. But the idea of addicted parents failing their children is one of the most emotive elements of the heroin discourse. It is a different kind of transgression to the alcoholic sort. A man beating up his wife and children in a drunken rage is only exceeding the limits of his authority. After all, many people would sanction his

121

exertion of power over the family to the point of using violence against the children; and the condoning of wife-beating, though not publicly acceptable, is hardly extinct. If he goes on to develop alcohol-related diseases, this is likely to occur in middle life. As a victim he is unpromising material. His condition is self-inflicted, and he is of an age associated with responsibility and parenthood. And the drug that causes the damage is regarded primarily as a normal pleasure by much of the population. It is also legal.

Illegal drugs, on the other hand, afford the media a whole host of little victims. The search is on for Britain's youngest junkie. Reports of a five-year-old glue addict in Birmingham have been trumped by the Newcastle three-year-old 'thought to be Britain's youngest victim of glue-sniffing'.[36] After the death of fourteen-year-old Jason Fitzsimmons, a senior police officer referred to the existence of thirty-five heroin addicts aged fourteen or thirteen in 'DRUGS CITY', as the *Daily Mirror* referred to Liverpool.[37] While the 'hushed' jury heard evidence which would show that the boy actually choked on his vomit after an overdose of Dalmane sleeping tablets, rather than the heroin to which his death was originally attributed, the National Association of Head Teachers 'revealed' that 'children as young as nine are becoming regular drug users'.[38] The jury returned a verdict of death through non-dependent use of drugs. 'We hope this will bring home to parents the responsibilities that they have and the constant risks that children are subjected to,' commented the foreman. The coroner's words underlined the point: 'I urge mothers and fathers to keep an eye on teenage children. Jason's death will not be in vain if we can draw lessons from it.'[39] The next day it was reported that 'teenage junkies' had turned the grave of the boy who had become their hero into a 'shrine', beside which they smoked heroin.[40] Whether these juvenile drug users had formed their image of Jason through friendship or through his representation in the press was not clarified.

A familiar story resurfaced. In the sixties, pushers were supposed to lurk outside school gates offering children ice creams or sweets laced with LSD. In 1983, the *Daily Telegraph* reported that a twelve-year-old user was 'a victim of drug pushers who waited outside Woodchurch High School, Birkenhead, offering "free gifts" to children'. Carole Wooley, an adviser to the Merseyside Drugs Council, was quoted as the source for the story. It reappeared a year later in the *Daily Express*, where she repeated the claim: 'A pusher will give them free smack three or four times, promising it will make them feel good. Then they have to start paying for it. And when they can't they turn to crime.' 'We've got the equivalent of the Black Death breaking out in the Wirral,' added the local MP Frank Field. Gifts and money may have played another part in the background to the original release of this horrifying story at that particular time. A few weeks earlier, the chairman of the Merseyside Drugs Council had appealed for funding. Subsequently a £305,000 plan to combat the heroin threat was announced.[41] Carole Wooley's claim was adopted cheerfully by the exponents of the tabloid technique of sensation through lazy generalization. Some of these journalists seem never to need to draw breath. 'Across the country, drugs are destroying lives like the plague. Kids no longer spend all of their pocket-money just on sweets and at the cinema. They are after glue, cannabis, cocaine and heroin. And when the pocket-money runs out, they'll lie, steal, prostitute themselves and even sacrifice their lives for the next fix. Pushers wait outside school gates offering heroin for £5 a go, tempting children with the dream of "chasing the dragon". They know the kids will soon be back for more. Teenage addicts are giving birth to heroin babies screaming in agony. And every day, the tragedy grows.'[42]

William Burroughs had seen it all decades before. Having fled an American drugs panic, he viewed its progress in his home country with his jaundiced junkie common sense. 'Safe in Mexico, I watched the anti-junk campaign. I read about child addicts and Senators demanding the death penalty for dope peddlers. It didn't sound right to me. Who wants kids for customers? They never have enough money and they always spill under questioning. Parents find out the kid is on junk and go to the law. I figured that either stateside peddlers have gone simpleminded or the whole child-addict setup is a routine to stir up anti-junk sentiment and pass some new laws.'[43]

The ultimate victims are infants. The *Daily Mirror* Shock Issue splashed a picture of an ordinary-looking baby splayed awkwardly on its back and labelled him 'BABY GAVIN: HEROIN ADDICT'. 'IS YOUR CHILD'S LIFE AT RISK?' it asked underneath. Adults, it seems, are immune to the 'modern Black Death'. All the big metaphors were deployed as the mighty tabloid swung into action. 'The *Daily Mirror* declares war on the drugs barons and the pushers. We want you – the ordinary people of this great nation – to help rid us of this evil epidemic.' Having ordered parents to initiate surveillance, it instructed this Home Guard of ordinary people to inform on dealers. Their finest hour was recalled by comparing major pushers to Nazi mass murderers. The courts were urged to sentence them accordingly. 'But most of all,' it concluded, 'parents, teachers, brothers, sisters and friends of victims should mobilise into a fighting crusade against this evil.

'It is, literally, a fight to the death. The death of young lives. Your kid or the kid next door.

'**No one is safe unless we all act now.**'

The *Daily Express* mounted a similar campaign some weeks earlier, playing heavily on the slang expression 'chasing the dragon', which has gained currency as an expression meaning 'smoking heroin'. This way of taking the drug has undoubtedly assisted its spread among youngsters whose idea of junkies inevitably involved needles, and who have none of the strong inhibitions about heroin that kept many of the children of the 'psychedelic' era away from opiates. It has also given papers like the *Daily Mirror* and the *Daily Express* the opportunity to indulge in a little chinoiserie. Both have used an Oriental dragon graphic as an emblem of the fight against the 'deadly flood'. The *Daily Express* brought another, rather unfortunate foreign connotation – using a phrase from one of the most famous Nazi films – into its own declaration of war on the pushers with its conclusion: 'We can ensure the defeat of heroin through the triumph of the will.'[44]

The *Daily Express* was delighted to announce the recruitment of allies to its cause.[45] 'The Prince and Princess of Wales have declared war against the tide of drugs now swamping Britain,' it proclaimed. The Princess, the second part of the 'exclusive series' related, was 'now one of the most effective personalities fighting the problems of drug abuse in Britain'. She has achieved this impact in a tally of four visits, a television appearance, an endorsement and a foreword written for a National Directory of Drug Services (which totalled some seventy-seven words).

Princess Diana had made her campaign début on the BBC's *Drugwatch* programme. Hosted by the popular television personality Esther Rantzen, of the *That's Life* light entertainment consumer programme, and Nick Ross of *Crimewatch*, it combined the two shows to come up with a populist concoction of information, tragic examples, punditry and testimony. The last was crucial. In true evangelical style, the fallen were enticed into testifying. The repentant also went through their paces. Ex-addicts, put in front of TV cameras and coaxed by an alliance between the overwhelming authority of that medium and the rehabilitation agencies who imposed the disciplines which replaced their drug dependence, tend to behave in the ways expected of them. There is no deception, simply the replacement of drug users' discourse by approved ones. The programme showed training for the battle on the borders of the law as role-playing schoolchildren gave the viewers some hints on ways to refuse drugs offered, as they usually are, by friends.

This was a different kind of drug campaigning. Its brief was to police families, and especially children, rather than to sell newspapers. The mythology of the pusher had no place in this project, though the excitement of the hi-tech drug interdiction programmes was illustrated by clips from American TV. *Drugwatch* was the flagship of an anti-drug campaign whose vested interests were those of the state rather than commerce. It used the techniques of mass-audience television to build up a crusade with a benign feel to it. The emphasis was on mutual help and a sense of community, not the pseudo-militarism of the tabloids' call to arms. A sense of momentum was generated by encouraging self-help groups to make themselves known to the programme while it was being transmitted. Periodic updates geared up the bandwagon in the manner of charity 'telethons'.

The psychological sophistication of the programme was in large part imported. The semi-official anti-drugs campaign was transplanted from the USA, where Nancy Reagan had been enthroned as Patron and what her husband called the 'motivational force' of the 'Just Say No' Movement. This simple command was the key weapon in the operation aimed at preventing the spread of illicit drug use. A slogan for the 1980s indeed. In the course of promoting it, the First Lady allowed herself to be photographed sitting on the lap of the actor who played Mr T in the pyrotechnic television series, *The A-Team*: such was the motivational force of the anti-drugs movement that it could induce the wife of the spectacularly reactionary President into such close proximity to a large black man with a Mohican haircut.

Drugwatch took the 'Just Say No' concept to its bosom. It needed a home-grown equivalent to Nancy Reagan. Thus it was that the Princess of Wales walked unannounced on to the set and nervously told her interviewer: 'The drug problem is something that worries me very much. I hope families will watch together so they can talk about it openly.'

The Finale was the scrawling of the Drug Wall. Her Royal Highness inaugurated it with her signature, and was followed by a motley assortment of famous people, all just saying No. What was rather lacking at the end of it were the signatures of people likely to have some influence over the kind of young people who were actually likely to try illegal drugs. In this context, the presence of people like the chat-show host Terry Wogan, middle-of-the-road pop singers the Nolan Sisters, and entertainer Rolf Harris, may have been counterproductive. But they helped bolster the sense of unity; and it was, after all, family television.

A number of television drama programmes have tackled the drug issue. Prominent among them are those inspired or controlled by producer Phil Redmond. In the Channel 4 soap opera *Brookside*, a stereotype snivelling junkie girl arrived – and disappeared just as suddenly, taking some of her hosts' property with her. The reaction of the characters Sheila and Bobby Grant on finding the tinfoil spoor of heroin in their home was well observed: they both took particular exception to their son bringing it into the house, polluting the hearth. They did not reach for a drink, though. *Brookside* differs from its rivals *Coronation Street* and *EastEnders* in its unwillingness to indicate moments of tension by such devices, and in not focusing its characters' social life upon a pub.[46] A second heroin addict in

Brookside Close, who appeared in the guise of a well-groomed professional man in the autumn of 1986, is probably the most implausible fictional addict of the whole panic. By now, it appears, the producers have put the need to educate the public about drugs second to the need for a sensation in the storyline.

Redmond, a non-drinker himself, developed the Merseyside smack-and-dole theme in a serial, *What Now?* Its characters were social-realist versions of Disney cartoons, bouncing off each other like misguided projectiles in search of a target. The watershed event in their young lives was the death of one of their number, a heroin user. 'Bloody drugs,' wailed his father, repeatedly, despite the fact that the apparent cause of death was the Ford Capri in which the youth had been doing some spur-of-the-moment racing. As if the crux of the drama were not enough, the message was reinforced down to subliminal level. One character wore a *Drugwatch* T-shirt. There were anti-heroin posters everywhere, even flashing through an action shot of a chase scene at an empty swimming pool.

By far the most effective of the anti-heroin productions from the Redmond stable has been the BBC childrens' serial *Grange Hill*, set in a school. Originally devised by Redmond, it has established a reputation for authenticity and a readiness to tackle controversial issues, as well as an enormous following among schoolchildren. It is decidedly brisk. There are none of the protracted will-she-won't-she story-lines designed to milk the ratings for all they are worth. You are liable to miss the dispatch of the teacher seen dallying with a pupil if you blink, and if you missed the very first episode of the series, you wouldn't know that the head teacher had been written out in a car crash. But the heroin story-line was carefully developed, and avoided stereotyping. It explored the psychology of the addict, his behaviour, and how others dealt with it. The alien quality of the addiction was diluted by comparisons with dependence on legal drugs. All in all, it has a strong claim to being the best of all the fictional television portrayals of heroin addiction.

Then came the 'Just Say No' Movement. Brought over as a package from America on to British soil, it hijacked the recognizable London schoolchildren and turned them into the all-dancing, all-simpering Kids From Fame. They recorded the 'Just Say No' theme song and released it as a single, with an accompanying video. Lee Macdonald, who played the addicted Zammo, was flown out along with some other cast members to see the American movement in full swing. They met a pre-teen monster rejoicing in the name of Soleil Moon Frye, apparently a local TV personality, and for the climax of the visit, were presented to Nancy Reagan. Back home, the record made the Top Ten, selling some 225,000 copies.

Genuine pop stars have proved harder to integrate into the campaigns. They are role models for youth, and members of the industry whose place as a responsible force in society has been confirmed by concerts for the Prince's Trust (its patron is said to attend wearing earplugs) and, of course, the global impact of the Live Aid charity events. It is not enough for Nancy Reagan, however. She refused to attend an anti-drugs concert at which Madonna, Ozzy Osbourne, George Michael and Aretha Franklin were billed to appear, because she considered the stars to be a 'corrupting influence'.[47] It might have been a prudent move. The 'growing army of pop stars ... warning of the grim realities of taking heroin'[48] are not the most reliable of troops. Although many allow their names to be associated with various anti-drug declarations, the benefit records and concerts have not materialized on the scale that might be expected. More publicity surrounds the fate of performers like Phil Lynott, a casualty in the war. Others fail to live up to their good intentions. 'It's up to us to play down the fashionable side of drugs. It's all very well asking teachers, doctors or even the police to remain vigilant over youngsters but they will always be seen as too authoritarian. Drugs are seen as very fashionable. So it stands to reason that rock stars should be the ones who make the most relevant statements against drug abuse.' That was Boy George's advice.

The public education campaign has infused the tabloids, helping to restructure and discipline it. But the battery of potent themes which could be brought into a drugs story remains an irresistible lure. 'A junkie mum who turned to vice to pay for heroin has made a solemn promise to Princess Diana to quit drugs and prostitution.'[49] This one had the lot: royalty, heroin, motherhood, sex – and that was all in the opening sentence. The junk story would run and run.

Notes

1   *Sun Day* (*News of the World* colour supplement), 6 July 1986.
2   *Daily Mirror*, 11 January 1986.
3   *Daily Mirror*, 8 January 1986.
4   *Guardian*, 11 January 1986.
5   *Daily Mirror*, 2 January 1986.
6   Thatcher used such formulations on more than one occasion,
    despite public outcry. A late example, 'there are, as we know,
    enemies of democracy both within and without', was part of the
    Second Carlton Lecture given at the Carlton Club on 26
    November 1984.
7   There are labels: 'Thatcher's drug war' (*Guardian*, 10 August
    1985). There are commands: 'Make war on pushers' (*Daily
    Express*, 22 September 1984). There are statements: 'Mums get
    the call in drug war' (*Daily Mirror*, 4 April 1986). And there are
    strings of alarm-signal words: 'Drug war jail crisis' (*Daily Mirror*,
    27 September 1985). The use of 'crusade' is less common. 'My
    Crusade For The Lives Of Our Children', by Margaret
    Thatcher (*News of the World*, 20 October 1985), shows how her
    supporters strive to build an image for her which combines
    aggression with compassion.
8   The concept of war was extended to give the military even
    greater powers. The Posse Comitatus law, which prohibits US
    armed forces from enforcing the civilian criminal code, had to be
    amended to permit drug interdiction forces to make use of
    technologically advanced military systems such as the Sentry
    radar surveillance aircraft and the famous U2 spy plane
    (Freemantle, *The Fix*, p. 101). See also *Air International*,
    December 1984, and Charles Clements, *Witness to War* (London,
    Fontana, 1985). The latter provides a memorable account, from
    a target's point of view, of the use for which the A37 counter-
    insurgency jets sent to bomb cocaine traffickers' airstrips (Ch. 5)
    were built, and deployed in Latin America.
9   *Sun*, 13 June 1986. The next quotation is also from this source.
10 *News of the World*, 15 June 1986.
11 *People*, 15 June 1986.
12 *Sun*, 13 June 1986.
13 *News of the World*, 15 June 1986.
14 For example, *Sun* 13 June 1986, *News of the World*, 15 June 1986.
    Subsequently Sebastian Guinness was gaoled for four months for

possessing heroin and cocaine, and Rosie Johnston received a nine-month sentence after being convicted of possessing amphetamines, cannabis and cocaine and of supplying heroin to Olivia Channon.

15 *People*, 15 June 1986.

16 'Of all the words written about the tragic death of Olivia Channon at Oxford last week, one fact beams through. She didn't like herself very much.' (Anne Robinson, *Daily Mirror*, 18 June 1986.) This was a thoughtful piece with a number of insights about growing up, but the point about personality theories still stands. An article criticizing the editing process that makes a nonsense of young people's accounts of drug-taking (glue-sniffing in this case) by removing references to its positive side appeared in the *Guardian*, 19 August 1986.

17 *News of the World*, 15 June 1986.

18 *Star*, 17 June 1986.

19 *Daily Mirror*, 12 June 1986.

20 TV-am broadcast, 17 June 1986.

21 *News of the World*, 22 June 1986.

22 *Sunday Times*, 16 May 1965.

23 Filmed interview, included in *The Rock'n'Roll Years*, transmitted 7 July 1986 on BBC 1.

24 *People*, 15 June 1986.

25 Dr David Owen, leader of the Social Democratic Party, was one who contradicted the Government's assertion that there was no causal relationship between illegal drug use and unemployment. He cited academic research in support of his claim, made in the 1985 Prime Lecture at St Thomas's Hospital in London (*Guardian*, 16 October 1985).

26 cf. Susan Sontag: 'In the Middle Ages, the leper was a social text in which corruption was made visible; an exemplum, an emblem of decay.' (*Illness As Metaphor*, London, Penguin, 1983, p. 58).

27   Then she did some smack with a Chinese chap, oh-oh,
        An affair began with Charlie Chan, oh-oh . . .

A song from the period of 'Chinese' heroin that began when heroin from the Golden Triangle of South-East Asia was supplied to meet the demand frustrated by the 1968 ban on prescribing. It was said to be smuggled by the Triad criminal organizations which had a presence in the British Chinese community. The Triads, incidentally, originated in seventeenth-century China as a secret

nationalist movement dedicated to the overthrow of foreign rule.
The foreign rulers were the Manchus.

> There's a Siamese cat in the council flat, oh-oh,
> The finest grains for my lady's veins, ooh-ooh . . .

('Plaistow Patricia', by Ian Dury and Chaz Jankel, from *New Boots and Panties*, Stiff Records, 1977. Published by Blackhill Music.)

28 'The way young people are being lured into debt is scandalous,' said the *Sun* in an editorial entitled 'Loan mania'. 'Getting into debt is really no different from getting hooked on drugs, with the money lenders acting as the pushers.' (23 June 1986).

29 cf. Christopher Lasch, the American social critic who argues that the traditional idea of a political Left and a Right should be abandoned: '. . . the model of ownership, in a society organized around mass consumption, is addiction. The need for novelty and fresh stimulation becomes ever more intense, intervening interludes of boredom increasingly intolerable. It is with good reason that William Burroughs refers to the modern consumer as an "image junkie" . . . Drugs are merely the most obvious form of addiction in our society. It is true that drug addiction is one of the things that undermines "traditional values", but need for drugs – that is, for commodities that alleviate boredom and satisfy the socially stimulated desire for novelty and excitement – grows out of the very nature of a consumerist economy.' (*New Statesman*, 29 August 1986).

30 *Daily Mirror*, 27 November 1984.

31 For example, *News of the World*, 30 September 1984, *Guardian*, 27 March 1986.

32 *Guardian*, 21 March 1986.

33 *News of the World*, 20 October 1985.

34 For example, 'VICARS SAVE BLONDE RAPED BY WITCHES: Ordeal of drugs and blood lust. A terrified blonde yesterday relived the nightmare of her initiation as a witch. The girl, who fears for her life, told how she was:
MADE to drink cockerel's blood mixed with her own.
RAPED by the coven's high priest in front of 200 people.
HOOKED on heroin handed out by the devil-worshippers to lure innocent youngsters.' (*Daily Mirror*, 16 September 1985.) Heroin is thus associated with secret conspiracies, satanism, violence, enslavement and the corruption of the young.

35 *News of the World*, 29 September 1985.
36 *Daily Mirror*, 7 December 1985.
37 *Daily Mirror*, 6 August 1985.
38 *Daily Mirror*, 31 January 1986.
39 *Guardian*, 31 January 1986.
40 *Daily Mirror*, 1 February 1986.
41 The foregoing material in this paragraph is derived from an outstanding, but unfortunately unpublished, 1984 Cambridge M.Phil. thesis by Tony Borzoni entitled *The Mythology of Heroin and the Press*, plus a *Daily Express* report of 20 September 1984. The *Daily Telegraph* piece appeared on 20 October 1983.
42 *Sun Day*, 2 February 1986.
43 William S. Burroughs, *Junky* (London, Penguin, 1984), p. 143. Originally published in 1953.
44 *Daily Express*, 22 September 1984.
45 The crusading papers displayed a vanguardist attitude towards their place in the struggle that would make the average Trotskyist grouplet seem self-effacing. Reporting a call by trade union officers representing Customs personnel for increased recruitment to improve the interdiction of cocaine, the *Daily Express* ran the banner 'Customs men join *Express* campaign' (11 December 1982). The officers of both sexes who had been stopping the smuggling of illegal drugs as long as they had been in the Customs service would perhaps have liked a little more emphasis on the conflict between their demand and Government public spending policy.

   The articles referred to in this paragraph appeared on 14 and 15 April 1986.
46 *Daily Mirror*, 26 April 1986.
47 *Daily Mirror*, 5 April 1986.
48 'Rock stars twist the Dragon's tail', *Daily Express*, 20 October 1984. The Boy George quote which follows is from the same source.
49 *Sunday Mirror*, 9 March 1986.

EIGHT

Da Da Da

It is not difficult to deconstruct the mythology of heroin. Part of this deconstruction has produced a small sub-caste of heroin stories in which it appears as the object – the *victim* – of a smear campaign. With such a massive tide of discourse as the one establishing heroin as a malevolent spirit which exists to make people its victims, perhaps a reaction which makes the drug the victim is inevitable.

This curious movement creates a counter-mythology for the drug which is plausible in detail but somehow unsatisfactory in general. In March 1986[1] the *Observer* devoted a page to a re-examination of heroin policy which showed signs of the magnetism of an alternative view. It cited some of the evidence suggesting that long-term heroin use does not cause physical damage in the way alcohol and tobacco do, but swiftly countered them with representatives of the traditional picture, and ended up wanly concluding that more research was needed. A more partisan production made for Channel 4's *Diverse Reports* series[2] painted a distinctly benign picture. Arguing the benefits of the system of prescribing opiates to maintain a stable, controlled habit, it showed addicts in their nicest clothes, suggesting that it would basically be all right to be an addict if the needles were clean and the drugs legal. Although it adhered to the protocols governing the representation of drugs in the media, expressing disapproval at the appropriate points, the programme produced a friendly heroin from which there was little to be feared.

The question of maintenance-prescribing really lies outside the scope of this book. It is the way that heroin is represented that is at issue. And there remains something distinctly insufficient about heroin cleaned up and cut down to size. There is an excess left over from this reduced meaning of the drug that begs the question, *what makes heroin so special?*

It isn't the most extreme form of intoxication. If intoxication is the trick of poisoning the body until the drug-taker is as near to a shambling subhuman as is possible without being dead as well, then barbiturates are the thing. The lethal ultimate stage is a vital element of a special drug, but heroin hardly has a monopoly on toxicity. Heroin is not the only drug to produce euphoria, nor does it do so automatically. Despite everything that says heroin is not unique, though, something keeps saying that it is.

It could be just the edifice of mythology and the protestations of addicts. Propagandists and addicts collude in inflating the myth of the drug as a kind of destiny, whether that destiny is rooted deep in the allegedly flawed personality of the addict, or in the terrible secret power of the drug itself. Some addicts, the cult addicts, they could be called, have a special relationship with heroin. A punk rock group of the late 1970s, expatriate Americans calling themselves the Heartbreakers, were able in the close world of punk to be more explicit about heroin than would be conceivable today. They played what they called 'love songs to objects'. 'Objects' belongs to the language of psychoanalysis, which may be the right language in which to describe as intimate an experience as heroin addiction. The objects were, of course, drugs; mainly heroin. The Heartbreakers' residual coyness pointed their phrasing towards the royal road to the heart of heroin.

Diverse Reports revived the image of the man who discreetly injects his morning dose of pharmaceutically pure heroin, rolls down his sleeve, disposes of the syringe and needle in a responsible manner, dons his jacket and goes off to a respectable job – the old maintenance image. The model is the diabetic, whose life is normal to the point of being exemplary, but who has to punctuate it with regular injections in order to preserve that normality. No shame attaches to the diabetic, and, it is implied, no shame would attach to the heroin addict if he were removed from the squalid black market, and the social stigma removed from heroin. The assumption is that the stigma is simply social, and irrational. But it can be contended that heroin for such an addict would always be a secret shame because unlike diabetes, it is far more than a physical dependency. The secret weakness puts our white-collar addict into the immeasurable class of Britons with something rattling in the cupboard; something like cross-dressing, paedophilia or fetishism.

Fetishism is a zone into which many heroin users find their way. The manner in which injecting the drug takes on a ritualistic form has become something of a drug platitude. The drug itself becomes something of a fetish for many of its users, as is to be expected in cases of monomania. A model of heroin addiction that derives from diabetes may serve to calm down a seriously overheated public debate, and it may be useful at a certain point to rescue the addict from being forever branded as a drug fiend. But, in reducing the relationship between addict and drug to a matter of adjusting a chemical balance, it reduces the addict as a human subject. The relationship between heroin and those who would sing love songs to it is bigger than both of them. What its vast bulk contains is the source of a shame that goes beyond the social.

Some analysts, looking at the classic young ghetto junkie, have gone beyond the trite observation that heroin addiction might not be as bad as an undrugged ghetto life. They point out its appeal to the immature and confused person who is faced with a range of unpalatable choices. If female, she may become pregnant and devote herself to the care of her child, a move which may bring her back to the comfort and support of her family. If male, he may survey the options and look for something as basic and simple. Deprived of the chance to move from school to a decent job with modest prospects, he may be frightened by the complexities and dangers of life in the urban badlands. Nothing is simpler than the personal economy of heroin. The complexities of the 'object choices', and relationships with other people can be bypassed. The prime relationship is with the drug.

At this level, it is possible to explain the explicit choice of addiction as a career.[3] The relationship is a deeper one, however, and it is one that lends itself to a very loose version of a psychoanalytic account of *desire*.[4] Beginning such a hazardous account is daunting. I shall shield myself with an excuse for beginning that echoes the plaint of the ghetto junkie in search of his object choices. 'Desire says: "I should not like to have to enter this risky order of discourse; I should not like to be involved in its peremptoriness and decisiveness; I should like it to be all around me like a calm, deep transparence, infinitely open, where others would fit in with my expectations, and from which truths would emerge one by one; I should only have to let myself be carried, within it and by it, like a happy wreck".'[5]

Desire says, let this fluid support me; let my experience be cut free from time, for time is anxiety. There is desire and it makes everything else into anxiety. Every time a gaggle of neurons signal hunger or fatigue, a demand for food or rest is initiated, and between the demand and its satisfaction there is anxiety. Yet the satisfaction of the immediate demand always leaves a sort of excess. The demand always 'bears on something other than the satisfaction which it calls for'.[6] The excess that is left when the demand is met can be named 'desire'.

Why should desire exist? It isn't really anything, and so it can certainly never be satisfied. It is no good trying to give it a reasonable explanation, because, being an empty space, it is not amenable to reason. Nor, as the example of hunger above shows, is there any point in treating it as a biological need, to be shut up as you would a pet cat, by feeding it. But it cannot be ignored, because it is always there. For the French psychoanalyst Jacques Lacan, it is the product of language.

The grave attention that Freud gave to the children he encountered, and who thus unwittingly donated parables to the original texts of psychoanalysis, was held by a boy of eighteen months in whose household Freud spent some weeks. The boy was unremarkable in most respects, not a fast developer, but considered 'good' by his parents. In particular, he would undergo his mother's absence for a few hours without crying. His one unruly trait was a habit of throwing small objects into inaccessible places, accompanying this with a long drawn out cry of 'o-o-o-o'. His mother and Freud agreed that this was the boy's version of 'fort', the German for 'gone'. One day Freud watched the boy throwing a wooden reel on the end of a string over the edge of the cot, to the 'o-o-o-o' cry, and reeling it in with a happy 'da' ('there'). Freud made a number of observations about the meaning of this game, but shrank from drawing definite conclusions from it. However, he was clear that 'it was related to the child's great cultural achievement – the instinctual renunciation (that is, the renunciation of instinctual satisfaction) which he had made in allowing his mother to go away without protesting.' To make up for this experience of loss, he re-enacted the experience using objects as substitutes – and included a happy ending.[7]

The highly suggestive, yet still provisional quality of the way Freud discusses this episode was to be impassioned by the hysteria that gives Lacan's work (and life) its seductive magnetism. The latter was transfixed by the first moment when an infant perceives loss. It learns to go beyond putting the reel in place of the mother: when objects are gone, it puts words in place of objects. The object only becomes an object for the infant when it is lost, and the use of language is a constant repetition of the operation that is needed to deal with loss. So loss is present throughout language; language is what makes humanity human, and so the human condition is characterized by loss. Like the background radiation which has filled the universe with background noise dating from the moment of its creation, desire is always present and uncontainable. Desire can not be satisfied.

Such starkness: it poses the question why? One of the advantages of this view of humanity is that it provides a way of explaining why any human being should want to do anything, an explanation that is fundamental to that person's being, but goes beyond the animal fundamentals of biological needs. The infant experiences loss: it is separated from the mother. What was untroubled, fluid, timeless and surrounding becomes fragmented, urgent and incomplete. By learning to substitute a thing for the lost object – the mother – it starts on the long path to becoming human. The entry into that humanity which is more than genetic is the moment when the infant learns to put words in place of things. But the word, or the cotton reel, are not the same as the lost object, and so the infant alienates itself from its desire by fastening on a stand-in. The process is one of displacement, and it can be used to account for any of a person's goals. They could all, had we a perfect view of the unconscious mind, be followed down the chain of substitutions to the initial loss that started the whole process.

It is an account of the human condition that includes a permanent, ever-present excess which confounds merely biological gratification. The consequence of this must be permanent anxiety: for the individual, a total, universal climate of tension. Stress could be thought of as being unconsciously measured against the primordial benchmark of original calm. The more a person's feelings stray away from his ideal state, the greater is the anxiety generated.

The desire to be static, or even to drift 'like a happy wreck', is one on which a civilization could founder. For Lacan the role of the father, or those various influences that could be said to add up to a symbolic father, is to introduce the infant to the symbolic order, the Law. And what a crisis, if we are to believe psychologists and social critics, the Western father is in! Christopher Lasch notes the general recognition among such observers that the father has absented himself, emotionally or actually, from the modern family, and bemoans the outbreaks of infantilism that have arisen in his absence.[8] Father is indicted in those character sketches beloved of psychiatric assessors who have set themselves the task of assembling a specification for the addict's unconscious. Harris and Isbell, declaring their findings in 1961, found that the addict showed a tendency to regress to the oral stage and regarded others as objects for his own gratification. His mother was overindulgent but showed him rejection in an inconsistent way, and what he lacked was a consistent father figure.[9] Bender's inventory of addict psychopathology (see Chapter 6) included maternal dependency, oral fixation, 'introverted schizoid and non-aggressive traits . . . ego pathology with poor reality testing, and an inability to delay gratification, low frustration tolerance and a marked tendency to retreat into passivity in frustrating situations . . . low self-esteem, depression and pessimism, difficulty in relating except on a manipulative level together with disturbances in sexual identification and rejection of the conventional American male role'.[10]

For Lasch, the most important effect of the father's absence is that he is not around to lay down the Law. The infant has yet to develop a sense of being separate from the rest of the world, or of having a place in the human order: the place in which the father and the Law will put it. The urge to regress – the desire for original simplicity – may turn these infantile misperceptions into fantasies of omnipotence. Heroin can stimulate such fantasies. Aleister Crowley: 'This sensation was one of infinite power . . . With heroin, the feeling of mastery increases to such a point that nothing matters at all.' Alexander Trocchi concentrates not on the illusion of power to affect the rest of the world, but on the complementary illusion of being complete: '. . . it is that the organism has a sense of being intact and unbrittle, and above all, *inviolable*.'[11] Here is the illusion that the fundamental split in the subject has been healed: the split that he undergoes when he puts a desire into words but inevitably leaves some of that desire unspoken.

Lasch is much preoccupied with illusions. Science and popular culture conspire to promote the illusion of omnipotence and 'reactivate infantile appetites' by presenting a myth of human power over nature, labour-saving technologies that obviate the need for human effort, and by electronically blurring the distinction between illusion and reality. In short, short cuts. Lasch is not simply echoing the vulgar hordes who think that young people have it too easy and could do with a stiff dose of discipline, but if the jargon were translated, parts of his work would have a lot of troubled traditionalist heads nodding in agreement. Into the picture of a world shaped by a consumer capitalism that promotes instant gratification and regression comes the short cut *par excellence*, a drug which creates the ultimate hallucination of satisfying desire.

Anxiety is diminished by a culture which prefers to acknowledge only its jagged edges. In that form, it means flutterings in the stomach and biting nails; overt anxiety that has got loose in the system. The drugs prescribed to deal with it are still widely regarded, despite mounting evidence of their pernicious effects, as about one notch up from aspirin.[12] This class of chemicals, the benzodiazepines (diazepam, or Valium, nitrazepam, temazepam and so on) were negligently dubbed the 'minor' tranquillizers. Their stated purpose is better described by the term 'anxiolytic' – anxiety-destroying. It is a term which doesn't seem to be applied to opiates, despite the fact that they are the supreme anxiolytics. If anxiety is conceived of at a more profound level than that of butterflies in the stomach, and its relationship to desire and the nature of being human accepted as it is considered here, then the especial power and danger of heroin becomes apparent. The other typical effects of the drug could not be better configured to add to heroin's primal allure. Those effects – warmth, comfort, the suspension of time, a painless drifting in and out of consciousness, and above all, a liberation from anxiety – may persuade users that they have found *the way back*.

The trap is then sprung: it wears off. The original loss has been re-enacted. The user moves in the pattern Freud grasped when he detected the compulsion to repetition. The addict chases the first high, and its elusiveness testifies to his primal experience. He learns yet again that you can't hang on to anything, but it doesn't stop him trying. One sort of junkie glamorizes himself as a tragic hero, without admitting the true nature of his quest.

Anika Lemaire plucks out the word 'hero' to describe the obsessional neurotic according to Lacan: 'Unlike the hysteric, the obsessional has felt himself to be loved too much ... A hero in possession of his mother, the obsessional feels himself to be irremediably guilty. Fear of castration requires the necessity of the death of the father if he is to avoid feeling guilty. Castration is avoided by assiduous, obnubilant work.'[3] In this light, what presents itself is the possibility that the junkie is a degenerate obsessional. Instead of being held in the grip of obsessive toil, he takes an illegal short cut to the abolition of guilt – and, as he knows this route to be 'wrong', heroin becomes even more necessary to overcome the guilt that the taking of it induces.

Such a junkie is an affront to conventional society in the most radical sense. The image of the drug-taking outlaw meandered into banality long before the dawn of the eighties, but heroin in its singularity re-presents that challenge by confronting the Law from a level deeper than consciousness. The question of legalization becomes laughable, because in this scheme of things heroin must always be against the Law. Heroin throws down a unique challenge to the symbolic order.

Heroin demonstrates the catastrophe that ensues upon the

stimulation of original desire and the short-circuiting of the chain of substitution. There is nothing left to live for. The economy becomes monopolistic: since everything desired is on an ever-proliferating chain of substitution stemming from the original loss, the illusion of making good that loss tends to destroy the infinite complexity of a subject's basic humanity. Personal relationships become superfluous, and the user becomes less and less concerned by the physical deterioration caused by self-neglect, as the ultimate goal recedes ever further from view.

This account concentrates on the pure essence of the matter, and it is not intended to reflect the patchy realities of drug-taking. Addiction is a less absolute phenomenon than is generally admitted. Users may, for instance, avoid drug-taking before appointments with officialdom, or even come off the drug so that when they restart, their tolerance will be lower and the habit cheaper.[14] They may drift into heavy use when supplies are available, come off when it is not, and relapse when conditions change again. The variations in the user's relationship to the drug produces a degree of autonomy that subverts such absolutist representations of the addict condition.

But the idealized image does walk free through the dingy streets, at least for a few onlookers. As the junkie stands for the antithesis of the police officer's values,[15] he (the generalization about gender is deliberate) forms an equally compelling figure for a very different kind of observer. There is a beautiful completeness about the self-conscious junkie. He needs but one thing, and as that thing is so tiny and minutely divided (it is only a small amount of powder, and that soon becomes part of the bloodstream, part of the organism), it can almost be overlooked in the pursuit of an image of a self-contained being. The closed circuit of gratification is an awesome thing, particularly if the circuit is closed by an intravenous needle.

It is also a phallic figure – but the phallus is a sham. It can never be had. The magnetic attraction of this figure is that of a perfection that is guaranteed to be unthreatening and inviolable. At the risk of sounding like *Viper*'s ghostwriter, there *are* smack groupies who persist in a *pas de seul* courtship dance. Such a relationship has the purity of perfect narcissism. The smack groupie recognizes in the object of her gaze (if the assumption about gender may be excused) a creature totally wrapped up in himself. The semblance of the phallus is a hologram unlikely to be conjured up in much actual sexual activity: the addict's loss of sexual drive is firmly entrenched in heroin folklore. She may approach him as nurse; mother, even, secure in the faith that her own sense of integrity and completeness is unlikely to be challenged by the complexities of the real relationship. The addict will monomanically continue to labour in his one-track personal economy, and she will protest her selfless desire to help.

Her relationship is at best voyeuristic. She may, after a formal ritual of coyness, be permitted to witness the ceremony. The passage from Lemaire about the obsessional quoted earlier continues: 'For the obsessional, therefore, the important thing is to fill in a crack, that of castration, in order that he may be the unfailing phallus.' The idea of a 'crack' in the body is fundamental to this area of theory. A hole in the body asserts the issue of incompleteness – a crack is there to be filled in, and the filling in will be attended by pleasure. The groupie is privileged to witness the needle-user creating a hole – 'o-o-o-o' – and filling it with the heroin that fills the hole of the whole organism. *Da!*

Within this perfect *fort–da* game for grown-ups, there is the drama of uncertainty. Will he find the vein? Will he have to withdraw and spill the dose into a battered sponge of subcutaneous tissue? The blood drawn into the syringe which confirms that the user's anatomical skills are adequate also makes the syringe part of the organism, a siding in the circulatory network, and thus transforms the nature of the instrument that made the crack. The needle junkie is a magician who can work the conjuring trick of making a hole and simultaneously fixing it.

In time, the viewer can withdraw, honourably admitting defeat, intact. It is a bogus relationship. The object of our gaze is always partly a mirror in which we ourselves appear beautiful; the smack groupie sees the beauty in the eyes of someone whose secret attraction is that he is as self-absorbed as she is.

This is high drama. It is a form of behaviour which assaults the essence of pleasure. Its prime medium is blood, rather than flesh. The risk of death from going too far is always present, as is that of possibly fatal infection. It is a heavily clandestine affair, whose nearest cousin is hardcore sex. There are other similarities: the obvious sadomasochism, the sexual symbolism of penetration and the needle, the investment with fetishistic qualities of the equipment and the ritual present. Both groups eschew conventional bodily sites and practices of pleasure. Hardcore heroin users – those who glory in it, not those who use it to express and seal their 'victim' condition – form an élite among drug fiends. They develop an enclosed and defensive subculture with codes of its own. Its mortality rate, and the other grisly consequences of the hardcore, hard drug way of life, are seen in terms of these codes.

William Burroughs is the hardcore poet. Although a literary establishment protects him by including him among the ranks of the greatest living authors, I find it difficult to believe he is actually alive. There must be some trickery, some voodoo neurology of the kind on which he has expended so much prose, that keeps the ancient drug and gun fetishist walking and talking. Our greatest undead author, certainly. He has survived by living the life of the outlaw while speaking the language of his pursuer. His fascination with pseudo-scientific fantasy reveals him as one of modern science's most enthusiastic groupies.[16] No professional scientist ever found deeper pleasure in pathology: 'You know how old people lose all shame about eating, and it makes you puke to watch them? Old junkies are the same about junk. They gibber and squeal at sight of it. The spit hangs off their chin, and their stomach rumbles and all their guts grind in peristalsis while they cook up, dissolving the body's decent skin, you expect any moment a great blob of protoplasm will flop right out and surround the junk. Really disgust you to see it.'[17] From the depths of the underworld, Burroughs relayed a commentary in the language of the heroin horror pamphleteers. It was a dialect more readily appreciated by the hipster, but recognizable none the less.

The most notable absence from Burroughs's revealing accounts of opiate addiction is affect. The expression of subjective feeling is as meagre as the first person singular is visible. On junk, Burroughs has one major line to peddle: the disease model and the myth of the Pusher. The latter is filtered through a counter-cultural suspicion of capitalism: 'Junk is the ideal product . . . the ultimate merchandise. No sales talk necessary. The client will crawl through a sewer and beg to buy . . . The junk merchant does not sell his product to the consumer, he sells the consumer to his product. He does not improve and simplify his merchandise. He degrades and simplifies the client.'[18] The former, the disease model, exists not only in his appropriation of medical terminology ('*The junk virus is public health problem number one of the world today*').[19] When he calls his dependency The Sickness, he is not speaking metaphorically. He argues that opiate addiction is a purely physical dependency, emphasizing the withdrawal syndrome as a demonstration of the power of junk over the body's cells. For all the aura of the underground, Burroughs is just a maverick disease-model theorist.

The rejection of emotion, and its science, psychology, is consistent with the hardcore attitude. The shocking lack of affect with which junkies discuss their pathology and mutual exploitation is diametrically opposed to the way in which outsiders represent the same phenomena. Part of this is attributable to the subculture shock that hits the conventional when they encounter a different way of life. There is also the difference in circumstances of the kind that shapes, for instance, the hopelessly incompatible attitudes of working-class families in English cities and their counterparts in the nationalist strongholds of Northern Ireland to the IRA insurgents. The latter see real people, not demons. But perhaps there is actually a pharmacological element at work too. Opiates act, as is fairly well known, upon neural receptors to which chemicals produced by the body normally bind. Speculation about this class of chemicals, known as endorphins (from *endo*genous m*orphine*), has flourished since they were first discovered in 1975. It has been suggested that jogging pumps up endorphin levels and thus rewards the exercise enthusiast with a dose of euphoria, and that childbirth would hurt even more were it not for the release of these intriguing compounds. It certainly seems sensible to suppose that endorphins are involved in the modulation of mood and affect. It might just be that chronic opiate intake disrupts a system of inconceivable subtlety to the extent that the capacity for emotion is impaired at the neurological level. To use a familiar line of imagery, exposing a nervous system to a lot of heroin might be like flooding the engine of a car.

Feeling is not just deadened by opiates. It is denied by those in the sphere of opiate influence. One of the more surprising family responses to the realization that a son or daughter is dependent on opiates is clandestine maintenance. Parents or other relatives actually support their children's habits. This may mean simply giving the child money, or, in some cases, actually going out and buying the drugs. *Drugwatch* featured a young Scottish woman whose mother and aunt had done just this, in order, as the family emphasized, to keep her alive. The family's assertions were not examined in any depth. The basis for the claim was not explained, and the possibility that heroin supplied by the older women might contribute to death by intoxication or by infection was not canvassed either.

A death threat is perhaps the most extreme formulation of the disease view of drug dependency. It dramatizes the family crisis, and can be used to justify criminal acts. A more restrained expression of the disease model is often used as a justification for family maintenance. Here money is used as a substitute for feeling and involvement. If parents can convince themselves that drug addiction is primarily a physical disease, it is easier for them to banish it to the category of externally inflicted woes, like polio or meningitis, for which they have little or no responsibility. Wealthy parents whose relationship with their children has always been primarily economic will simply find that the cash cost of parenthood is higher. For working-class families, the price of the disease model may cause far greater hardships.[20]

Disease is also a modern guise for sin. Both moralism and a medical model, which is by no means a matter of consensus in the medical profession itself, survive within organizations like Narcotics Anonymous. The fundamental principle that the addict is suffering from an incurable disease places a terrible blight on that individual's life. This reincarnation of the albatross hangs a burden round the addict's neck which is not unrelated to the stain of sin that churches use to reinforce their hegemony over their congregations. The NA member is inherently addictive in the way that man, in Christian

145

teaching, is inherently sinful. The task of the believer is to exercise free will in the struggle against temptation.

Narcotics Anonymous makes its spiritual foundation explicit in its affirmation of a 'Higher Power'. It is left to the individual to decide just what this phrase means, which seems to verge on the blasphemous. You don't obfuscate the Supreme Being. If the founders of NA and related movements believed that faith in God is essential to the resolution of drug problems, then they should be proud to proclaim that faith. Some religiously inspired drug charities do explicitly demand acceptance of Christ as a condition of treatment. This might severely restrict the number of people whom they can help, but at least this system of belief does not have to be unearthed from beneath a medico-mystical superstructure. While close co-operation between hospital drug dependency units and NA groups significantly strengthens drug treatment networks, it seems remiss of medical practitioners not to point out that when NA speaks of addiction as an incurable disease, it is expressing its belief, not objective fact. The same lack of qualification occurs in media coverage based on interviews with the proponents of such views.[21]

The main problem with spiritually based programmes is that they tend to be addictive. The pressure on their members to substitute the group for their former peers often leads to a simple transfer between enclosed subcultures. The hermetic world of Anonymity is often particularly noticeable to friends of problem drinkers, who, by contrast, are more likely to enter the subculture from a relatively open social circle. Former abusers of illegal drugs may warm to the new rituals and closeness of the NA groups, and will be spared the consequences of their former way of life. That may, of course, save their lives. But, in accepting their 'incurability', they condemn themselves to a permanent state of dependency.

Some social critics have explored the possibility that the so-called 'addictive personality' is, at least in part, the product of culture. Prominent among them is Stanton Peele, author of *Love And Addiction*.[22] Arguing in an American context, he describes a culture that trains the child to be dependent. Authority keeps itself separate from the individual, reluctant to let itself be internalized. An unsatisfiable desire is generated for external validation: the permanent student, forever huddling inside the institution, seeking the external affirmation of degree after pointless degree, is a prime example of the syndrome. A rigid and successful social structure which integrates such individuals into the machine may neutralize discontent; a more complex one, in which crisis is endemic, is liable to display the morbid symptoms of drug addiction.

Peele's ideas about the addictive nature of 'relationships' – sexual partnerships – gain immensely from his socio-political observations. His is a rare concern to follow the rhetoric of personal responsibility to its logical conclusion, rather than employing just enough of it to get children to say no. It also avoids the postulation of a transcendent form of dependency called the acceptance of God, the one good addiction in a world full of narcotic heresies.[23]

Notes

1   *Observer*, 16 March 1986.
2   Channel 4's *Diverse Reports*, 'A Bad Habit', transmitted 26 September 1984.
3   John Kaplan, *The Hardest Drug* (Chicago, University of Chicago Press, 1983), pp. 50–1.
4   See Anika Lemaire, *Jacques Lacan* (London, Routledge & Kegan Paul, 1977), and the Introductions to *Feminine Sexuality* by Jacques Lacan and the *école freudienne* (London, Macmillan, 1982).
5   Michel Foucault, 'The Order of Discourse', 1970; in *Untying the Text*, edited by Robert Young (London, Routledge & Kegan Paul, 1981).
6   Lacan, 'The Meaning of the Phallus', quoted in Lacan, *Feminine Sexuality*, p. 32.
7   Sigmund Freud, *Beyond the Pleasure Principle* (London, Pelican, 1984), pp. 283–7.
8   Christopher Lasch, *The Minimal Self* (London, Picador, 1985), p. 192. See also Lasch, *The Culture of Narcissism* (London, Abacus, 1980).
9   *British Journal of Addiction* 57 (1) (1961).
10 Cited by Joy Mott, 'The Psychological Basis of Drug Dependence', *British Journal of Addiction* 67 (1972), pp. 88–99.

11   Crowley and Trocchi are both quoted by Julius Merry in 'Social
     History of Heroin Addiction', *British Journal of Addiction* 70
     (1975).
12   Under US Food & Drug Adminstration rules drawn up in 1980,
     the following warning should be supplied with all prescriptions for
     such drugs: 'You can become dependent on Valium. Dependence
     is a craving for the drug or an inability to function normally
     without it. An overdose of Valium alone or with other drugs can be
     fatal. You should avoid drinking alcohol while taking Valium. The
     combination of alcohol and tranquillizers dangerously increases
     the effects of both. Studies indicate an increased rate of birth
     defects in children whose mothers took Valium during the first
     three months of pregnancy. If you have been taking Valium for a
     month or more, your doctor should reassess your condition and
     your continued use of the drug. The effect of these drugs for the
     relief of anxiety for periods longer than four months has not been
     studied.' Perhaps 'Valium Screws You Up' would have a
     reasonable paraphrase.
13   Lemaire, *Jacques Lacan*, p. 229.
14   Kaplan, *The Hardest Drug*, pp. 34–5.
15   An interesting discussion of this idea is to be found in Peter
     Laurie, *Drugs* (London, Pelican, 1984).
16   He must have felt particularly honoured to be asked to contribute
     some observations on his experiences to the *British Journal of
     Addiction*. Lacking academic qualifications, he devised a style for
     himself which appeared in the title: 'Letter from a Master Addict
     to Dangerous Drugs', *British Journal of Addiction* (53 (2)).
17   William Burroughs, *Naked Lunch* (London, Grove Press, 1982),
     p. 5. The article referred to in note 16 is reproduced in this
     edition as an appendix.
18   ibid., p. xxxix.
19   ibid., p. xliv.
20   I am obliged to Radehey Bentley of the ACCEPT alcohol and
     drug agency for bringing this phenomenon, and the analysis of it,
     to my attention.
         An interesting example of the way family maintenance is
     portrayed in the press is the case of Mrs Jean Bird, a Bristol
     woman who took a second job to pay for cocaine which she bought
     for her nineteen-year-old son. Drug addiction served as their
     background against which the strength of a mother's love for her
     son could be lauded. 'I weaned him off cocaine like a baby from

the bottle': such was the pitiful image of motherhood in the 1980s. The *Daily Mirror* report ('MOTHER TURNED DRUG PUSHER TO SAVE HER SON', 29 August 1986) defined love as the force which led her to 'descend into the squalid world of dope peddlers'. Yet further on in the copy was a glimpse of an uglier dynamic at work within the family: '. . . there was my son changed from the lovable boy he had always been into some kind of monster who would threaten to smash my face in if I didn't give him money for his damn drugs.' She explained her action by referring to doctors who 'told her he should not try to kick the habit until he could get special treatment'.

The police took no action against Mrs Bird.

21 'Death and despair litter the trail of the Dragon. But the monster can be beaten.

'Junkies are never cured, only reformed.' (*Daily Express*, 20 September 1984). This report also informed readers that 'Junkies set fire to anything from fields to schools.'

Similar disease-model assertions could be found in far wiser articles, such as one in *Sun Day* magazine (6 July 1986), which was full of useful advice supplied by 'experts James and Joyce Ditzler'. However, it also contained the flat statements 'Drug addiction is an illness like any other and it can be treated by experts,' and '. . . it is important to remember one vital fact – an alcoholic or drug addict is NEVER cured.'

Such ideas received an extensive airing in *From the Horse's Mouth*, a two-part documentary about the 'Minnesota Model' method of treatment (Focus Productions, 1985; transmitted by Channel 4 on 18 and 24 January 1986).

22 Stanton Peele, with Archie Brodsky, *Love and Addiction* (London, Signet, 1976).

23 Dr Meg Patterson's book *Hooked?* (London, Faber & Faber, 1986) discusses the relationship between addiction and spirituality from a committed Christian perspective. It is prefaced by the following entry from Webster's Dictionary:

addict: *addictus*: past participle:
addicere: to favour, to adjudge.

(i) to award by judicial decree; (ii) to surrender, to attach oneself as a follower to a person, or adherent to a cause; (iii) to surrender as a constant practice, e.g., 'we sincerely addict ourselves to Almighty God.' Thomas Fuller.

NINE

Narcomania

It was a story waiting to happen. The man on the early evening news made some wide-eyed remark about how the world of pop must have been shaken to its foundations. Frankly, anyone in the industry who was surprised by Boy George's implication in a heroin scandal deserved to be sacked for being irremediably out of touch.

It didn't take the tabloids by surprise either. Their movements around the George camp generated a second level of gossip. One major national tabloid pop columnist was said to be offering £35,000 to anyone who was prepared to spill the beans. A well-known musician was supposed to have accepted, but couldn't come up with the proof. The bounty was still up for grabs. Hints of something brewing began to bubble to the surface. The *Daily Mirror* secured a stool-pigeon and ran an exposé of George's alleged taste for cocaine.[1] This was in tune with shifts within the drug complex. Heroin, having served as a spearhead for the establishment of the drug issue, and as a paradigm of the horrors of drug abuse, had moved back into the shadows by the summer of 1986. There was only so much commercial mileage in heroin's initial image as a sort of miasma hanging above the urban wastelands. The public would watch one or two gritty kitchen-sink dramas, but glitzy soap operas are what sell newspapers. Cocaine is the kind of glamorous vice which could be used in the popular papers' double-action operation; tantalizing their readers with a vision of lifestyle nirvana, and simultaneously neutralizing the envy aroused with a warning of the price to be paid.[2]

The social history of the two drugs shows that where there is one, the other is usually not too far away. It was the *Sun* which got the big story. 'JUNKIE GEORGE HAS EIGHT WEEKS TO LIVE' was the stark message that took up nearly half of the front page of the *Sun* for 3 July. The death sentence had been pronounced by doctors, and brother David O'Dowd predicted a fourth heart attack by Christmas for his father Gerry. George himself was smoking up to nine grams of heroin a day, at a cost of £800. David described how his brother had tried to beat up his father and told his mother to ' — off out of his life'.

The story was massive – so massive that a picture of the androgynous singers George and Marilyn replaced the household institution of a picture of a half-naked woman on page three. It contained one gram of truth and eight grams of fantasy. The ensuing orgy of media attention led the *New Musical Express* to interview David O'Dowd in an attempt to sift the facts from the fiction.[3] David admitted to having organized much of the 'white-wash' that had contained the damage caused by the cocaine story. He felt that his brother had abused this respite. 'To George's mind,' David said, 'he'd got off the hook.' By David's account, it was his parents' distress and George's apparent lack of concern which spurred him to take the action he did. He received no payment for it. The death of rock star Phil Lynott had recently commanded tabloid headlines: David noted that Lynott's widow had expressed the wish that she had revealed her husband's condition while it still might have done him some good. 'The thing is, I'd run out of all ideas; the family had run out of ideas; there was nothing more we could do.'

Picking which unlovely organ would carry the exposé was unimportant. 'It wasn't really choosing, because all the papers are pretty much the same, the lot of them. To me, the *Mirror* pretends. The *Sun* are utter bastards, but they don't try and cover it up. Everybody knows they're bastards. You ask anybody – every person who reads the *Sun* – they don't believe it! They don't believe a word that's written.' This is a commonly expressed opinion: it is hard to accept that the state of the popular press faithfully reflects the nation's intelligence. But the trouble with drugs is that the checks that readers can normally bring to a story through a comparison with their own knowledge of the subject are drastically weakened by the fact that drugs remain completely alien to most people's experience.

David O'Dowd hit the *Sun*'s Nick Ferrari like a bolt from the blue with his phone call. It was on a plate and it wasn't going to cost News International a penny. Not that the truth was good enough. 'The stuff that was in the *Sun* that was true was that I said my brother was a drug addict; that is the truth. The rest, the times, how long he had to live and all that, I mean, that is a complete load of crap. All I said to them was, the reason for me doing it is, you know, it might be soon that he drops down dead.' He denied mentioning the eight weeks or the nine grams – 'I said that he was *spending* an average of £500 a day. I didn't say he was spending £500 a day on drugs.' The *Sun* even got the day of George's appearance at an Anti-Apartheid festival the previous weekend wrong.

George was special. Pubescent girls were paying for his habit, just as they pay the drugs bill for dozens of other pop stars, but George also had the knack of charming their mothers. Wittier and capable of better manners than most of his peers, he managed to win over parts of a generation which was bemused by his make-up and dresses.[4] He became a very English showbusiness personality: a family entertainer. The closeness of his own family lent itself to the development of this image – and put the story of his 'fall from grace'[5] firmly into the family category of drug stories. This was a particularly nasty example, which reached its nadir with the *Sun*'s member-by-member attack on the 'DOTTY O'DOWDS'.[6] There was hardly a shortage of angles. George's family, his psyche, his sex life, the decline of his career, the sordid side of the world of pop, the lesson for the nation's youth: all were grist to the mill. Heroin had given the popular press the ultimate story, and it was all too much for some of them. *Today*'s Bill Mouland resolutely put any residual literary fear of mixing metaphor behind him and launched into the tale of the fall from grace: 'The sleazy circus which cocooned outlandish pop stars Boy George and his friend Marilyn in a web of fantasy plunged deeper towards rock bottom yesterday.'[7] In the *Daily Express*, Roger Tavener and his sub-editor lost their tenuous grip on reality altogether, claiming that 'Once a strapping six foot one inch tall, George is now pale and haggard. His once famous long hair is cropped short and matted into dreadlocks.'[8] The curious idea of cropped dreadlocks unfortunately blurred the effect of the implicit assertion that the singer had lost height as well as weight. Despite stiff competition, this occupies a class of its own in the pantheon of heroin misinformation. The possibilities are surreal. Instead of 'Heroin Screws You Up', the Government could have blazoned hoardings round the country with the slogan 'Heroin Makes You Shrink'.

The furore forced the police into action. On 8 July, a squad of detectives operating out of Paddington Green police station raided George's St John's Wood house to the north and a flat in Westbourne Terrace to the west. Neither singer nor substances were found at the first address, but several people, including Marilyn, were picked up at the second. Four people, including another brother, Kevin O'Dowd, were charged with supplying heroin to George as a result of these and other raids. Marilyn emerged from Operation Culture facing a possession charge. The *Daily Mirror* congratulated itself by way of commending the Met: 'On Monday the *Mirror* demanded action from the police over the accusations surrounding this tragic pop star. Yesterday police swooped in an attempt to resolve the whole sad mess. The *Mirror* applauds their prompt action.'

The *Star* had been fatally slow to move on the original story, and had reported George's television denial of the heroin allegations with the prim note that it was 'the only tabloid newspaper yesterday not to join the hysterical clamour over Boy George . . . In the pop world you can trust the *Star* to get it right'.[9] Having got it wrong, it showed what a 1980s tabloid could do with its handling of the raid story. Just ten years before, such papers might have been content with a picture of a nubile woman and some accompanying copy about a conventional sexual indiscretion. Now, like an ageing roué, the *Star* found a young man could revive its jaded tastes. Under the headline 'STRIPPED NAKED!', it ran a picture of a scantily clad blond – the androgynous starlet Marilyn wearing a skimpy pair of swimming trunks. 'They made us all strip – and they searched us in places where I didn't think you'd be able to hide anything,' reported a coy teenager caught in the swoop.[10] Two days later, the *Star* led with an 'exclusive' report alleging that those ubiquitous, anonymous 'doctors' now feared that George was suffering from AIDS.

The police faced a problem. They had acted in response to the media clamour, and they had some prisoners. What they lacked was heroin. If they had found some, normal possession charges could have satisfied the demand for judicial action. As it was, Marilyn had to be charged on the basis of a confession, and the other defendants were on charges of conspiring to supply George. Unless it was to be the prosecution's case that they had not actually succeeded in their conspiracy, it followed that George had at some point been guilty of possessing heroin. There was also the undesirable possibility of the public perceiving that others were carrying the can while a rich and famous individual was escaping punishment. The case revealed the tension inherent in the dual status of the addict as both victim and criminal.

George was in camera at this point, being treated by Dr Meg Patterson, who had become well known for her work with other addicted pop stars. The border dispute between medicine and its neighbours, in this case the law, flared up when George was questioned and charged with possession of heroin before his course of treatment was complete. Dr Patterson pointed out that the precedent set by removing a drug user from a place of treatment could deter others from seeking such treatment, and that 'past possession' charges, laid in the absence of any material evidence of possession, could be brought against any illegal drug user in medical care – or ex-addicts talking about their past on television, for that matter.[11] By contrast, George's father took the news with historical stoicism. 'They have been arresting Irishmen for centuries,' he said. 'George is going to be alright.'[12]

He was. His co-operative attitude, and the shakiness of the evidence, resulted in a £250 fine at Marylebone Magistrates Court. (The case against Marilyn was dismissed for similar reasons, the prosecution offering no evidence.) After making his way out of the court with his mother, through droves of camera crews and screaming fans, George agreed that he had 'got off very lightly', describing the magistrate as 'very fair'. His television performance was mature and straightforward. Clearly reluctant to be dragged on to the bandwagon, he said what was proper for him to say, advising kids not to take heroin, and no more. He also endorsed the authenticity of the Government-sponsored copywriters' work, applying to his own case the lines about users thinking they can control the drug, and finding that it is controlling them. In other words, he joined the chorus of the dominant discourse. He also leaned heavily on the disease model in his warning, stressing the agony of withdrawal. Dr Patterson must have been none too pleased about this, since the whole point of her 'neuro-electric therapy' is that it provides quick and painless detoxification, thus eliminating the withdrawal syndrome as an excuse for not coming to grips with addiction. Perhaps George's use of the term 'hell' as an illustrative image indicated a certain moral dimension to his experience.

Anthony Burgess detected 'what the old-fashioned still call sin' in the aura surrounding modern pop stars. Drugs, he explained, grant the 'instant sin' necessary to achieve fame through shock. 'How old-fashioned the Beatles must seem now to the Boy George generation,' maundered the distinguished novelist. 'The Beatles were neat, clean, witty, cunning, undeniably Liverpool and undeniably male. Their talent was recognized through the whole spectrum of the musical world.'[13] How selective memory can be. Though Burgess could be forgiven for being unaware of the foursome's pill-fuelled nights in Hamburg, or reports of John Lennon's heroin addiction, he should hardly have overlooked the group's heavy involvement with the LSD-oriented culture of the late sixties; or Paul McCartney's more recent convictions for possessing cannabis. As far as drugs go, the Beatles make Boy George look wet behind the ears.

The whole episode has subjected pop to a lot of similarly off-target comment. The industry's recently consolidated status as a responsible part of society's cultural superstructure has made a clean-up campaign imperative. As the form of culture with the most influence on youth, and also the one most riddled with drugs, it is problematic. In a society whose responses to illicit drug use are dominated by the reflexes of prohibition or exclusion, it is inevitable that there should be calls to ban artists exposed as drug fiends from the airwaves. From the Conservative Party Chairman, Norman Tebbit, to the radio phone-ins, censorship has been the order of the day.[14] In a small brouhaha occasioned by a record which seemed to be trying to create the impression that it alluded to narcotics, Radio 1 DJ Mike Smith has gone further and recommended a ban on talking about drugs. He had, in his words, *suggested* to the producer of his record review programme that the single not be played, 'because I knew that the ensuing discussion would centre around the subject of drugs'. 'Why give any more publicity to a subject which is in danger of becoming acceptable?' he asked. 'Talking or writing about drugs (as opposed to drug problems) surely just serves to glamorize narcotics even more.'[15]

Meanwhile, the turn of events across the Atlantic makes the giddiest pronouncements from the old country seem like models of level-headedness. Urine tests for drugs have become all the rage. President Reagan, Vice-President Bush, and seventy-eight members of the White House staff took them, setting an example for the policing of employees across the United States. While 'jar wars' rage through the interior, the foreign army of smugglers have been challenged by a partial blockade of New York Harbour. Upstate, a school board has discussed allowing children to be strip-searched for drugs. State autonomy was threatened by White House proposals to withdraw Federal funds from states which did not have 'adequate' drug prevention programmes, or had decriminalized marijuana. Thirteen-year-old Deanna Young, of Tustin, California, handed her parents' stock of marijuana and cocaine over to the police, and won Nancy Reagan's praise. The girl 'must have loved her parents a great deal', said Nancy.[16]

Drugs, the Other of American consumer capitalism, and symbol of the alien Other outside her borders, seem to precipitate an inversion of all the civil libertarian principles on which America professes to stand. If Raisa Gorbachev had praised a Soviet child for turning her parents over to the state, every American prejudice about totalitarian oppression would have been confirmed.

Cocaine certainly seems to present the United States with problems, both as a result of its abuse, and because its illegality and profitability support large and well-armed criminal syndicates.

There is a historical precedent: that of Prohibition. Yet America has either failed to learn or chooses to ignore the lesson that mass drug use cannot be controlled by the crude device of a ban. Perhaps the period over which Reagan presides, making America 'feel good about itself' with wish-fulfilling Rambo fantasies, is not conducive to remembering the lesson of an unwinnable war. Both the profitability and the abuse-related problems of cocaine stem from a consumerist culture which exploits the pursuit of instant happiness and increasing intensity of sensation. Cocaine is a symbol and example of conspicuous consumption. Customs ordaining and regulating its judicious use have not evolved. One solution, therefore, might be to ditch its symbolic value as enemy, and come to terms with it. There exists a model for its controlled use, in the form of coca-chewing among South American mountain-dwellers. There, the modern metropolitan rush of cocaine-taking is absent; a moderate degree of stimulation is not. It might just be productive to subvert the illegal industry by legalizing (and taxing) similarly dilute preparations of cocaine which would lend themselves to benign use. In short, a hard drug might be softened. A practical solution, however, would not satisfy the covert urges gratified by 'jar wars' and informing on one's parents. The prime importance of these issues would seem to be confirmed by assessments which indicated that the number of regular cocaine users in the United States peaked at around five million in the late 1970s and has remained at that level.[17]

The American panic is infectious. In 1985, the all-party House of Commons Home Affairs Committee toured the United States to get a good fright, on the supposition that America's problems today would be Britain's five years hence. They duly returned to declare that drugs posed 'the most serious peacetime threat to our national well-being'.[18] The Committee called for the armed forces to be deployed against the 'warlike threat' which 'Western society' faces from the 'hard drugs industry', though this might seem injudicious in the light of the American services' chemical proclivities. When the matter of an experimental opium poppy crop grown in East Anglia (for the plants' non-narcotic, edible seeds) was raised in the House, the Committee's chairman, Sir Edward Gardner, did not inspire confidence in his knowledge of drug issues by claiming that the Government was trying to persuade Peru and Bolivia to destroy their opium crops.[19] The coca-growing peasants of those countries would, no doubt, be happy to agree to destroy crops that they never grew in the first place.

The Committee put the number of cocaine users in the US at twelve million. The numbers game, so effectively played by Hamilton Wright in the early years of the century, is rolling again. It flourishes in Britain, too, being particularly prominent in the early speculation that established heroin and other illegal drugs as a major topic of discourse. Illicit drug use lends itself to conspiracy theories and paranoid anxiety because of its invisibility and unmeasurability. Its extent can only be inferred by references to indices such as arrests for drug offences, seizures by the Customs & Excise, and notifications of addicts to the Home Office. Round numbers come into play: rules of thumb hold that the Customs intercept a tenth of incoming narcotic contraband, and that the number of addicts known to the Home Office is a tenth of the total. These proportions are no more than guesses, but that fact is often obscured in their presentation. A paperback on heroin published in 1985 bore the following rubric on the back cover: 'IN 1975 THERE WERE PROBABLY 4,000 KNOWN HEROIN ADDICTS IN BRITAIN: BY 1985 THE NUMBER WAS 50,000.'[20] The statement is confusing through and through. 'Probably' and 'known' are contradictory. The number of narcotic addicts known to the Home Office to be receiving drugs at the end of 1975 was 1,949. Of those notified during the year, 812 were dependent on heroin. The equivalent figures for 1984 were 5,869 and 6,611.[21] (The end-of-year total is derived by subtracting the number of addicts no longer recorded on 31 December from the total of new notifications and those known from the year before.) The absence of qualification from the second statement conceals still further the lack of a basis for the 50,000 figure.

The numbers game is a key feature of the 'immigration question'. Manipulation and partisan interpretations of the immigration statistics have become the central site of a debate in which anti-immigration propagandists seek to demonstrate the potential of the non-white population to overwhelm the indigenous British. Margaret Thatcher herself used the kind of anxious islanders' aquatic imagery so inseparable from characterizations of the illegal drug threat in her notorious words about people's fears of being 'swamped by an alien culture'. Racism is a most potent political asset, and part of the Conservatives' success in 1979 must have been due to their ability to appropriate some of the fascist National Front's less committed support. But full-blooded racial hatred is out of the question as an instrument for exercising hegemony over a jingoistic populace. The obvious substrate of national unity is unacceptable in a multi-racial society. The Falklands war was a one-off. The fact is that alien people were no longer the legitimate targets of overt hatred. The essence of being alien can still be attacked, however, when it presents itself in the right form.

With the heroin panic in full cry, animals rights campaigners have proposed a solution to the vexed question of fox-hunting. The ritual, the pinks and the chase could continue, but there would be no fox as quarry. Some sort of inert substitute would be provided. Thus the tradition would be perpetuated, without the need to address the questions of class and the impulse to kill that are at the heart of the custom. A sentimental notion of English tradition would be safeguarded, free from the contradiction posed by the equally sentimental notion of the British love of animals. The anti-heroin campaign is a bit like that. It is a pogrom fit for a civilized society. If it is a crusade, it is one in which the Saracens are pitied as victims of their Imams and the evil religion that enslaves them.

The black British population itself is dissociated from heroin. It is apparently culturally resistant to the drug, and that is probably just as well. If it had been identified with heroin, it would, no doubt, have been subject to surveillance and punishment rather than sympathy. Black and white addicts themselves would probably likewise be viewed in a harsher light. As it is, heroin still has its effect on the black community. The ravages caused by 'hard' drug abuse serve to justify the adoption of extraordinary policing measures wherever any illicit drug use is suspected.

The police enacted the prescription with which Derek Agnew concluded *Viper* using tactics and technology undreamed of in the

1950s. Drug dealers were blamed by the police for the Handsworth riot in 1985,[22] and drugs were identified as the new element in that year's phase of rioting which had been absent in 1981. There was almost a trace of nostalgia detectable. In fact, the trigger for the Handsworth riot was a spectacular drugs raid by 100 officers on the Villa Cross pub, which netted a small quantity of cannabis. David Webb, who had resigned from his post as a local police superintendent in 1981, because of what he saw as failure on the part of his superiors to back his community policing strategy, felt that there were plenty of subtler ways to stamp out unlicensed transactions in a pub.[23] The police, it would appear, chose this method to get a blunt message across to the black youth. The following year, Special Forces' fantasies seemed to be the inspiration for police tacticians. In Operation Condor, they borrowed a train which, 'with officers crouching below the windows, halted in the heart of the flashpoint area. Then police, some of them armed, poured out of the carriages commando-style and raided shops and houses backing on to the track.'[24] The target area was Brixton. Nearly 2,000 officers were involved, actively or in reserve, in the raids, which were officially described as being aimed at drugs dealers. A month later, the 'police "army" '[25] descended upon Bentley's pub in Canning Town. The style of Operation Brookland was similar to that of the Brixton raid, the gimmick in this case being a helicopter rather than a train. Again, a social centre for black people was the target, and the main drug involved was cannabis. Operation Delivery in Bristol afforded passers-by the spectacle, by now familiar, of officers leaping out of unmarked vehicles and descending upon premises favoured by young blacks. This time, they met resistance. Small amounts of cannabis and a few offensive weapons were seized. The immediate cost to the community was two nights of violence, in the area where the first of the modern inner city riots had taken place in 1980.

The post-mortem on the St Paul's events revealed the dynamics at work behind the police assaults. Local critics of the raid were challenged by a BBC Radio reporter to deny that drugs broke up families. Jagun Akinshegun, of the St Paul's Community Association, and Richard Barrett, a Methodist minister, both assented, but tried to suggest that cannabis might not be that kind of drug.[26] Akinshegun acknowledged the police obligation to enforce the law, but argued that less provocative methods were available. Barrett spoke of how 'areas like this, which experience deprivation and powerlessness, are experiencing shows of strength of an almost military kind, which are seen to be authority invading people's community.' The Chief Constable of Avon and Somerset, Ronald Broome, indicated the broad sweep of the action which was licensed by the duty to uphold the drug laws. 'The future lies with the people of St Paul's,' he said. 'Parts of that area were being taken over by drug pedlars, muggers, burglars and prostitutes and their clients.'[27] 'Drugs' are effectively synonymous with 'lawlessness', and the law charged in from its undercover vans to reoccupy the zone. 'Drugs' is also a codeword which authorizes extraordinary police action without the public discussion that other police objectives might provoke. Don't drugs break up families? The territorial nature of modern British policing was confirmed by Home Secretary Douglas Hurd. 'It was precisely in order to prevent it becoming a no-go area that the police took their action,'[28] he said, as if he were still in Northern Ireland.

Heroin and cannabis play complementary roles in the drugs complex. Heroin is the active ingredient and cannabis the filler. The debates of previous decades about the safety of cannabis are almost completely dormant, as is any serious attempt to present a case for its harmfulness. It is fairly frequently alleged to lead to heroin use, though the mechanism by which this takes place is not elaborated. Its main function, however, is to increase the bulk of the complex. When a new device for detecting drugs in urine samples was tested on a random sample of patients at a London hospital, 128 out of 400 were found to have taken cannabis in the previous fortnight. Four samples betrayed cocaine use. The results were reported as an 'alarming' discovery which had 'shocked' doctors.[29] The reasons for medical concern were not discussed: it is apparently axiomatic that illegal drug use of any sort should alarm doctors.

Surveys of young people's attitudes to drugs display a similar sort of pattern. Audience Selection found that, as the *News of the World* put it, a 'staggering twenty-seven per cent of people aged between 16 and 34 have experimented with illegal drugs'.[30] Some twenty-four per cent of the sample had tried cannabis. Four per cent had taken amphetamines and LSD; two per cent had tried cocaine, glue or barbiturates, and less than one per cent admitted to touching heroin. The report of the survey began: 'More than four million young people in Britain have been lured into risking their lives by dabbling with drugs.' A *New Society* survey of the 'Thatcher Generation'[31] found that sixty-five per cent of the young people it canvassed said that they had tried cigarettes, and eighty-five per cent alcohol. The figures for cannabis and heroin were seventeen per cent and two per cent respectively. The pattern is clear. Cannabis is fairly widespread, but other illegal drugs remain at a much lower level of use. Use of such drugs might be marginalized still further if the young people who have found cannabis to be relatively innocuous had not crossed the line of legality in doing so. Unless the law is reflecting some sort of pharmacological similarity which links the illegal drugs and separates them from the legal ones, the connection between cannabis and heroin could be broken by legalizing the 'soft' drug. Drug laws are hardly the most rational components of the legal code, though.

A liberal attitude to cannabis has also emerged from the follow-up studies carried out to assess the effectiveness of the 'Heroin Screws You Up' campaign.[32] Even the young people whom the investigators called 'drug resistant' are showing an increased interest in it. It is widely seen as being less harmful than cigarettes or alcohol, and the different varieties in which it is available are apparently tested and discussed in the same way as brands of lager or cigarettes. One area in which it is viewed less approvingly is the Wirral, where a popular backlash against heroin has affected attitudes to drugs in general. Here the connection between the two drugs is expressed in stories about cannabis being impregnated with heroin and, tellingly, customers being offered heroin when the cannabis they were seeking is not available.

The study found that young people were developing their understanding of drugs, and were learning which of them were relatively safe and controllable. Heroin invariably meets with strong disapproval, and its users driven further underground as attitudes have hardened. Increased police pressure has also put heroin users on the defensive. The rock culture image of the wanly glamorous junkie has faded in the face of the onslaught of Government posters depicting the addict as pathetic, unattractive and friendless. The report concluded that 'the primary campaign objective, "to reinforce young people's resistances to heroin misuse in order to discourage interest in trial" has, to a large extent, been fulfilled.'

There were caveats, however. The isolation of heroin as 'the drug to avoid' is tending to encourage complacency about the dangers of other drugs. The high profile of the campaign has led to the assumption that it reflected a continuing increase in the scale of the problem. And, now that rejection by family and friends has been compounded by the harsh reflections from giant posters, addicts themselves are feeling even more hopeless and isolated. The junkie is the unfortunate sacrifice within the grand project.

The survey also gathered information about groups for whom illegal drugs remain alien. Parents tend to lump all drugs together, and to see experimentation with any of them as the first step on the road to ruin. These are the people whose perceptions of the issue are populated with 'pushers' and menacing inner city blacks. Suspicion, ignorance and fear are the main elements of the parents' mood. It is regrettable, but predictable. The real revelation comes from a sample of general practitioners. It was as though Rolleston and Brain had never convened their committees: 'We're all looking at them as though they were ill. In fact, they're just anti-social.' 'It seems odd to speak of treating someone who is actually a criminal.' 'They have no moral principles whatsoever.' 'I like the American way . . . the cold turkey treatment . . . just lock them up.' 'Send them to prison!'

These members of a caring profession generally favour confinement and enforced withdrawal under what the report summarized as 'relatively harsh, oppressive regimes'. They blame heroin on 'personality disorder or a social aberration or possibly both'. Compassion for people with what they identify as non-medical problems is apparently to be considered beyond their brief. The expansionist impulses of medicine in the previous century have evidently lost their appeal for the modern practitioner, at least as far as drug addiction is concerned. The abandonment of the disease model by the profession which developed and exploited it, seems to have lifted the lid off a visceral reservoir of hatred. Perhaps the persistence of disease-model ideas in the lay population is a benign illusion, allowing the expression of sympathy for addicts and checking the hostility engendered by the criminal model of the drug fiend.

After the first year of the campaign, the Government decided to provide a further £2 million for its continuation. Giant posters cast the urban landscape as the background for depictions of the degradation caused by heroin, a move which emphasized the Government's determination of priorities, but was hardly calculated to brighten the visual impact of the inner cities. Anti-heroin posters and police patrolling in vehicles hardened for riot control would become dominant images of the mid-eighties metropolis. On the home front, the advertisers were preparing to draft mothers into the anti-heroin army.[33] In their role as 'sheet-anchor' of the family, they are judged to occupy key positions of influence. The move was in line with Government strategy, too, in that encouraging the policing of heroin within families would support the principles of privatization.[34] The Conservative ideologues have long preached the doctrine of parental responsibility for preventing minor criminal and anti-social behaviour. The extension of these principles to drug policing takes family vigilance into the realms of medicine and the social services. At the crudest level, it facilitates the Thatcherite impulse to cut public spending. On a loftier plane, it encourages the growth of surveillance. Electronics and authoritarianism have collaborated to increase the degree of technological surveillance, from the advent of machine-readable passports, to the seemingly continous presence above Londoners' heads of police helicopters. Police-sponsored 'neighbourhood watch' schemes and govern-ment-sponsored anti-heroin campaigns help to take surveillance into the home.

At the highest level of policing, the Government have made sure that drugs are prominent in the list of public evils. Leon Brittan, when Home Secretary, explicitly linked the two great contemporary symbols of horror when he announced the establishment of a National Drugs Intelligence Unit with Colin Hewett as its head. Brittan noted Hewett's former anti-terrorist responsibilities, and said that his appointment reflected the gravity with which the Government regarded drug trafficking. The missions were comparable: 'In drugs, as with terrorism, the need for good intelligence is paramount.'[35]

Amid the blaze of publicity, there has been scant sympathy or help for the most hopeless drug-abusing group of all. It first came to light in Edinburgh, a city whose heroin customs seem to belong to times gone by. Edinburgh junkies take the stuff the old-fashioned way, by needle; and Edinburgh judges have punished them with Old Testament simplicity. One told a twenty-year-old man whom he had sentenced to two years' gaol for the possession of ten pounds' worth of heroin that his treatment had been 'extremely lenient'.[36] The police have also pursued a simple policy of muscular law enforcement. In this case, the simplicity has proved lethal. A clamp down on the sale of syringes did have the effect of ensuring that legitimate pharmacists and medical suppliers were seen not to be collaborating with illegal practices, but this demonstration of symbolic purity has simply concentrated a far from symbolic pollution elsewhere. The needle famine intensified the practice of needle sharing, one of the most efficient ways of transmitting the Human Immunodeficiency Virus (HIV). Researchers estimated that, by 1986, up to eighty-five per cent of the city's heroin users had been infected with what has come to be known as 'the virus' in this manner.[37]

At present, the prognosis for those infected with HIV is highly uncertain. It may be that only a relatively small proportion of them will become ill, and that not all of these will develop full-blown AIDS. It is also possible that all those infected will eventually become ill. Much remains to be learnt about what causes the infection to lead to illness, and there is reason to believe that the reduction of stress and of further challenges to the immune system may do much to defend an infected person's health. Intravenous drug users are poor candidates for such palliatives. Every time a dirty needle is pushed through the skin and unsterile street drugs injected, the body receives an immunological insult. The challenge to the body may be compounded by mild immunosuppression directly caused by heroin itself. Nor is the addicts' self-neglect likely to increase their survival chances. The new menace has failed to register with many of the users: perhaps it is a heroin-induced deadening of emotion; perhaps their emotional reserves are exhausted by the stress of heroin dependency alone. The brevity of the heroin user's economic cycle does not favour forward planning, either. As one teenage addict put it, 'if you're sitting withdrawing, and you ken who has got the virus, if you've got a fifty-fifty chance of catching it, you're not going to stop and say, well, I don't want to catch the virus. You'll still take a shot.'[39] The virus is like the genetic code for the imaginary heroin of popular imagination. With HIV, heroin has finally become the horror it has so long been cracked up to be.

Drug workers dealing with intravenous users have had to rethink their priorities. The most urgent imperative is to stop the spread of the virus, which means preaching 'safer drug use' rather than abstinence. Schemes in which used needles can be exchanged for new ones have been met with a certain amount of official sympathy, though not from John MacKay, who was Scottish Health Minister when the problem first emerged. For him, it was unthinkable that the symbolic purity of the state be sullied by actions which might appear to condone illicit drug use.[40]

With a highly charged unreason on the loose among their elders, the young might be expected to deal with drugs in a similarly chaotic manner. The evidence of studies such as the anti-heroin campaign evaluation report suggests that, on the contrary, the young are managing illegal drug use rather better than their parents, whose guilt and anxiety about the world they have made for their children is organized so strongly around drugs. The abuse of statistics notwithstanding, a substantial increase in the use of illegal drugs must be beyond reasonable doubt. A similar process seems to be taking place in many other parts of the world, in countries as diverse as the United States and the Soviet Union. If this change is a lasting one, it may turn out to be one of the most significant cultural phenomena of the late twentieth century. Drugs which were once contained within dissident subcultures have now broken out of their ghetto, and this proliferation has given heroin back one aspect of its universal character. But, while it has penetrated all classes of society, this does not mean that the ranks of its dependants will swell indefinitely.

Ultimately, drugs can only be controlled by culture, in a complex relationship involving the evolution of guidelines for use which limits the associated damage to a level deemed socially acceptable. Some drugs are unlikely to be sanctioned in any form, and the reported attitudes of the young are consistent with the idea that heroin is one such pariah. The significance of drugs is distended with veiled social meanings; it is their status as Other which permits this overloading. Perhaps the adults of the next century will change this status, and in the process demonstrate that a society need not remain forever in the grip of heroin; or of narcomania.

Notes

1 *Daily Mirror*, 10 June 1986. The incriminating testimony was provided by David Levine, a rock photographer. Well-placed sources suggested that he received a fee of £15,000.

2 It also served as the start of a new invasion scare. Home Office Minister David Mellor spoke of cocaine 'waiting in the wings', alluding to a theory (dating back at least four years) that the US market was saturated, and the powerful Latin American syndicates were about to flood Europe with cheap and irresistible powder. Whatever the truth of this scenario, it served a useful propaganda purpose. (See *Daily Express*, 23 November 1982 and 11 December 1984; *Daily Telegraph*, 13 April 1984; *The Times*, 8 December 1984.)

3 *New Musical Express*, 12 July 1986. By Sue Joseph and Quentin McDermott.

4 For example, columnist Anne Robinson: 'Boy George was different from other pop stars. He was witty, articulate and gentle . . . I met him at the height of his fame when he was mobbed wherever he moved, and guarded by a charmless and aggressive manager . . . Yet he has that marvellous knack of appearing to have all the time in the world to talk to you.' (*Daily Mirror*, 11 June 1986.)

5 'In courtroom and clinic, the crumbling world of the pop star

who fell from grace' – front page headline, *Today*, 10 July 1986. The phrase seemed to strike a chord with the singer from an Irish (and therefore Catholic) background. He was quoted using it by the *News of the World* (13 July 1986). Having been tracked down to his cottage hideaway by the hack pack, he put the *Today* front page in a window together with a sign reading 'MORAL MAJORITY HAVE YOU COME TO RETURN MY GRACE!!' (*Today*, 12 July 1986).

6   'Junkie George's family are a clan of crackpots.' (*Sun* 11 July 1986).

7   *Today*, 10 July 1986.

8   *Daily Express*, 4 July 1986.

9   *Star*, 4 July 1986.

10 *Star*, 9 July 1986.

11 *Guardian*, 16 July 1986.

12 *Mail on Sunday*, 13 July 1986.

13 'The killing of Boy George', *Daily Mail*, 4 July 1986.

14 'THE DRAGON OF DEATH THAT MUST BE SLAIN
    'For once I agree with Norman Tebbit: the BBC should ban anyone in pop music connected with drugs. And if necessary start with Boy George . . . If someone as intelligent as George becomes a junkie, then there is no hope for any of our young people.' Alix Palmer, *Star*, 9 July 1986.

15 Letter to the *Guardian*, 29 July 1986. The record in question, 'Some Candy Talking', by the Jesus & Mary Chain (Blanco y Negro), seemed to be attempting a pastiche of the old veiled drug allusions popular in the 'underground' music of a bygone era. Lines like 'give me more of that stuff' set up such an effect with a bare minimum of subtlety.

16 *Guardian*, 23 and 27 August 1986; *People*, 24 August 1986.

17 *Guardian*, 23 August 1986.

18 Misuse of Hard Drugs, Interim Report; Fifth Report of the Home Affairs Committee, HMSO, May 1985.

19 *Guardian*, 19 May 1986.

20 Justine Picardie and Dorothy Wade, *Heroin: Chasing The Dragon* (London, Penguin, 1985).

21 'Official statistics on drug-taking in Britain', ISDD Library & Information Service, December 1985 (from Home Office Statistical Bulletin, 3 September 1985).

22 *Guardian*, 16 September 1985. The West Midlands Chief Constable, Geoffrey Dear, said: 'It is almost certain that major drug dealers were responsible and that investigations now going on will prove it to be so.' He went on to speculate that heroin and

cocaine dealers might want to create a 'vacuum' – presumably of
law and order – so that they could move in on 'established soft
drug routes'. The interpolation of the 'vacuum' into the well-worn
pusher conspiracy theory was a deft stroke. A vacuum has to be
occupied. That would counter the common complaint that police
often operated in areas with large black populations like an army
of occupation. Dear's elaborate hypothesis was promptly
dismissed by the Handsworth Defence Committee, who claimed
that local dealers were paying protection money to the police
(*Guardian*, 23 November 1985). An independent inquiry
conducted by Julius Silverman, a barrister and former Labour MP
for Birmingham Erdington, also rejected the notion that the riots
could have been initiated by a dealers' conspiracy. (*Guardian*, 28
February 1986.) Dear stuck to his guns in his final report, which
concluded that the riots were 'orchestrated by local drug dealers
who had become fearful for the demise of their livelihoods'.
(*Guardian*, 20 November 1985.)

23 *Observer*, 15 September 1985.
24 *Daily Mirror*, 25 July 1986. In a Parliamentary answer Douglas
    Hogg stated that 1200 g of cannabis, 34 g of cocaine and 42 mg of
    heroin were seized by police during the course of Operation
    Condor. (*Hansard*, 7 November 1986.)
25 'Moment police "army" pounced' – headline, *London Standard*, 29
    August 1986.
26 *The World at One*, BBC Radio 4, 12 September 1986.
27 *Guardian*, 13 September 1986.
28 *The World at One*, 12 September 1986.
29 *News at Six*, BBC 1, 29 July 1986.
30 Audience Selection canvassed 506 respondents by telephone on
    14 May 1985.
31 *New Society*, 21 February 1986. Interestingly, the proportion of
    respondents who identified heroin as the most dangerous drug in
    terms of its effect on society in general diminished with age,
    although overall it was far ahead of the field at fifty-six per cent.
    The dangers of alcohol and tobacco became more apparent with
    age. *New Society* felt that this trend, which would probably have
    been welcomed by the BMA, meant that 'the government clearly
    has a lot of educating to do'.
32 'Anti-Heroin Misuse Campaign: Qualitative Evaluation Research
    Report' (Andrew Irving Associates, January 1986).
33 'Mums get the call in drugs war', *Daily Mirror*, 4 April 1986.

34 Jeffrey Minson refers to a similar significance for nineteenth-century anti-masturbation campaigns in *Genealogies of Morals* (London, Macmillan, 1985), pp. 187–8.

35 *Guardian*, 19 July 1985. On the same day, the *Mirror*'s Paul Callan revealed that Hewett had served in the *Viper* zone: 'Colin Hewett knows about bare, torn streets where drugs and poverty meet like vile brothers. Back in the 1950s, when all policemen seemed Dixons of Dock Green, he patrolled sad Paddington as a young constable and was shocked by the human wreckage he saw.'

36 *Evening News* (Edinburgh), 16 August 1985.

37 J. R. Robertson *et al.*, 'Epidemic of AIDS related virus (HTLV–III/LAV) infection among intravenous drug abusers', *British Medical Journal* 292 (22 February 1986), pp. 527–9. See also Marek Kohn, 'The Virus in Edinburgh' (*New Society*, 2 May 1986). One of my strongest impressions of researching this assignment was the contempt and mistrust of journalists among drug workers that a recent flurry of media interest had inspired.

38 Kohn, *New Society*.

39 *Pulse* 46 (7) (1986), p. 8. MacKay's tenure as the Scottish Office Minister responsible for health ended with the autumn Cabinet reshuffle, shortly after he gave a controversial interview to *The Scotsman* (3 September 1986), in which he reiterated his position on needle supply and his view that AIDS was a 'straightforward moral issue'.

Index

Feldman's Club, 91, 92
fens, opium use in, 43–6, 55
First World War, 74, 76, 77, 79–80, 107
Fitzsimmons, Jason, 122
Fleischl, Ernst, 3
Fleming, Alexander, 2
fluid imagery, 2, 3, 12, 24
Folkestone, 79
Fliess, Wilhelm, 32
Fordham, John, 91
Foreign Office, 76, 85
Foucault, Michel, 51
Frankau, Lady Isabella, 100–1
Franklin, Aretha, 128
Freud, Sigmund, 3, 32, 136–7, 140
Frye, Soleil Moon, 128
Fu Manchu, Doctor, 28–9, 77–9, 85

Galdston, Iago, 32
Gardner, Sir Edward, 157–8
Garrison, Fielding H., 37–8
George IV, 42, 54
Giordano, Harry M., 103
Gladstone, William Ewart, 42
glue-sniffing, 122, 123, 130
Goldsmith, Oliver, 16
Grange Hill, 127–8
'Great Depression', 7
Guinness, Daphne, 106
Guinness, Sebastian, 112, 113

Hague Conferences, 72–3, 76, 80, 85
Handsworth, 160
Hanway, Jonas, 16–23
Harris, Rolf, 126
Harrison Narcotic Act, 73, 74
Harrods, 80
Hastings, Warren, 26
Hearst, William Randolph, 84
Heartbreakers, The, 134
hemp, *see* cannabis
heroin, 2–7, 34, 47, 74, 82, 85, 86, 95–
    103, 107–10, 112–16, 118–28, 130,
    131, 133–45, 150–5, 158–9, 161–7;

medical use of, 4, 5, 86, 97–8;
    naming of, 3; 1980s Government
    publicity campaign against, 110,
    118–20, 153, 155, 162–4;
    physiological action of, 6; *see also*
    injection, addiction
Hewett, Colin, 165, 170
Hobbes, Thomas, 60
Hobson, Richmond P., 74–5
Hollywood Babylon, 112
Holmes, Sherlock, 9, 11, 37
Home Affairs Committee (House of
    Commons), 27–8, 157
Home Office, 45, 85, 96, 100, 104, 120;
    notification of addicts to, 97, 99, 100,
    101, 158
Hood, Thomas, 43
100 Club, *see* Feldman's Club
Hunter, Dr Henry Julian, 42–3
Hunterian Society, 42
Hurd, Douglas, 161

India, 25, 26, 31, 47, 57, 76
inebriety, 59, 66
injection, 9, 31, 37, 94; introduction of,
    64; fetishism, 141–3; and AIDS,
    165–6
Invasion of the Body Snatchers, 71

Japan, 22, 76–7
Johnson, Samuel, 16
Johnston, Rosie, 112, 113
*Journal of the American Medical
    Association*, 5
'junkie', origin of term, 74
'Just Say No' movement, 126–8

Keats, John, 41
Kerr, Dr Norman, 59, 66
Knopf, Dr S. Adolphus, 84
Kolb, Lawrence, 83–4
'Kubla Khan', 33–5

Lacan, Jacques, 136–8, 140